D0275143

Th

T
a

The Dogs of Littlefield

The Dogs of Littlefield

SUZANNE BERNE

FIG TREE
an imprint of
PENGUIN BOOKS

FIG TREE

Published by the Penguin Group
Penguin Books Ltd, 80 Strand, London WC2R ORL, England
Penguin Group (USA) Inc., 375 Hudson Street, New York, New York 10014, USA
Penguin Group (Canada), 90 Eglinton Avenue East, Suite 700, Toronto, Ontario, Canada M4P 2Y3
(a division of Pearson Penguin Canada Inc.)
Penguin Ireland, 25 St Stephen's Green, Dublin 2, Ireland (a division of Penguin Books Ltd)
Penguin Group (Australia), 707 Collins Street, Melbourne, Victoria 3008, Australia
(a division of Pearson Australia Group Pty Ltd)
Penguin Books India Pvt Ltd, 11 Community Centre, Panchsheel Park, New Delhi – 110 017, India
Penguin Group (NZ), 67 Apollo Drive, Rosedale, Auckland 0632, New Zealand
(a division of Pearson New Zealand Ltd)
Penguin Books (South Africa) (Pty) Ltd, Block D, Rosebank Office Park,
181 Jan Smuts Avenue, Parktown North, Gauteng 2193, South Africa

Penguin Books Ltd, Registered Offices: 80 Strand, London WC2R ORL, England

www.penguin.com

First published 2013
001

Copyright © Suzanne Berne, 2013

The moral right of the author has been asserted

Poems: 'Parliament Hill Fields', from *Collected Poems*, by John Betjeman © 1955, 1958, 1962, 1964,
1968, 1970, 1979, 1981, 1982, 2001. Reproduced by permission of John Murray (Publishers)

All rights reserved
Without limiting the rights under copyright
reserved above, no part of this publication may be
reproduced, stored in or introduced into a retrieval system,
or transmitted, in any form or by any means (electronic, mechanical,
photocopying, recording or otherwise), without the prior
written permission of both the copyright owner and
the above publisher of this book

Set in 12/14.75pt Dante MT Std
Typeset by Jouve (UK), Milton Keynes
Printed in Great Britain by Clays Ltd, St Ives plc

A CIP catalogue record for this book is available from the British Library

HARDBACK ISBN: 978-0-241-14566-1
TRADE PAPERBACK ISBN: 978-0-241-00382-4

www.greenpenguin.co.uk

MIX
Paper from
responsible sources
FSC
www.fsc.org   FSC™ C018179

Penguin Books is committed to a sustainable
future for our business, our readers and our planet.
This book is made from Forest Stewardship
Council™ certified paper.

For Maxine Rodburg

ROTHERHAM LIBRARY SERVICE	
B53070297	
Bertrams	05/12/2013
AF	£14.99
BSU	GEN

I.

No one was very surprised when the signs began appearing in Baldwin Park. For years people had been letting their dogs run free in the meadow to the west of the elementary school and no one had said much about it; but once an authorized off-leash 'dog park' was proposed and a petition presented to the Littlefield Board of Aldermen, fierce arguments erupted over whose rights to the park should be upheld and the town broke into factions, those who loved dogs and those who did not, at least not in the park.

At first the signs were polite reminders to dog owners to curb and pick up after their dogs, but as the off-leash proposal gained support among the aldermen, several of whom owned dogs themselves, the signs became more pointed. 'Respect the Park,' they read. Or 'The Park is for All of Us.' On St Patrick's Day, a sign was posted on a telephone pole at the frontier of the elementary school playground where wood chips gave way to grass and dog-walking parents often congregated after escorting their children to school. Printed in black ink on the kind of thin, flexible cardboard that comes slipped inside of men's dress shirts, it read:

> Pick up
> after Your Dog.
> Aren't You Ashamed
> that You Don't?

This sign created a small uproar among the parents, who objected to its tone, and it was taken down by the custodian. Then, on March 21st, according to the 'Crime Watch' column in the *Littlefield Gazette*, an unidentified man threatened to shoot an unleashed dog for colliding with his bicycle while he was riding in the park; the dog owner reported this threat to the police. The man had dark facial hair, 'scruffy' was her actual term, and was between eighteen and twenty-five in age. A description, she acknowledged, that fitted half the young men in Littlefield. Not long after the collision between dog and cyclist, another sign appeared overnight on a telephone pole, this one at the eastern edge of the park, bordering Endicott Road:

Leash Your
Beast

It was also quickly taken down, though not before being seen by two gardeners, several dog walkers and a woman out jogging.

A week later the aldermen voted to postpone discussions of the dog park proposal until an independent task force could conduct a site review, and for a while the controversy quieted.

Soccer season resumed in mid-April and once again whole families sat together in the park, wearing sweaters and baseball hats and fleece lap rugs against the chilly morning air, cheering from folding nylon chairs on the sidelines, mist rising from the grass at their feet, many of them holding dogs tightly on leashes while children flew back and forth across the damp green field, hair backlit by the low morning sun.

On weekend afternoons as the weather warmed, families strolled down Brooks Street with ice-cream cones from the Dairy Barn. Soft-hipped mothers wearing large dark sunglasses stopped to exchange greetings and to share mild mutinous jokes about driving to Manhattan one of these days instead of doing the three o'clock school pick-up in the minivan. Elderly women from Avalon Towers wandered slowly past in turtlenecks and boiled-wool jackets and elastic-waisted slacks, holding onto each other's thin arms, shaking their heads at flocks of flamingo-like girls in black leggings and oversized hooded sweatshirts texting each other in front of Walgreens. Now and then the trolley rumbled to a stop at the old fieldstone station, people stepped onto or off the platform, and then the trolley rumbled on again. Almost always a dog was tied by its leash to a parking meter outside the Dairy Barn or the Bake Shoppe or the Tavern, looking hopefully at passers-by, or cringingly, or indifferently, but as much a part of those busy village afternoons as anybody else.

Spring turned to summer. Families went away on vacations to the Cape or Maine or Martha's Vineyard, taking their dogs with them or boarding them at kennels. The park was quiet and hot and smelled of mown grass and faintly of car exhaust. Gardeners in sun hats and rubber clogs worked in the collective gardens; young parents who could not afford to go on vacation pushed strollers to the elementary school playground and then across the soccer field and into the park for a picnic or to nap on a blanket under the big spreading maple tree that stood alone in the bowl-like meadow. In the background floated the oceanic roar of the Massachusetts Turnpike. No new signs about dogs were posted; the old ones faded in the sun and eventually were torn down or blew away.

In September, just after school was back in session and the evenings turning cool, the aldermen voted to grant a three-month trial period to dog park proponents. The meadow of Baldwin Park would be 'off-leash' between eight a.m. and ten a.m. on weekdays, and for two hours on Saturday and Sunday evenings. If all went well, these hours would be expanded. An editorial in favor of the dog park appeared the next day in the *Gazette*, pointing out that Littlefield had historically embraced free-thinking. Collective gardens occupied half an acre of Baldwin Park; Clean Up Littlefield Day was an institution, as was Celebrate Your Heritage Day (twenty-two different countries with tables last year in the elementary school gym), and for the past six years the high school had celebrated Gay Pride Day with speeches and banners. *Let us not be guided by visions of what could go wrong*, wrote the editorialist, *but by what could go right. Certainly we are tolerant enough of our fellow creatures to designate an off-leash area in Baldwin Park.* That same morning, a woman named Margaret Downing drove her dog, Binx, into town for a walk in the meadow.

On her way to the park she stopped at Whole Foods grocery to pick up a loaf of bread for dinner, parking near the store entrance where a bearded young man in a yellow T-shirt stood with a clipboard, shaking a ballpoint pen that appeared to be running out of ink. Canvassers often hovered outside the glass doors and on her way back to her car Margaret made a point of signing their petitions for Green Community initiatives or to ban plastic bags, though usually she declined requests for donations. She contributed online to three charitable organizations and was trying to keep an eye on which ones did what with the money; but after being asked twice this morning for a donation to the Nature Conservancy, she did offer the canvasser a pen from her bag. He was thin, morose, dark and foreign-looking in his yellow T-shirt, and was being avoided by other shoppers.

'Here's to a better world,' she said, handing him the pen.

He frowned as if she'd made an off-color remark and took the pen without thanking her. Walking quickly to her car, she passed a small fat black woman in an orange turban; normally Margaret would have made an effort to smile at the woman, even more out of place in the Whole Foods parking lot than the canvasser, but she kept her head down, feeling his eyes on her still as she climbed into her Volvo station wagon, the back window decorated with Audubon Club and Sierra Club decals. Had he thought she was being snide?

She was glad to find she had the park all to herself; by ten o'clock the dog owners and professional dog walkers who visited each morning had come and gone. Against a taut blue sky the heavy crowns of oaks and maples were dark green, interrupted here and there by a few gold leaves.

Her dog was a black Lab, still a puppy at ten months old, a big handsome sleek animal, already almost sixty pounds. She didn't often let him off his leash; despite months of puppy kindergarten, he didn't come when she called, he rolled in dead things – during their two weeks at the beach he'd found every decayed seagull carcass, every washed-up fish – and he jumped into any kind of water. You accept certain responsibilities, the breeder had told her, when you have a large dog, and one of them is simply holding onto it.

But the day was so lovely, and he was whining and pulling hard, dragging her across the grass, making the gagging noises dogs make when they lunge against their collars. Sometimes a dog needs to run away with itself – an unruly thought that might not have occurred to her had she not been brooding about the incident in the parking lot. She'd only meant to be encouraging. Why was even the simplest gesture so complicated? *You worry about everything*, Julia was always telling her.

'Oh, for God's sake, Binx.' She bent down and unclipped the leash from his collar, watching as he shot away across the meadow, immediately realizing her mistake.

He ran toward the woods, divided from the rest of the park by a shallow creek where primordial-looking skunk cabbages flourished greenly in black mud along with greasy clusters of poison ivy, just turning scarlet. Ignoring Margaret's cries, he leapt into the creek and wallowed for a few moments before clambering out of the mud and up the opposite bank. Then he shook himself and galloped toward where the pine trees cast jagged shadows onto the bright grass.

But instead of running into the woods he stopped to nose a boulder under a tall clump of sumac, his back legs muddy and gleaming. The creek smelled like water in a vase of dead chrysanthemums as Margaret hurried across the little wooden footbridge, calling his name, knowing that she would have to catch him by the collar and drag him away from whatever he had found.

The sun was in her eyes and at first she noticed only sumac, the stalks already turning the chalky lavender that comes to sumac in the fall. Underneath was not a boulder at all but something enormous and pale, its coat so short as to make it seem hairless. Teeth bared, huge furrowed face contorted in a snarl. Bloodied yellowish foam had collected around the folds of its muzzle.

A breeze brushed Margaret's forehead and stirred the tasseled grasses and a spray of goldenrod at the verge of the woods. From deep within the trees came the high igniting sounds of small birds and the stirrings of insects in the bracken. In a moment it would come to her what she was seeing and what she should do about it. But in the vast divide between one moment and the next, she could only stare at the creature, white and motionless, almost too big to be believable, the smooth skin of his underbelly spotted with wide pale freckles, so exposed, so tender-looking, so innocent and perverse.

2.

Bill Downing was eating Goldfish crackers, shirtsleeves rolled partway up his forearms, describing a crisis with the network server at his office while he and Margaret sat on the patio by the pool, having drinks and waiting for the lasagna in the oven to finish baking. A tall, balding man with light blue eyes and a blade-like nose, he often wore pink button-down shirts with his gray summer-weight suits. In the dusk his shirt was nearly the same color as the pink sky lowering into the trees, while at his feet the patio flagstones had turned a pale aquatic blue.

'Everything went dead. Roche was going nuts.' He noticed a daddy-long-legs scaling his trouser leg and brushed it away. 'The IT guys got us up again after about twenty minutes. But for a while we were all just sitting there. Passano kept joking that it was some kind of hostile takeover.'

'Weird,' said Margaret.

His office had a seventh-floor view of the Charles and during those twenty minutes he'd looked down at the plaza below the building, at Storrow Drive and across at the river, glassy and full under the afternoon sun, winding past green banks and the stone bridges and brick buildings of Cambridge. While he was staring out of the window, the strangest thing happened: he saw himself walking across the plaza below. There was his pink shirt, crossing the street, walking toward the stone walkway that stretched above Storrow Drive. Hands in his trouser pockets, he strolled across the walkway and then took the steps down to the Esplanade, where people were sitting on the grass, having lunch or sunning themselves by the water as sailboats tacked back and forth. For a minute or two he'd stood by a bench, still with his hands in his pockets, gazing at the sailboats. It looked as if he might be whistling. Then he walked across the grass to the river and threw himself in.

'Well, I'm glad it all got fixed,' said Margaret.

'Yeah,' said Bill, staring at the pool.

The pool had come with the house; it was small and oval, more like a reflecting pool, ringed by fieldstones. Margaret never liked the idea of owning a pool – she thought it required too much upkeep and later worried about Julia falling into it as a toddler – but he'd always wanted one. A pool was a sign, his father used to say, of 'having it made'. The summer before Julia was born Margaret had added an electrically powered waterfall trickling down rocks at one end, banked by tall hydrangeas tumbling with pink and blue flowers. It had been a kind of mania with her, planning that waterfall. 'Margaret's Niagara', Bill's father had called it. Yet he was the one who helped Margaret build it, first wiring the pump, then spending days piling up rocks and taking them down until Margaret was satisfied. Already the waterfall had been switched off; in a week the pool would be drained and covered with a tarp.

An acorn caromed off a patio slate. Binx had been asleep beside Margaret's chair. He scrambled to his feet and began barking at the pool. Margaret grabbed his leash and ordered him to lie down and with a reluctant groan he obeyed, metal tags clinking.

'So, how was your day?' he asked.

She sighed and lifted her wine glass. 'I'm trying not to get too freaked out about it.' The chardonnay in her glass caught the light, a minute twin to the sun going down behind the trees. 'I found a dead dog at the park.'

'A dog?'

'A huge dog. A white bullmastiff.'

'That's terrible.' He watched a black line of ants emerge busily from a crack in the patio slates. 'Had it been hit by a car?'

'The animal control guy said it looked like the dog had been poisoned.'

'Poisoned?'

'That's what the guy said. I had to call the owner.'

'That can't have been easy.'

'No,' said Margaret. She was rubbing Binx's belly with her foot. 'It wasn't.'

The pool lights had come on. For a few minutes they sat looking at the shifting web of reflected watery light thrown across the hydrangeas. When Margaret began speaking again her voice sounded disembodied, as if it were coming from a dark margin beyond the hydrangeas, somewhere at the edge of the yard below the oak trees.

'I can't stop seeing that dog. How could someone do something like that? And of all the people who could have found it, why did it have to be me?'

Bill shook the ice in his Campari and soda, listening to the low whine of the pool filter. Noticing also a smell mixed with the scent of chlorine. Earthy, dank, slightly fecal. The daddy-long-legs he'd brushed off a few minutes ago was now delicately ascending the side of Margaret's chair. From near the back steps, a cricket had started up.

'Well,' he said finally, 'I'm sure there's a reasonable explanation.'

Another acorn ricocheted off the patio. Binx tried to scramble up again but Margaret held him down with her foot. He jumped into the pool at every chance, so he had to be kept on his leash even in the yard.

A long silence followed, broken only by the steady creak of the cricket. Bill could sense Margaret waiting for him to go on, to say things were never as bad as they looked and a dog being poisoned wasn't a sign of anything else. Instead he kept staring into the depthless turquoise glow of the pool; from where he sat, a single underwater light was visible, round and convex, like an enormous unblinking yellow eye.

Something is wrong with me, he thought.

But he didn't know what it was. He didn't know why every time he looked at Margaret, for instance, he noticed the faint puckering above her lips or the moth-colored spots dappling the backs of her hands. On the side of her neck was a small dark mole. It appalled him. Even her gallantry in carrying on despite these indignities, in getting manicures and facials, buying lotions, taking yoga classes – even that appalled him. He couldn't help it. Just as he couldn't help flinching when she put her hand on his back at night, or straightened his shirt collar. Hoping she wouldn't notice, knowing that she did.

And yet once she'd been all he could think about. Every evening that first spring he'd walk across the Back Bay to meet her for dinner, repeating her name like an incantation, each step a syllable, *Mar-gar-et*, as he strode through the rinsed air of late April, passing magnolias along Commonwealth and the wide front stoops of brownstones, their brass door-knockers shaped like pineapples and fox heads, smiling at girls and women on the sidewalks. Smiling especially at the homely ones, the ones with big noses, heavy legs, pitted cheeks, smiling at the pains they took to fix their hair, wear earrings. He'd wanted to sleep with every woman he saw, the unbeautiful ones most of all – for their hair and their earrings, for their continued brave hopefulness despite not being Margaret, despite not being loved by him.

Often when he arrived at the girls' school on Exeter Street where she taught English, Margaret would be playing the piano at the back of the old building, in a hall used for assemblies. She liked to practice at the end of the day, so he would wait for her by the open front windows in the high-ceilinged wood-paneled parlor where the school secretary had a desk and cork boards held school announcements that rustled whenever anyone opened the door. Ivy hung over the window casements, leaves glowing in the evening sun, turning the light greenish. As he stood reading announcements for auditions and swim meets, listening to quiet piano music from within, he felt suspended within that greenish light, surrounded by a sweet lucid membrane, like being inside a grape. By the time Margaret appeared, walking quickly, shyly, smoothing her blonde hair as she crossed the uneven parquet floor, he was often trembling.

At dinner she liked to talk about her students and whether she should go for a master's degree in English or music. Sometimes she talked about Schumann, whose music she loved because, she said, it was full of heightened awareness of the world's beauty and pain. Wine made her categorical and vague. 'Musicians are the true poets,' she might declare. Or 'Human loneliness is literature's only subject.' Becoming more ardent as she drank glasses of wine, making pronouncements, pausing to qualify them, describing emphatic arcs with her hands, cheekbones finely outlined beneath her fair skin, the pulsing hollow at the base of her throat the exact width of his thumb. As he watched her talk he would find himself holding his breath. Once he even passed out in an Italian restaurant. Woke up with his forehead pressed against brown wallpaper garlanded with gondolas and Venetian palazzos, and to Margaret's hand on his shoulder, a hurt look on her face.

Now and then, in bed in her apartment, as he drowsed against the pillows, she would read aloud poems she'd assigned to her class or poems she liked. There was one poem he used to ask for, though it put him to sleep; he could still recall a snatch of it:

Oh the after-tram-ride quiet, when we heard a mile beyond,
Silver music from the bandstand, barking dogs by Highgate
    Pond . . .

He remembered the bright spacious feeling those lines had opened within his chest, a feeling that he was heading toward exactly the life he wanted to have. He was going to find a good job that paid good money and come home to a nice old town in the evenings; someday he was going to say 'my wife', and have those words mean Margaret.

All of which happened. He got his job with Roche Capital.

13

Margaret quit teaching when they moved out to Littlefield, planning for the child on the way.

But that part had not happened.

The losses, Margaret used to call them, which to him sounded like 'the lasses', little girls in white nightgowns, although it had been too early, in all but one case, to know. 'Don't talk about it to anyone,' she'd said fiercely, after the first. 'I don't want people feeling sorry for me.' Tests, procedures, on and on. Until the summer night when she turned to him, face gleaming like wet stone, and said she could not take anymore. Not knowing there was going to be Julia. And then there was Julia, and he thought it was all going to be all right.

But they had done something to her. Not aged her, exactly, although of course she had aged, but turned her apprehensive, fretful. Overly sensitive. For years now at dinner she mostly talked about worries. Julia was eating too much candy. Wasn't wearing her bike helmet. What if she got a concussion while playing soccer? He found it hard to listen, which she took as lack of interest. But it was something else, some imbalance in her that had become permanent, something unreasonable, morbid, a persistent boring dread. When Julia started middle school, he'd suggested that Margaret find an outside interest, get a job, do volunteer work; she'd seemed almost frightened at the idea of leaving the house.

'Well, wish me luck,' she often said, even when heading to the store for milk. Thank God for that dog. At least it got her out of the door.

She was still Margaret. She loved him. He still loved her.

But he couldn't bear it.

14

Mostly he tried not to think about it. Or when he did, like this afternoon when he'd stared out of his office window at the glittering Charles, shot with racing sculls and white sails, he thought only: *I can't bear it.*

He shook the ice in his glass again. What *was* that damned smell?

Margaret was talking again about the dead dog, worried that it might have been diseased. From down the street a lawnmower started up, drowning out the cricket. He thought of his father mowing the grass on warm evenings in an old pair of dungarees and a white undershirt that turned blue as the evening deepened, later coming into the kitchen to drink a beer by the sink, tipping his head back to drain the bottle. Again he pictured the river from that afternoon, winding along its banks, while Roche scuttled around the office in his shamrock tie, using Post-its to leave messages on people's computer monitors. When Passano started joking about the Post-its, saying, 'What is this, the Dark Ages?' Roche had stared up at him like a newt under a rock.

'Something's going down,' said Passano in the elevator.

'I should probably tell Julia,' Margaret was saying. 'She might hear about it at school. But I hate to say anything. She's already so nervous about Binx.'

Under the hydrangeas bristled a row of popsicle-stick grave markers: one for the parakeet scared to death when Freckles the cat climbed onto its cage, another for Elvis the guinea pig, which keeled over after surviving for several years with a disfiguring eye condition that had to be treated with ointments (not by Bill). The two goldfish in a bowl above the kitchen sink died biannually; Freckles disappeared last fall, most likely eaten by a coyote. He had a memorial marker. Every time a pet died, Julia conducted rituals and burial ceremonies with somber devotion, the animal conveyed to its grave on a little red plush pillow Julia reserved for this purpose, covered by a handkerchief. Happy memories were recounted, followed by the Lord's Prayer and a poem, then the interment. Later, a moment of silence at dinner, a candle lit in honor of the dead. She even buried mice and toads that drowned in the pool. Now there was that lunatic Binx: chewing up shoes and chair legs, barking at every squirrel that ran across the lawn, sending rugs flying as he skittered from room to room. Heart failure, probably, in store for him.

He was starting to worry about Julia himself: how she went around with hair hanging in her face, plugged into her iPod, shutting herself for hours in her room to read books about girls falling in love with vampires. (*What?* she said, whenever he knocked on the door.) Once when he was in her room, he'd found a little china box full of fingernail parings. Hardly seemed to laugh anymore, except when she had a friend over. That little Hannah Melman, for instance. Always a lot of laughing and joking when Hannah was around. 'Hi, Mr Downing! Hey, I like your pink shirt! Is it Valentine's Day?' That kind of kid. Fresh, but fun. Decked out in some cute outfit, little shorts and T-shirts. Margaret kept deploring how short the girls' shorts were, how their T-shirts showed off their stomachs, but he found them charming. Trying out their powers. Skin so pure, eyes so clear. The clean sweet scent of them – kiwi, mango, some fruity shampoo. Maybe he could suggest to Julia that she invite Hannah over more often.

'Absolutely criminal.' Margaret was lying back in her Adirondack chair, waving a hand at a cloud of gnats. It took him a moment to realize she was talking again about the poisoned dog.

'What kind of person even *thinks* like that? I'd honestly like to know. Whoever it is needs help. That dog is going to give me nightmares for months.'

A gust of wind blew into the tree; acorns strafed the roof of their house and then rattled into the gutters. Binx stood up and started barking until Margaret called to him to stop. The smell was getting stronger.

He missed whatever she said next. 'I should go back to school,' she was saying now, as Binx settled once more by her chair, panting. 'Become a therapist. Everyone else around here is a therapist. You know, I bet if you ran out of the house yelling "Help!" doors would fly open and people would rush out with handfuls of Prozac.'

'Jesus.' His forehead was starting to perspire. 'When is dinner?'

Once again he forgot to listen, belatedly realizing her comment about therapists had been a joke. Ever since they'd started seeing Dr Vogel, Margaret had been making jokes about therapists.

'Anyway –' she sat back in her Adirondack chair, stroking Binx's broad head with one hand – 'it really was terrible telling that guy his dog was dead. He couldn't get over it. That's what he kept saying. George Wechsler. Know who he is?

'The novelist,' she said, when he didn't reply. 'He won a prize. He comes to the park sometimes. I've seen him there once or twice.'

'Oh, right.' He had no idea who she was talking about.

'The Fischmans rented out their carriage house. Some-one from Chicago, Hedy said.'

'That's nice.' He watched a bat swoop over the pool.

'Well, that's that,' she sighed. 'That's my news. Julia,' she called out, raising her chin toward the house, 'dinner's almost ready. Are you doing your homework?'

Julia did not answer.

He knew he was not making enough of an effort. Marga-ret, with her news, her reports and small jokes, her flying starts at conversation, was trying so much harder. Every evening she had some disastrous item to offer up. Tonight the dog, but often it was a story from the news online: 'Did you hear about –?' a tornado carrying away a trailer park in Nebraska, pirates kidnapping a family off their sailboat, the stoning of schoolgirls in Kabul, as if to say, 'See? What's happening to us is not so bad.' Then again she might offer something she'd heard on the radio while making dinner, a little mystery explained, how habits are formed or why people applaud after theater performances.

She was trying, he realized with a stab of grief, to be interesting.

Candles on the table, a vase of flowers, something baked for dessert. It was graceful of her, it was valiant. And all he wanted was for her to stop.

How could these feelings be explained, even admitted? And yet they were his feelings. He so wished they were not.

The lawnmower from down the street quit and he could hear the cricket again. Margaret was gazing up at the oak trees, leaves dark now but trunks banded with gold.

'You know –' he stood up to collect their glasses – 'I was

thinking I might mow the grass tonight. I might really enjoy something like that.'

'Oh, I wish I'd known, Bill. It's already done. The landscape guys were here yesterday. I got them to put more mulch around the hydrangeas.'

Mulch. That explained the smell.

Another fusillade of acorns, hitting car roofs along the street with a sound like gunfire. This time Margaret had her hand on Binx's collar, holding him back as he lunged forward, toenails scratching the patio slates.

'Did we need more mulch?' he asked despairingly.

Margaret gave another sigh that for a moment he thought had come from him.

'Hear that cricket,' she said.

3.

Over the park floated white skyscrapers, now and then blocking out the sun which shone superbly as soon as it came out again, gilding rocks, blades of grass, plastic water bottles, scraps of foil, every head of clover. On the green hillside a bush had turned magenta: burning bush it was called, a vivid burst against the cloud-thronged sky.

From eight to ten on most weekday mornings the meadow between the soccer field and the collective gardens fizzed and boiled with dogs – dogs chasing other dogs; dogs running in circles; dogs digging, barking, eating grass, sitting and staring, apparently at nothing. Today there were only the basset hound Lucky, Skittles the Labradoodle and Boris the Old English sheepdog, all on their leashes, hanging their heads under the wide maple tree in the middle of the meadow. Their owners spoke in subdued voices, gazing at their sneakers. These were a few of the regulars, a small battalion who brought their dogs to the park in every kind of weather.

Already rumors of a poisoning had got out, and Naomi Melman was telling the story of how Margaret Downing had discovered George Wechsler's dog beneath the sumac by the woods. Margaret had recounted the story on the phone after dinner last night when Naomi called to talk about the soccer carpool.

'Poor George.'

'I can't even imagine it.'

They all knew George Wechsler from mornings when he brought his white bullmastiff, Feldman, to run with the other dogs. Not that Feldman did much running. He was too big and too afraid of the other dogs – Ferdinand the Bullmastiff, George had sometimes called him. He spent most of his time trundling gently around the edge of the woods like a small white rhinoceros emerging from the jungle. But since last spring, George had begun hiring Wayne the Happy Paws dog walker to bring Feldman to the park. Wayne drove a rusty black van without a back bumper, but it was equipped with dog seatbelts and was capable of seating eight. Occasionally he lost track of one of his dogs; apparently he'd lost track of George's dog yesterday. No one blamed Wayne for trying to make money – he was a graduate student at BU who lived in his parents' basement; he was overweight and had psoriasis and kept scratching his beard; Naomi thought he might be clinically depressed – but he took on too many dogs. They were always running away, jumping the chicken-wire fence and getting into the collective gardens, digging in the soccer field or wading in the creek and afterward shaking mud onto people. Several times his dogs had jumped on elderly residents from Avalon Towers, out walking, and nearly knocked them down. He wasn't always careful about cleaning up after them, either. It seemed pretty clear that Wayne and Happy Paws were a big reason why all those signs had been posted, why there was so much resistance to an official dog park.

Resistance, repeated Emily Orlov, and now maybe worse.

'That's a little paranoid,' said Naomi.

The sun vanished behind another metropolis of clouds. The burning bush faded. Everyone under the old tree shivered. It was that unpredictable time of year when the sun was warm, but the air was cool.

'I'm just glad I have a fenced-in yard.' Sharon Saltonstall creased her wide, chapped-looking face. 'That's what I'm glad of.'

All this time the dogs had been whimpering and groaning, straining at their leashes. Naomi's Skittles was growling at Sharon's Lucky. Now there was an explosion of snarling.

'Skittles!' cried Naomi. 'No!' She pulled Skittles against her legs and made him sit while Lucky hung his head, long flat brown ears trailing on the ground.

'They're so jumpy today,' observed Emily.

'They know something's up,' said Sharon.

The conversation returned to George. George had taught Freshman English to Naomi's son Matthew at the high school before he quit teaching. Impatient, sardonic, unexpectedly emotional: that was George's classroom reputation. Lobbed chalk at his students when they fell asleep but also wept while reading aloud from *Of Mice and Men*. Naomi herself found George complicated, 'a good-enough guy' but also 'arrogant'. She had read parts of his novel on the Amazon website: a mystical Jewish baseball novel. Talmudic references mixed with meditations on the aerodynamics of the knuckleball.

'Wow,' said Sharon. 'Sounds intense.'

George and his wife had recently separated. Last week Naomi had spotted him in Starbucks with his arm around a blonde in biking shorts and a white Spandex top with no bra. But she suggested now that they propose George's novel to their book club. In light of what had just happened, it would be a nice thing to do. She'd mentioned this idea last night on the phone to Margaret, who agreed.

A small round figure had appeared near the collective gardens while they were talking, a black woman accompanied by an old yellow Lab on a leash. Instead of the shorts, T-shirts and sneakers favored by most dog walkers in the park, the woman wore a striped caftan, white and green and shot through with a metallic thread that glittered in the sunlight. A dress that seemed out of season despite the warm sun. Even more noticeably, she wore a red turban.

'Who is *that*?' Emily planed a hand over her eyes.

'She looks like a fortune-teller,' said Naomi.

'I think she's wearing heels.'

The woman in the turban moved closer to the collective gardens, unattended this morning.

She appeared to be examining a patch of staked cherry tomatoes bordered by orange marigolds. They watched as she bent down and murmured something to her dog, her hand a dark starfish on its yellow head. The dog wagged its tail.

'Anyway –' Emily lowered her voice – 'what else did George say?'

'That was it. He was shocked.'

'What a shock for Margaret, too.' Sharon extracted three liver treats from a pocket of her cargo shorts. 'Sit,' she told the dogs, then fed each one a treat. 'Where is Margaret, anyway? I haven't seen her here much lately.'

Naomi slowly shook her head.

'Oh no.'

'Husband –?'

'Not an –?'

'I don't know,' said Naomi. 'Maybe. Midlife crisis.'

'God, the world's a hard place. Does she work?'

Naomi shook her head again.

'Poor Margaret.'

'They're seeing someone, so here's hoping.' Now Naomi lowered her voice. 'But she says she can't eat, can't sleep. I saw her last week at a soccer game and she looked like a ghost.'

Emily said a ghost was exactly what she'd call a middle-aged divorced woman with no job. 'Especially,' she added, 'in this economy.' Emily's husband was an economist. She herself was a professor of Russian Studies. The other women sometimes called her The Pessimist.

'Well, she's not divorced,' said Sharon, who was a social worker.

Out in the meadow the grass shuddered in a sudden breeze.

Now the woman in the turban was walking slowly around the perimeter of the collective gardens' chicken-wire fence, stopping to examine a row of club-sized zucchinis, then moving on to a pumpkin patch, the yellow dog lumbering along beside her.

'I know I shouldn't hold it against George,' Sharon said, returning to their earlier subject, 'but I really think he should have walked that dog himself, instead of hiring Wayne.'

'It was an accident,' said Naomi.

'But if someone did it on purpose?'

'Who would do such a thing?'

'A monster,' said Emily.

The dogs began barking at a squirrel in the tree. Out in the soccer field, the woman's striped caftan rippled as she walked toward the blazing stand of aluminum bleachers and then slowly passed out of sight.

4.

The towering clouds from earlier that morning were gone and the sky was a brilliant vacant blue above the park as Margaret walked Binx across the footbridge. After arriving late on purpose to avoid Naomi, to whom she'd confided too much on the phone the night before, Margaret had then felt ridiculous standing alone in the meadow and decided to take a short walk in the woods. Binx couldn't get into trouble if she kept him on his leash, and anyway Bill had convinced her that whatever had happened to that poor dog yesterday must have been an accident. Coyotes, he thought, were the answer. If it was poison at all, someone had been trying to poison the coyotes.

The woods of Baldwin Park were said to be full of coyotes. Occasionally they materialized at the edges of people's backyards during evening barbecues, dark and bony and somehow accusing, hovering behind rhododendrons and swing sets. Whenever someone's cat disappeared, posters would be thumb-tacked to telephone poles with a grainy photocopied picture: *Have you seen me?* Deer also lived in the woods and flocks of wild turkeys that sometimes bobbled down Brooks Street, like an official delegation with their dark feathers and bald-looking heads, and someone last winter saw a black bear, though the bear turned out to be Mrs Beale, head of the Baldwin Park Garden Collective, examining the chicken-wire fencing in her old mink coat.

But the coyotes were what people minded, and not just because of the cats. It was their howling, demonic and miserable, and their eyes that shone yellow if your headlights caught them at night and how they seemed to appear and disappear right as you were looking at them. They were said to be multiplying. People were afraid one day they might snatch a child, or maul a jogger, and periodically letters were printed in the *Gazette* proposing ways to get rid of them.

Today the woods seemed quiet and unremarkable, wide leaves sifting overhead as Margaret crossed the footbridge and turned to where the woods curved past the soccer field. Three geese flew overhead honking, wings spread like boomerangs.

A man's voice said, 'Hi.'

It was George Wechsler, in a red baseball cap, standing in the shade by the clump of sumac where yesterday she had discovered his dog.

The animal control officer must have described for George the exact location where the dog had been discovered. Yes, look – a strip of yellow caution tape was tied to a sumac branch. Feldman. That was the dog's name.

'You're George, aren't you?'

She introduced herself as the person who had called him yesterday and said how sorry she was. They established that they had met once or twice at the dog park, where Margaret and Binx had only recently become regulars and where George no longer came very often.

He tipped up the bill of his baseball cap. His face was puffy, but perhaps that was how it always looked. He was holding something in his other hand.

'I don't want to bother you,' she said, after apologizing again. 'I was just walking by.'

'Visiting the scene of the crime?'

He was shorter than she was. Green T-shirt, tight enough to emphasize his biceps, denim pants, cowboy boots. There was a stolid pugnacity about him, an exaggerated maleness enhanced by the burnish of dark stubble on his cheeks and a way of sticking out his chin when he spoke. His voice was peculiar: harsh, sand-papery, bordering on derisive.

Binx was sitting at her feet panting, his pink tongue lolling out of the side of his mouth.

'I'm really sorry,' she said again.

'What do you have to be sorry about?' George crossed his arms. He was holding a brown paper bag, patchy with grease. When he saw her looking at the bag, he opened it and pulled out an enormous blood-streaked bone.

'Beef shank. I got it at the meat counter at Whole Foods.'

'Were you planning to bury it?' she asked politely.

'I don't know what the hell I was planning.' He stared at the bone for several moments. Then he made a disgusted noise and tossed it under the sumac bush.

To restrain Binx from lunging after the bone, Margaret began walking backward toward the trail that led into the woods. George followed, asking businesslike questions about how exactly the dog had been positioned when she found him and whether she had noticed anything nearby, a container of some kind, any evidence that he might have eaten something.

'No. Nothing.'

They arrived at the opening to the trail. Actually, two trails, one heading right and one left. She stopped, thinking that George would say goodbye and head back to the meadow, but he took a step or two into the woods, then turned to look at her. 'Going this way?'

They took the trail to the right and for several minutes they walked along in silence, Binx as usual pulling hard at his leash, forging ahead and gagging.

'You can't let him off?' George said finally.

'I'm afraid he'll run away.'

But she bent down and unclipped the leash from Binx's collar. Off he went, bounding down the trail ahead of them. Amber light filtered through the trees and from somewhere a bird cried out. How cool the woods were after the heat of the meadow; she felt herself appreciate the leafy privacy and the subversive sense of being, for a few minutes, where no one would look for her or expect her to be. In another minute they would turn around and the day would flow back into itself.

They walked on, George trudging along in silence. He walked heavily, with his fists cocked backwards; she wondered if he got into fights easily – or if he only wanted to look like someone who got into fights easily.

'So,' she said at last, 'this probably isn't the best time to mention it, but my book club is planning to read your novel. And we were hoping maybe you'd come talk to us? Maybe about how you get your ideas and what you're working on now?'

'Sure,' he said, hardly moving his jaw. 'Be glad to.'

Binx had returned to amble beside them.

'It's so amazing, what you do, making stuff out of nothing.' She was embarrassed to find herself blushing. 'Sort of like being a wizard.'

George gave a snort and kept staring straight ahead, stumping along in his cowboy boots. They had come to a narrow part of the trail, where the trees grew closer together and the underbrush was a tangle of saplings struggling through briar and creeper. A dead tree had fallen across the path; they had to take turns stepping over it.

'So what do you do?'

She pushed aside a whip-like branch and held it for George. 'Me?'

'Husband? Kids? Job?'

'I used to be a teacher before I had a family. Then, you know, I took time off, and then it's hard to get back in once you've been out for a while.'

She listened to the squeak of her leather sandals as they walked along the trail, heading back now to the meadow. The breeze had stopped and the leaves were still. From deep within the woods came a low insect vibration.

'My husband keeps telling me to develop some outside interests.'

He was walking behind her now, twigs cracking and popping under his boots. In her imagination, she continued to talk about Bill, hearing even the timbre of her voice – detached, unguarded, pitched at a reasonable middle register – describing in detail their marriage counseling: Bill saying that he loved her but that something was missing, and that for now they were following Dr Vogel's advice to be honest but kind to each other; in six months they would see where that landed them. It was the uncertainty of everything she was finding so terrifying. Bill wasn't a big talker, lately he hardly talked at all, so she found herself reverberating to every change of mood, every shift in tone. Any disturbance affected her. It had gotten habitual. She couldn't stop herself, even when she wasn't with Bill. It was like being a human tuning fork.

'He suggested tennis,' she said. 'Or squash.'

'Sounds exhausting,' said George.

'You have no idea,' said Margaret.

But he did. When she asked if he had a family he revealed that his wife had left him last spring. 'For two months,' he said, 'I had a heart attack every morning.'

Margaret stopped walking, so abruptly, in fact, that George almost walked into her. She had been staring at the ground, but now out of the corner of her eye glimpsed something large and white flickering through the trees.

'What was that?'

'What was what?' said George in his peculiar harsh voice.

'I thought I saw something.'

George squinted and then turned to look at her, his hands at the back of his belt, hitching up his denim pants.

She smiled apologetically and said she was very sorry to hear about his wife, waiting for him to say more about his separation, but he only made a small, open-palmed 'after you' gesture with one hand.

As they resumed walking she thought how surprising it was that he had confided something so personal to a near stranger and again imagined herself confiding in him, being as frank as he had just been. Well, for Bill it's mostly about sex, she would say coolly. He says he doesn't feel anything. He says he feels dead. His father died in March and, according to our couples therapist, death makes men think about sex. He probably wishes he could be with someone younger. That's what I'm afraid of, anyway. But I'm trying to give him some space, I want to help him go through whatever he needs to go through.

What a remarkable person you are, George would say to her.

Once more she found herself blushing and called for Binx. He came trotting back to the trail to stand by her legs while she fastened the leash back onto his collar. 'A miracle,' she said. 'He never comes when I call.' The trail was now wide enough that George could walk next to her, Binx trotting ahead.

'He's kind of an anarchist,' she said.

'All dogs are anarchists,' George said, 'at heart.'

'Well, some dogs hide it better than others.'

George laughed and said it was a miracle that any dog ever listened to human beings, given that dogs were the ones with big teeth. Then he reached over and rested a hand on her shoulder.

The trail was again stippled by sunlight, a complicated pattern that shifted with the tree branches. She felt the warmth of George's hand against her bare skin, a mild but insistent pressure. And then it was gone; the shade of the woods drew back and together they walked out into the ordinary humming light of day.

5.

The morning after her walk in the woods with George Wechsler, Margaret looked out of her kitchen window to see the door to the Fischmans' carriage house propped open with a battered-looking blue canvas suitcase. On the front stoop were woven baskets of varying size – each filled with books or colored scarves or embroidered pillows alight with tiny mirrors – along with a glossy jade plant in a red glazed pot.

Every fall for the past decade the Fischmans had rented their furnished carriage house to a visiting professor at Warren College, a mile to the south, an easy walk from Rutherford Road. Mulberry-colored and gabled, a smaller version of the Fischmans' house, the carriage house sat at the end of their cobbled driveway separated from the Downings' driveway by a privet hedge, though a gap in the hedge allowed for foot traffic between the two driveways. The carriage house had once been divided into two home offices – both Fischmans were psychoanalysts; she was Israeli, Polish originally – but since their retirement they'd put in a kitchen and an upstairs bedroom. Rental income was nothing to sneeze at, and they liked the idea of having someone to call on in an emergency, especially since Marv's stroke, which left him with a palsied hand and slurred speech. Generally their tenants had not mixed much with the neighborhood. Last year's tenant was a tall gaunt man from

Brussels with grayish teeth who wore dark suits, even on weekends, and never opened his window blinds; his subject was the Dialectic of Counter-Enlightenment. Not exactly a guy to invite over to watch the Super Bowl, Bill had said to Margaret.

That afternoon she and Julia walked across the driveway with a paper plate of chocolate chip cookies, as they always did whenever a new person moved into the carriage house. Even the man from Brussels got a plate of cookies. Julia had not wanted to go and had to be persuaded.

'It's neighborly,' said Margaret.

'People don't do that stuff anymore.'

'Of course they do.'

'No,' said Julia. 'Only you do.'

A small plump black woman met them at the door wearing a green turban, feathery pink mules and a peach-colored silk robe embroidered with dragons. It was two o'clock in the afternoon. She smiled broadly, revealing large front teeth with a gap between them, and introduced herself in a supple gravelly voice as Clarice. Then she thanked them for the cookies and said that they'd have to excuse her, as she was just about to have her bath, thanked them again and shut the door. Margaret and Julia walked back through the hedge.

'Well,' Margaret said as they reached their back steps. 'She seems interesting. I feel like I've met her before.'

'She's black,' noted Julia.

'African-American.'

But Julia wanted to know what if she wasn't: what if she wasn't American *or* African? What she should be called then?

Margaret opened the back door to the kitchen. 'I suppose you'd say person of color.'

'But who *says* that?' Julia loitered in the doorway, voice rising. 'Who says, "Hey, guess what, today I met a person of color"?'

'Let's talk about this inside,' said her mother.

The Downings had since learned that Dr Clarice Watkins was an assistant professor at the University of Chicago. Hedy Fischman said she wasn't sure but she believed Dr Watkins might be a friend of the Obamas. She'd told Hedy she was from Hyde Park, where the Obamas used to live, and mentioned that her mother also lived in Hyde Park. Hedy was slightly hard of hearing, a difficulty compounded by her tendency to talk over other people during conversations, so Margaret thought it was possible that Dr Watkins had said 'Mama', not Obama. What Hedy knew for certain was that Dr Watkins was this year's Talbot Scholar at Warren College, where she was scheduled to deliver a series of lectures on something, Hedy couldn't remember what.

Bill wondered aloud if they might invite Dr Watkins to dinner one evening. It would be interesting, he said, to meet someone who knew the Obamas.

'She *might* know the Obamas. It's not clear. She wears a turban.'

'Is she Muslim?'

Margaret didn't know; she thought inviting Dr Watkins to dinner was a nice idea but worried that an invitation so soon after her arrival might be perceived as too friendly, as if they were trying to ingratiate themselves. Also they had never invited Hedy and Marv Fischman to dinner. Bill found conversations with Hedy in particular to be heavy weather. 'Always analyzing everything.' Her field had been trauma therapy. Dr Doom, he sometimes called her.

The Fischmans would have to be included in any dinner invitation that involved their new tenant. And with Marv's trouble walking, and barely understandable now –

'Forget it,' said Bill.

They were having this discussion as they loaded the dishwasher after dinner. As she was pulling out the box of detergent powder from below the sink, Margaret mentioned that Dr Vogel had sent an email message that afternoon saying that she was going on vacation but would return on October 10th, and she could see Margaret and Bill for a counseling session the following Monday at ten thirty a.m.

'I'll be at work,' said Bill. 'Can't she see us in the evening?'

'That's her only free hour all week.' Margaret shook detergent into the wash and pre-wash compartments of the dishwasher. Dr Vogel had not been able to find a regular time for their sessions, but offered them cancellation slots. She had been recommended by Naomi Melman, who said they were fortunate to be able to see Dr Vogel at all. Often couples stayed on her waiting list for months. Sometimes they were already divorced before she could see them.

'For God's sake.' Bill was checking his iPhone calendar. 'I've got a meeting with Roche that day at ten thirty.'

'I think this is pretty important.'

'I'm not saying it isn't. I'm just saying it's inconvenient.'

Margaret kept shaking out detergent, which spilled across the door of the dishwasher.

'Fine,' said Bill. 'Ten thirty is fine.'

'I'll confirm the appointment, then.'

'Fine.'

Bill started the dishwasher and began wiping down the granite counters while Margaret finished rinsing a pot in the sink. Binx lay at her feet, head between his paws, scolded earlier for licking the plates in the dishwasher while it was being loaded. In the bowl on the windowsill, one of the two goldfish was lurking at the base of their crenellated ceramic castle. Its crisp-looking gills opened and closed; otherwise it wasn't moving.

'One of the goldfish looks sick.'

'Which one?'

'I don't know. Mike or Ike.'

'Better tell Julia. She can get the grave ready.'

'Oh, stop it.'

'*You* stop it,' he said, tossing the dishtowel he'd been using onto the counter.

Margaret heard him head for the hallway and then go up the stairs. Well, there it is, she thought, looking at the dishtowel.

Lights were on inside the carriage house next door, glowing through gauzy saffron-colored curtains that had recently been hung. On the carriage house's back porch, visible above the darkening hedge from the kitchen window, sat two peeling white wicker rocking chairs, one with a new orange African-print cushion. The porch overlooked a simple garden: a patch of grass, a grandmotherly bed of white begonias, a few striped hostas and two leathery laurel bushes in a wash of pachysandra ending in a gray stockade fence.

As Margaret stared out of the window, thinking of Bill's cold shut face and wondering when she had started to be afraid of him – not of him, exactly, but of his impatience with her, which lately seemed to border on aversion – she saw something glide behind the laurel bushes. An instant later a white shape flared up against the fence, like the illumination thrown by headlights of a passing car, and then slid away. But when she turned to look at the street it was dark and empty.

Dr Watkins also had a dog. Aggie, an old yellow Lab, sleepy and benevolent-looking.

Unusual for the Fischmans to rent the carriage house to someone with a dog. They had a dog themselves, an old gray toy poodle named Kismet, as fragile as a Fabergé egg. Kismet had her own chair in their living room and on rainy days wore a pink plastic raincoat; when Hedy encountered someone with a big dog while she was out walking Kismet she often crossed the street, casting reproachful glances at the other dog. People with big dogs did not always take into account that little dogs and their people might be afraid of them.

Hedy and Margaret happened to meet on the sidewalk with their dogs a week later. It was one of those mellow, lingering New England fall afternoons, the light turning apricot as it settled onto hedges and into the tops of the trees, while the air held a brisk sharpened scent, like pencil shavings.

Hedy pulled Kismet away from Binx, but stood close enough to talk to Margaret. Margaret asked after the new tenant.

'Do you know,' said Hedy, 'I was supposed to rent to somebody else, but the college called and asked could I please take Dr Watkins. She was looking maybe three weeks for an apartment. Everyone *said* it was the dog.'

Her small face was deeply wrinkled; but her eyes were dark and bright beneath a cap of thin, soft-looking gray hair that curled much like Kismet's. As usual she wore a black velour tracksuit and black sneakers; she said Marv called it her Geriatric Ninja uniform.

'Do you know what Marv thinks?' she said now. 'It was racist.'

A word she pronounced with relish: ray-*shist*.

'Oh, I don't think so,' said Margaret. 'Not around here.'

Hedy screwed up her face.

'In any case, it was nice of you to rent to her.'

'Yes,' said Hedy. She toyed with her reading glasses, which dangled from a chain of jet beads. 'Dr Watkins is very interesting. She likes Littlefield very much, even though no one would rent her an apartment. An enchanting village, she says. So *heimlich*, she says. A turban and she knows German? Do you know what I told her?'

Margaret did not know.

'I said it was a suburban shtetl.'

Hedy often made provocative statements along these lines – to test her listeners, Margaret had decided. If you smiled, you were thoughtless. If you frowned, you were an idiot.

'Well, most of us are pretty assimilated,' sighed Margaret.

Long blue shadows fell across the sidewalk. Up in a tree a mourning dove was calling out its sad wooing call. *Ah-lone? Ah-ah-lone?*

By hunkering down onto the sidewalk, Binx had managed to creep close enough to nose Kismet's hindquarters. Kismet growled.

'Hah,' said Hedy. 'Look at them. Beauty and the Beast. No, you, Binx. Get away.' Binx sat back, pink tongue hanging from the side of his jaws. 'I heard another dog was poisoned. Yesterday at the park. A terrier. It ate something.'

'Oh, please no, not again.'

'Poisoned hamburger, maybe.'

'I can't believe it.'

'I said to Dr Watkins, don't take that dog to the park. It is too dangerous. Maybe she doesn't listen. Her dog seems well-behaved. But *you* should not take *him*.' Hedy pointed at Binx sitting on the sidewalk panting at Kismet. '*He* wants into everything.'

Binx raised his head, panting more widely.

As they stood talking, Dr Watkins came out of the carriage house with her yellow dog on a leash and made her way down the cobbled driveway, which was littered with acorns like minute cannonballs. She was wearing red patent-leather pumps, a green silk print dress and a mustard-colored turban, and in the poignant evening air these colors, too, seemed saturated, superimposed on the scene behind her. Despite the cobbles and the acorns, she walked easily in her red pumps, swaying from side to side, her dog plodding in front, head down like a cart horse.

'Dr Watkins,' called out Hedy. 'Hello. Have you met Margaret?'

Dr Watkins called back that Margaret and her little girl had brought over cookies. So kind. She didn't know people did such neighborly things anymore.

'Now please, you must stop calling me Dr Watkins,' she said to Hedy as she drew close to them, scowling with mock severity and shaking a finger. 'I am not a cardiologist. Please call me Clarice.' Looking up at Margaret, she smiled. 'Such a beautiful evening.'

Binx and Aggie sniffed each other.

'It certainly is a beautiful evening,' said Margaret.

'We are talking about dogs being poisoned,' said Hedy.

Dr Watkins said it was a terrible thing and she had read about it in the *Gazette*. Then she said to Margaret, 'Dr Fischman here tells me you're the lady who found the dog? That must have been very disturbing.'

'Yes, it really was,' said Margaret. 'To be honest, I can't stop thinking about it. I feel like I keep seeing it.'

Dr Watkins laid a hand across her chest.

'And now it is *two* dogs,' Hedy went on. 'One is an accident. Two is strange. And three, God forbid, would be –'

'A phenomenon,' supplied Dr Watkins.

'It is that no-leash business. People let dogs run in the park with no leash and suddenly people who hate dogs think dogs are taking over the town.'

Margaret reached down to scratch Binx between the ears. Pink cloud bergs drifted above them in the still-blue sky.

Dr Watkins remarked that it was true she had never seen a town with so many dogs. And with so many mixed breeds: golden doodles, schnoodles, cockapoos, puggles. Years ago when she read Dr Seuss books she'd encountered these same creatures and thought they were imaginary.

'Hah!' Hedy turned to Margaret. 'You are right. That is what is happening.'

'I'm sorry?'

'Assimilation.'

Dr Watkins smiled again, showing the gap between her teeth.

'Maybe we could all have dinner sometime,' Margaret said quickly. 'I'd love to have everyone to dinner and, Clarice, maybe you could tell us about your lecture series.'

Dr Watkins said she would be delighted and then she and Aggie went off down the street on their walk.

Hedy watched them disappear around the corner. 'I don't care. I am going to call her Dr Watkins. I like the way it sounds. Or maybe just Watkins. My dear Watkins.'

'I think you should call people what they want to be called.'

'Oh, yes? What should we call you?'

Margaret said Margaret was fine.

'Yes? Well.' Hedy was shaking her head. 'You wait and see. Do you know what I am saying? With all these dogs, these are very strange times.'

6.

The leaves of Littlefield had turned red, yellow and deep bronze, drifting across glowing green lawns, onto hedges and doorsteps and the gleaming roofs of parked cars. As they walked to school, children ran to catch falling leaves before they hit the ground. In the collective gardens, purple aster and ragweed bloomed where the gardeners quit weeding and the pumpkins were fat and orange. Soccer season had reached its apex and in the afternoon squads of girls in yellow jerseys, black shorts and black knee socks sprinted back and forth in the park, while coaches blew whistles and soccer balls flew into the bright air. Houses, stop signs, bicycle fenders, all wore a precise gleaming look, a clarity brought on by the cool dry weather, and in the evenings the light turned gold as it was gathered into the harlequin trees, caught within nets of branches and leaves.

On Rutherford Road, white cobwebs stretched across the rhododendrons in houses where children lived and construction-paper witches and black cats decorated the windows; houses without children had at least a Hubbard squash on the front steps, or hanging from the doorknocker a spray of red and yellow bittersweet.

Three more dogs had been poisoned since Margaret Downing found George Wechsler's dog in the park. A Bellingham terrier, a rescued greyhound and a malamute named Violet that was a registered Canine Health Aide and visited bedridden residents at Avalon Towers. Photos of each dog had appeared in the *Gazette*. Last week the police issued a statement that someone trying to poison coyotes was accidentally poisoning dogs instead and warning the public against taking coyote control into their own hands. Two letters to the *Gazette* put forward other theories: one suggested that the poisoner was trying to frighten supporters of the off-leash dog park; the other, written by a local biologist, pointed out that bittersweet was deadly poisonous: the dogs might have ingested autumn decorations. People should be careful about what they bring into their houses. A public hearing had been scheduled at the town hall to address the off-leash dog park proposal and it was expected that the poisonings would be addressed as well.

These notes and impressions were recorded into Dr Clarice Watkins's laptop, along with what she'd overheard at the Forge Café, where she had taken to sitting at a window table with a view of Brooks Street. The Forge Café occupied a storefront on the site of what was once a blacksmith's shop; a rusty anvil was displayed in the front window, often topped with a wicker basket of plastic daisies. Today the front window had been painted for the Halloween Window Painting contest: within a taped rectangle two white ghosts played soccer with an orange pumpkin, using tombstones as goalposts. She regarded the ghosts closely for a moment before sitting down at her usual table.

Just an hour before, she had attended a Littlefield girls' soccer game, borrowing a fleece lap rug and a folding nylon chair from her neighbors the Downings, who, when she'd expressed interest in local youth sports, had invited her to watch their daughter Julia's team play a team from Walpole.

She sat on the sidelines cheering with the Downings and other families at the park as pink-cheeked girls with muddy knees thudded past, ponytails wagging. Julia Downing was on defense and hung back, often contriving to be elsewhere when the ball hurtled toward her. She was smaller than the other girls. Thin brown hair straggled from her ponytail and stuck to her pale neck. Her expression was tense, wary, at the same time disbelieving, as if she were baffled by everyone else's urgency as they rushed back and forth on the field.

'Come on, Julia,' shouted Bill Downing, less encouragingly as the game went on.

Margaret Downing said, 'Don't yell at her. She doesn't like it.'

Halfway through the game, as Littlefield tied the score, Bill said, 'Look at that Hannah. She's amazing. Three goals.'

And Margaret said, 'You're always watching Hannah.'

Dr Watkins noted down these comments on a steno pad, along with typical exhortations:

'Good hustle, Annie!'

'Get up there, Katie!'

'Go, Rachel, go!'

Only when a pair of gray F-15s from Hanscom Field streaked low overhead, like a pair of flung darts, did the encouraging cries cease for a minute or two.

'Where are they going?' one father wondered as the shattering noise receded.

'They're going somewhere,' fretted a mother.

The game continued on; a Littlefield forward charged the goal with three minutes left. 'Shoot! Shoot!' screamed the crowd. The ball circumscribed an exquisite arc to land just behind the leaping Walpole goalie, her gloved hands reaching, while the cold sun gleamed along the antennas of parked cars and clouds rushed across the bright blue sky.

'Great game,' called Bill Downing a few minutes later, when Julia and another girl trudged across the field. 'Give me five, Hannah. You were on fire!'

'You played well, honey,' Margaret told Julia.

'No, I didn't,' said Julia. 'Did you hear those planes?'

After ordering a cup of coffee, Dr Watkins opened her laptop to read the news online. She subscribed to four newspapers and scrolled now through each of them, clicking first on an article about a Libyan militia attacking a school with rocket-propelled grenades, then on an account of hearings on Afghan war atrocities. In the past hour, the sky to the east had turned a bruised purplish color above Brooks Street while the sun continued to shine in the west; behind the glowing red and yellow leaves, the shining telephone poles, the chimneys and rooftops, the sullen sky hung like a flat scrim, as if the village were a stage set illuminated by klieg lights.

Outside the café's window, beyond the soccer-playing ghosts, a red-faced young father in a royal-blue fleece vest was trying to quiet a crying toddler on a bench in front of the Dairy Barn. A thin, dark-haired boy pedaled furiously past on a green bicycle, eyes narrowed, bike chain rattling, brown and orange leaves flying up from the gutters in his wake. Several yards away two young girls were texting on their cell phones under a crimson maple tree, both frowning, sunlight patchy on their shoulders.

As she sat watching this mildly absorbing scene, it came to Dr Watkins that behind the young father, behind the crying

45

toddler, the texting girls – behind even the boy on the bicycle, that blank-faced boy, with the wind in his face, eyes narrowed, bike chain rattling, brown and orange leaves flying up from the gutters in his wake – behind all of them trailed shadows of previous citizens, previous lengthening restless autumn Saturday afternoons.

She opened a new document and began typing:

For nearly three hundred years people have passed along these same streets. It seems almost possible to glimpse them, those vanished residents: a booted plowman with his oxen, his goodwife in an apron feeding her chickens. It is almost possible to hear them, the plowman shouting at his oxen by the dry cleaners, the woman soothing her chickens in front of the nail salon. For nearly three hundred years this village, like Sleeping Beauty's castle, has remained largely undisturbed by events consuming the rest of the world . . .

Littlefield had come to her attention one morning six months earlier, when it appeared on a *Wall Street Journal* list of the Twenty Best Places to Live in America, each a small city or large town, most around fifty thousand residents, all boasting 'natural beauty' and excellent public schools. 'Good quality of life' was the general descriptor, along with 'Quiet and safe'.

As she read through the *Wall Street Journal* list at breakfast, she reflected that all around the world sociocultural anthropologists like herself were embedded in traumatized places, examining the effects of violence, oppression, need, fear. Why, she wondered, at first idly, then with quickening interest, was no one studying good quality of life?

Littlefield was sixth on the list. Leafy streets, handsome old Victorian houses, fine public schools and a small liberal arts college, and a pond in the middle of town, with a bath-house and lifeguards in the summer. Littlefield was also, she discovered, home to roughly one percent of the nation's psychotherapists.

Three years ago she had received high praise for her study of the effects of global destabilization on urban matriarchal structures, based on her fieldwork in Detroit's inner-city neighborhoods and in the labyrinthine *vecindades* of Azcapotzalco, in Mexico City. ('A thoughtful new voice,' read a review in *American Anthropologist*.) But she'd published little since, engulfed by her teaching duties and by her students, who emailed her day and night with questions and pleas for extensions, visited her office to complain about their grades, then stayed to talk about demanding parents, drunken boyfriends, suicidal roommates – all of this so distracting that she had not been able to settle on a subject for another book. A critical issue for an assistant professor up for tenure in two years.

How did global destabilization, she wondered, register among what must be the world's most psychologically policed and probably well-medicated population?

Over the next months, she held lengthy discussions with Dr Awolowo, her department chair, who, after some hesitation, approved a sabbatical and helped her obtain a fellowship at Warren College. It had been hard to leave her mother, who was getting old and melodramatic, and who had objected strenuously to that year in Azcapotzalco. Still harder had been leaving Dr Awolowo, whom she loved silently and hopelessly (not even her mother knew how she felt about Dr Awolowo), but with dignity, allowing herself a single expression of her feelings: adopting a turban headdress after overhearing the department secretary mention that Mrs Awolowo wore a turban. But by the end of August she had sublet her apartment, packed two boxes of books, along with a set of curtains and several embroidered throw pillows to recreate a homelike atmosphere, also a rubber plant she had nursed through two blights, said farewell to her mother (who at the very end turned up the volume on her TV and pretended not to hear) and drove east with Aggie the dog to Littlefield.

She'd begun visiting the Forge Café after the first dog was poisoned, deducing that she might listen discreetly to conversations in such a central location; earlier she had attempted to eavesdrop on a small group at the park and felt herself observed. The goal was to blend in with the local population, difficult in her case; the only other black people she had encountered in Littlefield so far had been a cashier at Walgreens and a bagger at Whole Foods.

According to a brass plaque beside the cash register, the Forge Café had been owned and operated by the Jentsch family since 1957. Coffee was served in thick white china mugs; hamburgers and club sandwiches came on thick white china plates, with a side of potato chips, whether you wanted them or not, and a pickle spear. In a Lucite container on the counter sat thick hand-cut doughnuts, glaze hardening throughout the day. The Forge Café was neither as clean nor as efficient as Starbucks across the street, and some people said the coffee tasted like scorched bicycle tires, yet older businessmen and even a few of the aldermen considered it necessary to spend half an hour or so every week perched on the rounded stools at the gold-flecked linoleum counter, eating Mrs Jentsch's hand-cut doughnuts, no longer made by Mrs Jentsch, who now lived in Boca Raton, but by a Pakistani law student who came in at five in the morning.

Equilibrium was what she was hoping to investigate, so by the second dog poisoning, which prompted a torrent of outraged and worried letters to the *Gazette*, she was concerned about her fieldwork. By the third dog, which elicited so many letters to the *Gazette* that an extra page was added to that edition, she emailed Dr Awolowo asking for advice.

'I am afraid,' she wrote, 'that the population, which I was counting on to be contented, is instead becoming frightened.'

Fear and doubt may elevate the quality of your work, he wrote back. He advised her to follow the inhabitants around, not ask questions but simply listen to them talk about themselves. He also reminded her that anxiety manifested itself differently in different populations. *Consider this a lucky stroke*. The village was under an assault of some kind and she was ideally positioned to study its coping mechanisms and apparent laws.

It was another stroke of luck, she now realized, to have moved in next door to the Downings, whom she could monitor unobtrusively at close range, especially Margaret Downing, who was so often at home.

Margaret played the piano for an hour every morning in the living room of her big yellow Victorian house. Something classical and melancholy. Afterward she moved back and forth past the tall uncurtained downstairs windows, picking up books, dishes, clothing, whatever everyone else had left behind in their rush to school or work. She walked her big black dog, got in and out of her silver station wagon.

Her clothes were loose-fitting, tasteful, middle-aged: beige, gray or black, brightened by a patterned scarf or an arty hand-knitted cardigan. In the afternoons, when it was time for Julia to return home from school, she stood at the living-room windows looking out toward the street until Julia turtled up the sidewalk under her enormous red backpack.

Almost always, Margaret opened the front door even before Julia gained the steps, each time smiling and saying something that did not arrest Julia's passage, or even cause her to look up. Sometimes Margaret continued to stand in the doorway for another moment or two after Julia had disappeared inside, still smiling, looking into the street.

An ordinary yet oddly disquieting woman. That alert posture, the air of determined grace, like a retired member of a corps de ballet. Her eyes widened whenever anyone spoke to her, even children; often she clasped her hands together against her breastbone as if accepting compliments. Yet whenever Margaret felt herself unobserved, her expression became tremulous, ambiguous, but also attentive. She appeared – besieged. But by what? The Downings had money; Bill was a kindly-looking man (too interested in adolescent girls?); Margaret was slender and attractive, an ash blonde with lightly freckled skin, only faintly lined. (*Another whiny white person*, her mother would say.) But there was something about Margaret's anxiety, if that's what it was, that was unsettling. She seemed to be attending to something just beyond the range of human hearing, something normally audible only to dogs, or bats.

For Halloween the Downings had studded their lawn with plastic tombstones and hung a six-foot glow-in-the-dark plastic skeleton in the dogwood tree by their driveway. Margaret was in charge of most family activities (she had offered the fleece rug and folding nylon chair, for instance, and knew the correct time of the soccer game), but it was Bill who insisted on decorating for Halloween. Usually they didn't do much beyond carving a pumpkin, he'd informed Dr Watkins last week as he was stringing up the skeleton on a sunny Sunday afternoon, but Julia wouldn't care about Halloween much longer and it was time to make the most of what they had left. The skeleton swayed in the breeze above their leaf-scattered yard, casting a long narrow shadow.

7.

Julia was practicing her oboe upstairs. She had a band concert in two weeks, in which she had a short solo, and Margaret had been hounding her about practicing. No trick-or-treating on Friday, she'd finally threatened, if Julia didn't practice half an hour a day. Julia and Hannah Melman were going trick-or-treating together. Supermodels this year. Feather boas and lip gloss and skirts the size of cocktail napkins. Margaret was insisting on pants. Why couldn't they be Gypsies or a pair of dice?

Margaret had just said all this to George Wechsler.

She and George had been in touch by email since their walk in the woods so that Margaret could schedule his visit to her book club in March. But after the third dog had been poisoned, Margaret had emailed George: *I don't think this is about getting rid of coyotes.*

George emailed back: *Neither do I. What we're seeing is essentially a domestic fear campaign. I think town officials have their heads in the sand.*

He said he intended to speak about the effect of the poisonings on the community at the upcoming hearing. In a brief reply that took her almost an hour to compose, Margaret said she agreed with him, and offered to listen to his speech if he wanted to stop by before the hearing, and sent him her street address; but he had not emailed her back after this invitation. The hearing was scheduled for that evening at seven o'clock, and in spite of telling herself that George was not going to stop by – that it wasn't even a real invitation, her email to George, only something she'd offered because like everyone else she was disturbed by what was happening at the park, and of course he'd probably forgotten – she had made a special trip to Whole Foods to pick up wine and a wedge of cheese, and mixed olives, taking so long to decide between Brie and Camembert that she'd had to hurry home, arriving just before Julia's bus dropped her at the corner. Had even gone upstairs to brush her hair after slicing an apple for Julia's afternoon snack, put on eyeliner and lipstick, and changed into her black cashmere sweater.

So she was surprised, but not as surprised as she pretended to be, when her doorbell rang at six o'clock, sending Binx into paroxysms of barking, and there was George, in jeans, a denim shirt and a brown wool jacket with suede elbow patches, and his cowboy boots.

Now he was sitting on a stool at her kitchen island, eating olives from a blue Andalusian bowl and dropping pits into a smaller matching bowl, a wedding-present set, and sipping a glass of pinot noir.

'The problem is,' she said now, running a hand through her hair, 'they have no idea how they look to other people.'

'My boys have given up trick-or-treating.' George spoke grudgingly. 'Though they're pretty much in costume every day, big baggy pants and baseball caps on sideways. Pretending to be "gangstas".'

Margaret had also sent George an email after reading his novel, *Pitch Zone*, about a blind Yeshiva student in Brooklyn who dreams of being the Yankees' designated hitter and spends every weekend in a batting cage in Red Hook teaching himself to hear the difference between a ball and a strike coming over the plate. She'd found the novel sad and funny, genuinely moving, if at the end maybe a little predictable, everything figured out. She had so many questions for George. When you're writing do you live in two worlds? Have you ever met one of your own characters? She'd always thought of writers as reserved, serious. Possessed by their stories, carrying with them small black notebooks, in which they might suddenly stop to write a few words even in the middle of an ordinary conversation. Were they more or less lonely than other people?

Not that she put any of this in her email.

'So, hubby at work?' George was looking around the kitchen as if Bill might emerge from one of the cabinets.

'Yes,' she said, straightening up. 'He works downtown.'

Dr Vogel had suggested that Bill and Margaret each keep a journal about their feelings and then once a week exchange them. In Margaret's journal, a blank book with a nineteenth-century painting of swans on the cover, she had written: *This is a confusing and difficult time, but in times of emotional intensity there are new possibilities for intimacy. More than ever I realize that marriage is a joint adventure, with its own deep mysteries.* Bill had not written much in his journal, which he kept in an old spiral notebook he found in Julia's room; the first few pages were full of math problems, which he did not bother to tear out.

I don't feel anything, he wrote on one page.

'Some kind of money guy?' George was asking.

'Investment planner.'

George smiled and sat back, hooking his boot heels on the rungs of his stool. 'That can't be much fun right now.'

'His office is going through some turmoil, with the new government regulations.'

'About time there were some regulations.'

What an ass, she thought, relieved and disappointed to find that she wasn't attracted to George after all. Those cowboy boots were laughable, for instance. So was his puffed-out chest. And yet it had been a distraction, these past few weeks, to have George to think about. She wondered what his wife looked like.

'So, you were saying your sons are gangsters?'

'Well, no, hard as they try. Just nice boys taking too many AP courses. Though one of their friends got in trouble last week for carrying a plastic pencil sharpener shaped like a pistol into math class. Full lockdown at the high school.'

'Well, people are trying to be careful these days.'

'There's careful and there's crazy.' He ate another olive.

After their walk in the woods, Margaret had spent considerable time picturing their next encounter as somehow heightened, sympathetic. His warm hand again on her shoulder. Herself explaining that she was in the middle of a difficult and confusing time. But now she realized that George had not been entertaining similar fantasies, had most likely shown up at her house tonight because he did, actually, want to practice his speech before the hearing.

'Speaking of crazy –' she twisted the top button of her cashmere sweater – 'I keep thinking I see your dog.'

'Me too,' said George. 'Every time I open the front door.'

Julia's oboe squawked from upstairs. Binx was looking hopefully at the olives.

She stopped twisting the button and cleared her throat. 'I mean, I really think I see him. Every so often I'll be looking out the window or taking a walk, thinking of something else, and then I'll see something that looks like him.'

George drummed his oily fingers on the island's granite surface, leaving small dark prints.

Margaret waited another moment. 'It was pretty upsetting, finding him like that.' Sighing, she poured herself some wine. 'And now three more dogs. It's just scary, knowing someone is out there –'

'Crap,' interrupted George. 'What's out there is a giant piece of crap.'

Together they stared at the bowl of olive pits. A few low notes sounded again from Julia's oboe.

'So,' he said, 'an oboe concert.'

'Well, a band concert. Julia's not very musical,' admitted Margaret. 'But I wanted her to play an instrument and she won't go near my piano. I played all through college. Chamber groups, mostly. Do you play an instrument?'

'Air guitar,' said George.

Margaret looked at the clock over the stove and saw that it was not even six thirty. She asked if he would like more wine.

'Maybe half a glass. Loosen my tongue for my big speech about striking back against fear and paranoia.'

'Do you have notes?'

'I thought I'd warm the crowd up first with a few jokes. Mention that dogs and humans have a lot in common and we should try for some sort of bipartisan agreement. Reach across the aisle.' George selected a large Greek olive.

'No, really.' She was smiling at his forehead, which was high and broad, capped by short reddish curls. 'How are dogs and humans similar?'

'Did you read that study in the *Times* yesterday? Asking married women if they could cheat one time on their husbands without them ever finding out, would they do it? Seventy-three percent said yes.'

She felt her face get hot.

George himself was looking mystified at this turn in the conversation, but he forged ahead. 'Even the women who say they love their husbands. Seventy-three percent. If they had one free pass to sleep with someone else, they'd take it.'

'Now why is that?' she asked unwillingly.

'Because,' he said, 'nobody ever has enough of anything.'

To give herself time to recover from the blush scalding her face, she fetched a package of rosemary crackers and set them out on a plate with the wedge of Brie cheese, which she had left by the sink.

From their glass bowl on the windowsill the two goldfish floated above their ceramic castle, regarding her emptily, opening and closing their mouths.

Perhaps it was only the wine, but now that George had begun talking he became unstoppable, moving on from his speculations about married women to baseball, and then on to the main character of his second novel, a baseball player who had come back from the dead to help his old team win the pennant, while Margaret sat with her hands folded in her lap, wondering what had happened between George and his wife, and Binx lay snoring on the wide honey-colored floorboards by the stove.

The baseball player in his novel was named Moses Finkle. A minor league outfielder who'd had a single season with the Kansas City Royals in 1962 before running his Pontiac into a tree. In the draft George was working on now, Moses Finkle is summoned from the grave by a kid who owns a signed Moses Finkle baseball card, given to him by his grandfather, who always said the world needed more Jewish baseball players. The grandfather dies and a year later, while saying Kaddish at his Kansas City temple, the kid finds the baseball card in his jacket pocket, takes it out and instead of the mourner's prayer starts chanting, *Moses Finkle, Moses Finkle* –

'Oh no,' said Margaret.

'Yeah, so Moses returns and he's a zombie, but he's now an amazing outfielder – shoestring catches, one-handed grabs, dives into the stands and comes up with the ball. Hits ninth-inning home runs in every tied game. But the thing is –' George paused to eat another olive – 'other stuff's got to happen. I can't just write a novel about a dead Jewish baseball player making clutch plays.'

Then he said, 'I'm eating all your olives.'

'That's okay. They're just for us. Bill hates olives.'

Just for us. Had she really said that?

A low quavering note trembled from above.

Margaret poured more wine for George and a second glass for herself, struck by the situation, which had become heightened after all. Sitting in her kitchen drinking wine with a man she hardly knew. Talking about adultery and zombies, surrounded by her blender, her blue enamel Le Creuset pots arranged on a shelf in descending order of size, her stoneware canisters on the counter labeled Flour, Sugar, Tea, all of which now seemed to be watching her. Especially watching from the refrigerator door were magnetized photographs of Julia in a bathing suit on the beach at Wellfleet; Julia on a pony in Wyoming; Julia with Bill in front of the Statue of Liberty, both holding aloft ice-cream cones.

George was finally talking about his soon-to-be-ex-wife, Tina. A personal injury lawyer. Tina was a partner at Weitz, Wilberding. Margaret must have seen their ads on the back of telephone books. No? *We Want Your Auto Accidents, Brain Injuries, Nursing Home Negligence! When You Need Us, We're There for You!*

'That's quite an offer,' said Margaret.

In April, Tina had left George for a massage therapist. Told him that for the first time in her life her needs were being met. At last someone was really there for her.

'I mean, could the joke get worse?' he demanded.

Tina was balking at the amount of alimony George's lawyer had requested, though George was the one with the house and the boys. She was living with her mother until she could find an apartment near her office; the boys spent almost all their time with him. When they were home, that is. Even when they were home, they were slovenly and distracted and practically mute.

'We don't talk at dinner. We masticate.'

He chose another Greek olive and squinted at it. 'She took me completely by surprise, I'll tell you that. I thought we had a pretty good marriage. I mean, we talked. We still had sex. We've got two kids who aren't in jail or rehab. What did she want? Whose needs are ever met? If your needs are being met –' he was pouring both of them the last of the wine – 'you're probably dead.' He set the bottle on the counter and then leaned closer to Margaret, close enough that she could smell him. Ever since her pregnancy days, she'd remained very sensitive to smells and George had a dense odor compounded of perspiration, soap, the oil of his hair, wine, olives, the wool of his jacket, and something warm and moist and faintly mineral, like a whiff of blood.

It was quarter to seven. Julia had quit practicing her oboe. As Margaret put on her coat she called up the stairs to tell Julia she'd be back by eight thirty. 'Your dad will be home soon. He's bringing a pizza. Don't let anyone in, okay? And don't go outside. Promise?'

A long oboe-ish groan from above.

'Binx,' said Margaret, looking down at the panting dog, 'you're in charge.'

Outside, a scimitar-shaped moon hung in the sky. The air was raw and the wind had picked up, scuffling dry leaves across the dark driveway and making the plastic skeleton sway in its tree. It grinned at Margaret as she locked the front door.

George was talking again about money. Despite winning a prize, his first novel had not sold well. He was broke; Tina was going to kill him on alimony; he was borrowing from his father, who was eighty-six and living in a retirement village in Bayonne, New Jersey. It was too expensive for a regular person to live in this town. Did she have any idea how expensive it was? With his second book he was selling his soul and going commercial.

While she listened, Margaret looked up into the shadowy plumage of the oak trees above her. It seemed the woman walking down the driveway with George Wechsler was not her but someone else. She was still in the kitchen, rinsing the wine glasses and setting the bottle in the recycling bin. Now she was sitting down again at the counter, waiting for Bill to come home so she could ask about his day at the office and then, when he was done talking, reach across the counter for his hand and tell him how much she appreciated him and everything he did for his family, that she was lucky to have him in her life, no matter what, that she would try to be less worried about everything, and that whatever needs he had she would try to meet them. Though whose needs are ever really met?

George had offered to drive them both to the hearing. He was a little drunk, she realized, but so was she, so they climbed into his sports car, an old green MG with rusted wheel wells; it stank of damp wool socks and cold French fries despite the pine-tree-shaped air freshener dangling from the rearview mirror.

'I need to appeal more to women,' he was saying as he released the clutch.

Margaret watched as George reversed expertly out of her driveway. His own competence seemed to calm him and he began to talk more reasonably.

'Women buy books. Thirty- to fifty-year-olds, that's the demographic.'

He was thinking of adding a female rabbi baseball fan to his plot, a character who solves religious crimes with her poodle and falls in love with Moses Finkle despite recognizing that he's dead and therefore likely, among other drawbacks, to be impotent.

'A regular putz, in other words.

'You think I'm kidding,' he added as they reached the street.

'You don't have to write a book like that,' she said quietly.

But George's voice had begun to rise once more. 'Kugel the poodle. Kugel barks whenever the rabbi is on the right track with one of her religious crimes. Except Kugel doesn't bark at Moses, because he's a big bone pile. Kugel loves Moses and that's why the rabbi starts to love him, too. The Kugel Krime Kaper. That's what I'll call it. Women love books about romance and dogs. I'll write a whole series. Pink covers with dog bones in the shape of a heart.

'So, whaddya think?' he said savagely, turning on her. 'Is it a sell?'

Lit by the dashboard lights, his face was ghastly, exhausted, like someone who'd been wandering for hours in a vast dark parking lot hunting for his car, resigned to never finding it, yet knowing that it was there. And at that moment, as she gazed back at him with pity and dismay, something enormous and white reared up in the window behind his head. Its nails clicked against the window, its breath fogged the glass. She heard the heavy chain jangle around its neck. A rank earthen smell invaded the car and clung to the membrane inside her nostrils: old leaves and coffee grounds, fish heads and mice, and something dark and secret, fetid, like the underside of rotting mushrooms. Behind it on the black road stood another creature. Smaller, darker, with eyes that glowed yellow in the headlights.

By the time she screamed whatever she'd seen was gone.

'What? What?' George swerved to the right and jolted the car up over the curb a few yards from her driveway, sideswiping a rhododendron bush.

'Nothing,' she said, clutching her hands together. 'Nothing, nothing.'

Then before he could ask her anything else, she leaned across the emergency brake and, in full view of whatever might be out there, she kissed George Wechsler hard on the mouth.

8.

Mrs Elizabeth Beale had been born in the house at 36 Endicott Street, overlooking the park, and there she lived still, at seventy-nine. Built by Mrs Beale's father, president for thirty years of the Littlefield Savings & Loan, the house was a lofty white Greek Revival with two Doric columns, situated in such a way as to suggest that the park was *its* park, a demesne, and that any visitors were either guests or trespassers.

In this house Mrs Beale raised her own children, Tina and Fred, with her husband, Dr Beale, an ophthalmologist, a tall quiet man with a tonsure of brown hair who wore black horn-rimmed glasses that had been in style during the Cuban Missile Crisis. One of his few enthusiasms was new dress shirts – he'd liked their smell – and he had bought so many that even now a stack of new shirts remained in his bureau drawers, shrouded in plastic. Otherwise he was modest to a fault, often apologizing for offenses no one else noticed, like leaving a closet door ajar. For the past ten years his widow had lived in her big white house alone.

Then, six months ago, Tina left her husband – left him with the house on Leverett Circle and their twin teenage boys – and asked if she could move in with her mother.

'I'm done with taking care of everyone. Let George be in charge for a while.'

Mrs Beale, as she was known to everyone, sometimes even herself, had welcomed her daughter back into the house, though she did not endorse the idea of women leaving their families, and worried about the effect their mother's defection would have on her grandsons. She also worried about the loss of privacy sharing her house would entail. She, too, had once taken care of 'everyone', and though she missed her children when they left home for college, she found other concerns to occupy her. For two decades she had contributed a monthly gardening column to the *Gazette* and she chaired the Baldwin Park Garden Collective, an administrative burden that carried with it remonstrations with gardeners whose tomato plants went unstaked and their zucchini unharvested. She had also taken as her personal mission the protection of the park that stretched beyond her windows. A mission that required daily visits to look for litterbugs, teenagers smoking marijuana in the woods, and unaccompanied dogs and children. When she encountered human malefactors, she addressed them with hushed disapproval ('I believe you have discarded a gum wrapper') which she realized was more unsettling than if she had shouted. She also realized that the sight of her battered panama hat and wraparound sunglasses often inspired a frenzy of weeding in the collective gardens.

She had a handsome predatory nose and long, pale, flat weathered cheeks; she looked something like a trout and also something like Margaret Thatcher, though she smiled more frequently than either, displaying long, crowded teeth; altogether her face had a rather daunting charm. She was aware of herself as a charismatic figure on Endicott Street, not entirely popular, but respected. Especially now that she was leading the battle against the proposed off-leash dog run at the park. A ruinous idea, as she had remarked to her neighbors. The park was a haven, not a kennel. Out of this conviction she had conceived last spring of posting signs where dog people tended to gather. Reminders that the park did not belong to them, no matter what they might think. But then someone else had taken up her idea and begun posting crude, ugly signs. Not what she would have written.

And now dogs poisoned left and right, the park turning into a no-man's-land. Horrible, horrible. Ban dogs from the park altogether, for their own good, that was the only answer. She'd devoted her latest column to outlining this position; tonight she planned to defend it.

If only having Tina in the house wasn't such a strain and a distraction. Tina was so unpredictable, in a way Mrs Beale recalled from Tina's adolescence: fogs of brooding alternating with spells of sultry good cheer, alternating with frosty petulance. Also self-indulgent: she turned up the heat, left on the lights. Bottles of chardonnay crowded the refrigerator door where Mrs Beale liked to keep her Lactaid milk; peculiar foods lined the shelves: yogurts and a green vitamin powder that Tina mixed with orange juice and drank at breakfast. Mrs Beale's own daily breakfast was an apple, of which she consumed even the core, and a glass of milk. She did, however, allow herself a finger of Scotch every evening. Sometimes two.

Worst were visits from Tina's new beau, whom Mrs Beale could only bring herself to refer to as 'the Hairy Man'. He wore musky cologne and jackets with Nehru collars. He had big white teeth and a thicket of black hair on his head. He had hair even on the backs of his hands, like a werewolf. Last week he snuck up behind her while she was reading the paper at the dining-room table and put his paws around her *neck*. To get her to loosen up, he said. She'd almost had a coronary.

With all the recent upset she found herself missing her husband. Several times since Tina's arrival, Mrs Beale had opened a shirt package in his dresser. Took out the shirt, shook it. Breathed in a whiff of starch.

She'd even found herself missing George. Two weeks ago he stopped by to fix a gutter that had become detached from the side of the house, said he noticed it while out for a walk. Tina, however, was adamant that she was relieved to be free of George. A monster of self-involvement. A narcissist. Talked about himself *ad nauseam*. Didn't help enough with the boys. She'd had to do all the planning for their bar mitzvahs, for instance, even though George was the one who was Jewish. Never mind that it was Tina who insisted on the bar mitzvahs, George claiming to be agnostic. 'They need something spiritual,' Tina had said at the time. 'This is a frightening world.'

Mrs Beale was fond of her grandsons, but could not detect anything spiritual about them after their bar mitzvahs. If anything they seemed somewhat more material, having received a good deal of money and several electronic gadgets apiece as a reward for those Saturdays spent at Hebrew School.

Final indictment of George: selfish in bed.

'Performance issues,' confided Tina one recent evening when they were sitting at the kitchen table, Tina drinking wine, Mrs Beale nursing a mug of warm milk, while rain smacked against the windowpanes and the radiators clanked. 'So you'd think he'd be willing to try something else. I've got needs, too. But I can count on two hands in all the years we were together that he agreed to –'

'Please,' Mrs Beale said in a small voice.

Tina shook back her lion-colored hair. 'Oh, come on, Mother. Do you even know what I'm talking about? Don't be such a prude.'

Mrs Beale looked deeply into her mug. She had become adept over the years at knowing certain things while simultaneously not knowing them, especially when it came to her own flesh and blood. (Fred, after all, lived with a man.) But she was not stupid or a prude. She knew that people desired things and each other and if she had largely put such desires aside herself it did not mean that she condemned them. But it was also true that she had become slightly afraid of Tina and her needs, which lately seemed to her rapacious and unreasonable and threatening to the rights of those around her. Twice in the last two weeks Tina had mentioned that her mother 'might want to think about moving someplace smaller one of these days'. An apartment in Avalon Towers, for instance.

Tonight Tina was off somewhere, thank goodness, after leaving a wine glass on the kitchen counter instead of washing it and setting it on the drain board. This evening, very soon, in fact, Mrs Beale would be speaking at the town hall. Accordingly, she had two fingers of Scotch while sitting at the kitchen table. At twenty to seven, buttoned into her Burberry trench coat, a Liberty scarf knotted at her neck, she was waiting under the fan light above her front door for her friend Sybil Forrest, who at quarter to seven pulled up in her moss-colored Audi.

'Look at my sedum,' Mrs Beale commanded from the steps. 'Still blooming. Should have died back ages ago.'

'I forgot to take my blood pressure medication,' shouted Sybil, opening her door and emerging partway from the car. 'I don't know if I should go to this hearing.'

The week before, Mrs Beale, Sybil and four others had filed their proposal with the Littlefield Parks Commission to ban all dogs from the park.

'It will be an opportunity to clarify our views, that's all.' Mrs Beale settled herself into the front seat of Sybil's car. Sybil was wearing her raccoon coat, a relic from her days of attending Yale–Harvard games, trotted out for important occasions, otherwise hung in a closet strewn with moth-balls. Stoically, Mrs Beale lowered her window. 'And in *my* view, people have become far too self-indulgent,' she continued. 'Especially with dogs. I saw one in a raincoat yesterday, and four little rain boots.'

'Is that what you're going to say at the hearing?'

'Of course not. I'm simply going to remind everyone that the park was designed for *people* to enjoy nature.'

'Well, good luck,' said Sybil.

Once they arrived at the town hall parking lot, they had to circle twice before discovering a spot by the Dumpsters. Above them loomed the town hall, a turreted granite build-ing that resembled a Bavarian keep. The camphorous smell of Sybil's raccoon coat had made Mrs Beale queasy and as she climbed out of the car she took several deep breaths of chilly air. Gazing at Sybil in her pelts, she could not help feel-ing as if she were about to face a barbarous uprising.

'Of course poisoning dogs is terrible and I urge the police to do everything in their power to catch the perpetrator and bring him to justice,' she said. 'But none of this mayhem would have happened if dogs were kept leashed.'

'Well, I think it's scary,' said Sybil.

'I do not believe in giving in to fear.' Mrs Beale fingered the knot of her Liberty scarf. 'Or to dogs.'

Once inside the two women followed signs to the downstairs meeting hall, a wide, bare room lit by fluorescent lights. At the far end, a low wooden dais was furnished with a long table and padded swivel chairs; below, rows of folding metal chairs were already almost filled. As she scanned the hall, Mrs Beale recognized many people without remembering who they were, and then she caught sight of George. He was at the front of the hall beside a slender blonde woman who seemed to be unwell; she had a hand on her forehead and was very pale. Mrs Beale had forgotten that one of the poisoned dogs had belonged to George, a huge smelly white drooling dog that used to shed all over the furniture. She tried to catch his eye, intending to give him a brief wave, neither friendly nor unfriendly, but George was talking to the poorly blonde and did not look up.

Sybil found them seats to one side of the hall, next to a gentleman with scanty hair dyed the color of aged cordovan; he wore a red and white diamond-paned sweater over plaid slacks and a pair of sneakers.

'Steven,' cried Sybil. 'Betsy, it's Steven Karpinski. Carolyn's husband.'

Carolyn Karpinski had been a member of the Littlefield Women's Club Executive Flower Committee, on which Mrs Beale served for two years as president. An enthusiastic but lazy gardener. Fond of big blowsy sentimental flowers, peonies, cabbage roses, that in their pale fatheaded way resembled Carolyn herself. Weedy garden. Aphid problems, Mrs Beale recalled.

Clasping her hand between both of his, Steven Karpinski leaned over and bussed her damply on the cheek. 'Ceci's dear friend! How she would have loved to be here.'

'Such a loss,' muttered Mrs Beale, withdrawing her hand with difficulty. 'Are *you* here tonight, Steven, because you have a dog? Or are you of the other persuasion?'

'Hah?' said Steven.

'We're talking about dogs,' shouted Sybil.

'It's a dog's life,' he agreed in a loud, triumphant voice. 'We're all going to the dogs! You bet!'

Mrs Beale looked at him with disapproval. 'We are *not* going to the dogs,' she said, 'if I can help it.'

A woman sat down on the other side of her. A black woman wearing an orange turban and a long greenish raincoat of some sort of iridescent material that gleamed like beetle wings.

Mrs Beale greeted her cautiously. 'Pro or anti dog?'

The woman fixed her with a brilliant smile. 'Impartial observer.'

'Hah?' said Steven.

'We're talking about the hearing,' snapped Mrs Beale.

'My hearing's fine! It's a dog's life, that's all I'm saying! I bet *you* agree with me.' He winked at the woman in the turban.

All the chairs were taken, and people lined the walls, by the time six aldermen filed onto the dais from a side door. They settled into the padded swivel chairs, fiddling importantly with their red or blue striped ties, sipping coffee or nodding to people they knew; one of them grinned and cocked his finger at someone. Mrs Beale eyed his expensively cut gray hair, large brown eyes and long, straight nose; he resembled a lanky television actor she'd seen in truck commercials. While the other aldermen glanced through their notes, this one lounged in his swivel chair, chewing a toothpick, a small American flag pin affixed to the lapel of his dark suit.

Politicians, she thought, are an indulgence.

By seven o'clock the doors were shut. One of the aldermen, a dark sorrowful-looking man with eyebrows like Leonid Brezhnev, announced that the hearing was now under way and that the topic was Baldwin Park. After reading aloud a police report on the poisonings at the park, then a description of the proposed ban 'on all canine visitors', as well as the ordinance for a designated off-leash area, he invited residents to state their support or opposition to either one. Chair legs scraped against the floor as people left their seats and waded into the aisle, lining up for their turn at the microphone, Mrs Beale last among them. She was startled to see George in line five or six people ahead of her.

The first speaker, a white-haired woman in a magenta sequined sweater, identified herself as a resident of Avalon Towers, and began by saying she loved dogs and was appalled by recent events, but that she felt the park should be for everyone and not just dogs. A few boos sounded from the audience.

'Dogs often don't come when they are called,' insisted the woman into the microphone and then described being knocked down by a Weimaraner. 'They are out of control when off their leashes. They're frightening. I'm sorry about those poor dogs being killed but I think it's their owners' fault.'

More booing from the hall. The chief alderman banged his coffee mug against the table for order. Mrs Beale watched the woman stumble back to her seat, a crimson spot high on each cheekbone.

Next a burly bearded young man wearing an old green MIT sweatshirt that appeared to be covered with dog hair. What *he* thought was at fault were the mean-spirited signs posted in the park. 'Put a muzzle on whoever's behind those signs,' he mumbled, scratching his beard. Several people shouted, 'Hear, hear.' Mrs Beale stiffened.

A spiky-haired woman in a potato-colored jacket approached the microphone. 'Do *children* always come when they're called?' Her silver nose ring glinted under the fluorescent lights. 'If you want dogs leashed, why not leash children, too?'

Stepping back from the microphone, she plunged a hand into the satchel slung over her shoulder and brought up a handful of yellow buttons, which she passed around: KIDS ARE FOR PEOPLE WHO CAN'T HAVE DOGS.

Absurd, Mrs Beale muttered to herself, shocked to see how many people reached for the buttons. It was getting very warm in the meeting hall; she loosened the knot of her Liberty scarf.

She had begun to lose track of the speakers when a small man in a teal-blue suit, a knobby-faced fellow with a dark goatee, introduced himself as Mr Eric Dibler. A strange look to him, both seedy and superior; he reminded her of a hillbilly preacher. In a mechanical voice, Mr Dibler explained that he had a master's degree in environmental science and had conducted a study of dog waste in the park. After exhaustive calculations, he estimated that three tons of canine 'sewage' was being deposited there every year based on the number of dogs per capita in Littlefield, at the moment roughly point six. He spoke of 'contaminants'. He referred to dogs as 'producers'. He frequently wetted his lips with his tongue, his mechanical voice becoming strangely mesmerizing, so that Mrs Beale found herself both embarrassed and enthralled, waiting to hear what he would say next.

At last he stopped speaking and gave a motoric twitch that shook his entire body before moving aside for the next speaker. Then he changed his mind and pitched back toward the microphone.

'And for your information,' he shrieked, almost knocking the microphone out of its stand, 'KRAP is PARK spelled backwards.'

'All right, all right.' The chief alderman waggled his black eyebrows. 'Thank you very much. Next.'

She was really beginning to feel hot standing in the aisle under the fluorescent lights of the hall. Her feet hurt. She should never have worn her black shoes with the Cuban heels, but she had wanted to dress respectably for this evening. A shame that no one in line was well-mannered enough to recognize that an elderly woman should be allowed to move up to the front.

A woman testified that she would like to see a leash law for cats, to keep them from killing birds in her yard. Then it was George's turn. He spoke in defense of dogs that, like humans, needed a chance once in a while to be free. The pursuit of happiness should be a dog's right, too. After the grating tones of Mr Dibler, George's voice sounded deep and even as he described how he had raised his dog, Feldman, from a puppy and how Feldman used to greet him whenever he came home, his whole body wriggling with joy. Happy to wait for him in the car, sitting right behind the steering wheel. Happy to sit on the couch to watch TV. Happy just to be alive. That was what it was like to have a dog. They reminded you of the basic joy of being alive, which, God knows, was easy to forget.

'Dogs are dying out there,' he said. 'For no other reason than somebody's sick fantasy of what a park should be like. Is this the kind of town we want for our children? Do we want to be driven by fear, not even knowing who we're afraid of?'

Several people stood to applaud. 'Who's sick?' Steven Karpinski could be heard asking. Mrs Beale felt light-headed and found herself squinting as if through smoke.

Alicia Rabb, her neighbor from two doors down, took command of the microphone. Alicia was small and sharp-featured, with black spiky eyes and a blonde pageboy; she was given to what Mrs Beale thought of as 'ethnic accessories'. Tonight she wore a white chinchilla vest over her turtleneck, tight denim pants and long feather earrings. Alicia leaned too close to the microphone and, through a painful squeal of feedback, said that because of the poisonings, *her* children were afraid to visit the park, which was why, after a lot of soul-searching, she had decided to support the ban on dogs.

'Children have a right to their games,' her quavering voice boomed through the microphone. 'They have a right to feel safe in the world and wonder at nature. Native Americans have a phrase for childhood, it's the Time of Awe.'

75

'Or the awful time,' said a disrespectful person, quite audibly, from near the front row.

It sounded like George. That was the sort of thing he would say. Mrs Beale was sure it was George. What a boor. A narcissist. Tina was right. Perfectly understandable why she'd left him. At that moment Mrs Beale was visited by an image of Tina splayed naked on a bed wearing her reading glasses, pointing instructively at the dark figure of a man poised above her. The nausea quivering in the pit of her stomach took a lurch.

'We are all children in this world.' Alicia turned and gave the hall a black spiky look. 'Please.' She turned back and took hold of the microphone with both hands. 'Protect the park. Protect us all. Give our children back their childhoods.'

Very moving, thought Mrs Beale faintly. She began to feel sorry for the Rabb children, until she remembered who they were: a pack of skinny blue-eyed youngsters with chaff-colored hair and scabby legs, who were often barefoot, regardless of the weather, and wore expressions of malevolent innocence that frightened even the postman. They threw pine cones at bicyclists riding by and squirted them with squirt guns, and one of them, the oldest boy, had been sent to counseling for something to do with a gerbil. Neighborhood cats avoided their yard. In September two of the Rabb girls ran through the neighborhood stealing flowers and ferns from people's gardens, then tied them into sloppy bouquets to sell for five dollars each at the Harvest Fair – in some cases hawking flowers to the very people from whom they had stolen them – before being apprehended by Sybil, whose entire bed of dahlias had been decimated.

Alicia sat down, looking proud and saddened in her chin-chilla vest. The two people in line ahead of Mrs Beale each spoke, both members of the Off-Leash Advisory Group, but she was too preoccupied with her own increasing physical discomfort to listen.

'Have we had dinner?' Steven Karpinski was asking.

Mrs Beale was the final speaker.

She gazed at the microphone with distaste. A long thrusting metal thing with a dark, globular foam knob.

'Littlefield is being overrun by dogs,' she heard herself say in a thready amplified voice, 'and we seem to feel there is nothing we can do about it. That is why this terrible person is acting in such a dreadful fashion. But we *can* do something.'

A good start. The crowd, which had grown restive after Alicia Rabb's speech, now settled down and seemed to be listening. Her energy returning, she went on to outline her proposal for a general ban on dogs in the park, enumerating the various ways in which dogs had not behaved like good citizens in the past, pointing in particular to several occasions when the collective gardens had been ravaged. The latest offense,' her voice was getting raspy, 'is a large hole that was dug in a gardener's pumpkin patch.'

She caught sight of Mr Dibler's stern knobby face; he was looking at his watch.

'But I'll tell you what I really mind,' she said, and paused to breathe into the microphone. Her heart was thumping. What did she really mind? Aphids. Tina's unwashed wine glass. The mothball smell of Sybil's raccoon coat. Those unopened packages of her husband's shirts and the thought of moving someplace smaller one of these days.

George's great pale slavering dog appeared before her: that dog, sitting in the front seat of George's car behind the steering wheel.

'What I *really* mind –' she grasped the microphone stand with a trembling hand – 'is the way *dogs* are being allowed to run things. A lot of very *high and mighty* people around here would tell you that dogs have as much right to the park as we do.' She turned to glare at where she imagined George to be sitting. 'But let me ask you, do *dogs* pay taxes?'

Someone began to shout from the audience. Other people shouted back. She touched the knot of her scarf. Her feet ached in her Cuban heels and she really was very hot. She had said what needed to be said. Nothing more could be expected of her. She must sit down, and yet her chair was so far away and everyone seemed to be yelling. A roaring reached her as the combined voices of the audience swelled fiercely and incoherently, like the sound of waves breaking on rocks, and out of nowhere that dog came leaping, white and enormous, its great red jaws opening wider and wider so that she could see all the way into its black gullet where there was nothing left for her in the world.

The alderman with Brezhnevian eyebrows banged on his desk with his coffee mug, banging so hard the coffee mug broke and flew into pieces. George had appeared beside her and now offered his arm.

'Allow me,' he said, his breath wreathing her ear, smelling of olives. She clutched gratefully at his arm with both hands and allowed herself to be conducted back to her seat.

Sybil was waving as if hailing a taxi. The black woman in the turban had moved over to give Mrs Beale her seat on the aisle; George said something friendly to the woman as he helped Mrs Beale sit down.

'Are *you* sick?' Steven Karpinski bellowed from the other side of Sybil. 'You look like you ate a mouse.'

'No, no,' she said gruffly. 'I am quite all right. Thank you,' she tried to say to George, but he had already moved away and was heading back down the aisle.

The hearing ended with the chief alderman declaring that they would consider both proposals, for a dog park and for a dog ban, at their next meeting. Everyone gathered their coats. At the front of the room the tall, actorish alderman was speaking to Alicia Rabb, his hand on his chest as if reciting the Pledge of Allegiance.

'Well, I hope we'll all survive until then,' said Mrs Beale aloud.

'Do you think we will?' The woman in the turban gave a gap-toothed smile.

'I suppose.' Mrs Beale felt dizzy again. 'I don't know.' She closed her eyes. And yet it was true that when she opened them she found that she was still in her metal folding chair and everything was very much as it had been.

9.

Dr Watkins was making progress in getting to know the inhabitants of Littlefield, as she had written to Dr Awolowo. In addition to her observations of the Downing family, she had met quite a few residents at hearings at the town hall, which she attended weekly, including hearings on the school budget and most recently at a hearing on what was now referred to as 'the situation' at the park. As a result of attending so many hearings, she had been invited to join a Save the Park task force and to attend a planning meeting of Celebrate Your Heritage Day ('We're especially interested in tribal cuisine,' the chairwoman told her. 'Any favorite dishes you might like to prepare?'). Most recently she had accompanied Margaret Downing to a cocktail party reception at the home of Dr Naomi Melman, who lived in a brown-shingled Dutch colonial behind an octopus-like forsythia bush on Ballard Street.

For the last four years Dr Melman, a family therapist at the Jewish Community Center, had given a popular once-a-month lecture on improving personal happiness, advertised in the *Community Center Bulletin* as the Live & Love series. These lectures had just been collected in a self-published book with a matte pink cover titled *The Bright Side: Feeling Better About Bad Things*, the letters picked out in scarlet, available at each lecture, $10.95 apiece, and on sale at the reception, twenty percent of the proceeds going to Walk for a Cure. A young woman in a trim black caterer's uniform that buttoned down the back took guests' coats as they entered the house. A crowd of well-wishers and friends pressed into the dining room, where Dr Melman sat at a table covered with a pink cloth and stacked with her books. She had a short wedge of black frizzy hair and a long, sallow face that appeared and disappeared as she signed copies of her book and accepted personal checks, each time dropping them into what looked like a metal tackle box and closing it with a snap.

When Dr Watkins held out her copy to be signed, Dr Melman looked up briefly and gave her a thin-lipped smile. 'Life is Good,' she wrote across the title page. 'Cheers, Naomi.'

The living room was decorated with pink balloons and six small, round, pink-draped tables; pink pillar candles flickered on each table set with a bouquet of small pink roses and sparkly pink swizzle sticks, plastic champagne glasses, a bottle of pink champagne and a tray of crackers topped with salmon paste. Margaret had found two seats at a table with a broad-faced social worker named Sharon, who had a pink blaze in the front of her short gray hair.

Sharon began talking about town budget cuts as soon as they sat down, especially cuts to the elementary school budget which had wiped out all kindergarten field trips along with the third-grade recorder concert. 'I usually *do* look on the bright side,' she insisted, making the flame of the pillar candle sputter. But it was getting impossible these days. So much wasteful spending. Take, for instance, the lavish new high school and the school superintendent's exorbitant salary. And look at the epidemic of pulled fire alarms at the middle school – six hundred bucks every time the fire department had to be dispatched, because some kid wanted to get out of a math test.

'But what if that's not it?' Margaret was toying with the candle, dipping a swizzle stick into the pooling wax surrounding the wick. She'd drunk two glasses of champagne while Sharon was talking and now her hand seemed a little unsteady. 'What if they're pulling alarms because they really are alarmed about something? Kids are like dogs with earthquakes. Isn't that true? They can sense something's wrong without knowing what –'

Just then her swizzle stick caught on fire, blazing up with an acrid stink and almost singeing her fingers before Sharon doused it with what was left in the champagne bottle.

'Sorry,' said Margaret, looking at her fingers. 'I don't know what I was thinking.'

Added to these concerns, the weather. Cold weather had arrived in New England earlier than usual. A few nights after Dr Melman's reception, a storm rushed through the village, hurling rain against windows like handfuls of gravel; the next morning almost every yard was covered in a sodden half-frozen mat of brown leaves. What leaves remained on tree branches rattled in the breeze with a ghostly papery sound in the evenings when Dr Watkins walked Aggie down Rutherford Road toward the village after dinner, peering into the lit windows of houses as she passed by. Such unremarkable houses during the day, sunlight falling flatly against painted front doors, raked lawns, empty driveways. But at night the same houses floated behind their shadowy shrubs and walkways, hushed, battened, as mysterious and provisional as ships moored in a dark harbor.

Sinister shapes loomed up at her only to be revealed the

next morning as rhododendron bushes, garden sheds, bicycles. Why were the suburbs felt to be safe? They seemed more unsettling, at least at night, than any Chicago neighborhood, where at least there were streetlights. *Never trust a place without sidewalks*, her mother always said.

One night she passed a parked car and there was Margaret Downing, kissing a man who was not her husband.

The following week, out with Aggie later than usual after typing up her notes, Dr Watkins spotted Bill Downing in a dark overcoat and a black wool cap on Ballard Street.

He was standing in the street with his big black dog, in front of the Melman house. Standing just beyond the reach of yellow light thrown by the Melmans' windows, but his face was visible to Dr Watkins as she approached in the darkness – and on it she perceived a look of such monstrous suffering, as if it were not a man who stood there, but something that had consumed the man and now occupied his body. It was a look of wooden self-consciousness, fraudulence, vacancy, a kind of flat-line anguish that was almost frightening. Even when he turned, startled, to say good evening to her, that look did not quite leave his face.

10.

He recognized her from his mornings at the park: the owner of Boris the sheepdog. She was standing with a little boy on the sidewalk outside of the Forge Café, the dog with them. George stopped to pat Boris's shaggy head, wondering, as people always do with English sheepdogs, how Boris could see anything.

He straightened up, smiling guiltily. She smiled back, understandingly.

'Emily.'

'Yes, of course.'

Christmas lights were already blinking from a few store windows though it was still a week before Thanksgiving. A cardboard turkey with a burnt-orange accordion-pleated tail had replaced the basket of daisies atop the anvil in the café's window. Soon enough the turkey itself would be replaced by a white plastic Christmas tree sprayed with glitter and decorated with frayed green and red silk balls, but for now the turkey kept a beady vigil as passers-by walked back and forth on their way home or out on errands. Door chimes tinkled as people went in and out of shops, while in the distance rattled the trolley. It was just past four thirty but already the trolley lights were on and shop windows were lit, the sky had a dull rosy-amber tint above the rooftops and the air smelled fresh and cold and watery, as it does just before snow. Here and there the sidewalks were rimed with ice.

Emily wore a long black wool coat that blew about the tops of her black boots; long blonde curls blew about her face and small pink nose, catching on her little round gold-rimmed glasses.

'And this is my son,' she was saying, 'Nicholas.'

Nicholas was in a red parka, a red fireman's hat and blue sweatpants tucked into a pair of yellow rubber boots. 'Ready for any emergency,' said Emily. 'Right, Nicky?' Nicholas nodded solemnly.

'And where are you off to, George?'

He was on his way to meet Margaret for coffee at the Forge. She had requested this meeting. Her email had read: *We should talk.* One of the worst sentences in the English language, in his opinion. Second only to: *Who do you think you are?* Always followed by what someone else thought you were, rarely a happy definition.

He hadn't seen her since the evening of the town hall hearing, when she'd thrown herself at him in his car. He had kissed her back. They'd sat kissing in his car at the bottom of her driveway for maybe five minutes. He tried to be muscular and commanding with his tongue, as he imagined her investment-planner husband must be. Then they broke apart and drove to the town hall in silence. She was trembling hard, pulling at the fingertips of her leather gloves. He figured she felt guilty about kissing him, and after the hearing, as he drove her home, he resolved to let her make the next move. In the car she began talking in an unnaturally high voice, reviewing what had been said at the hearing, and marveling at how, after so much discussion and event, nothing had been accomplished. It had started to rain.

'Politics.' George was looking at the road through his

windshield wipers, trying to decide whether to forget about his strategy and kiss her again.

He understood she was rattling on because she was nervous, because she was waiting for him to say something about their kiss in the car. Maybe he'd made a mistake by waiting for her to explain why she had kissed him. She must be hoping for some kind of declaration. But what could he say? Love me? Save me? Feed me olives? At the very least, could you call my wife and tell her I'm not such a bad guy?

Her face was turned toward her window, as if she were searching for something in the dark. By now she must be desperate to be rid of him, already picturing herself safe at home with her husband and daughter: her husband who worked 'downtown' and her oboe-playing daughter. Back in her house where the laundry was folded, the bills paid, extra toilet paper stocked in the cabinet. A palace of order and solvency.

As they pulled into her driveway, light from the house's tall front windows spilled onto the wet front steps and the privet hedge, illuminating pale tombstones on the lawn and the skeleton hanging from a dark tree. He could already see her hurrying up the front steps. She would shut the front door behind her, take off her coat and hang it neatly in the closet. Walk down the polished floorboards of the echoing hall, set her purse on the kitchen island where the last olives would be in their bowl and the plate of Brie and crackers not put away, and the two empty wine glasses on the granite counter by the sink. Call out that she was home and lean down to pat her big black dog as he ran at her legs. Tomorrow morning she would sit at her piano, reassured that no real harm had been done by her drunken impulse to kiss a man two inches shorter than herself, who needed a haircut, and a new pair of shoes, and whose novel, which took five years to write, had earned less than what her husband must make in three weeks.

All of this was so plainly before him that George was almost surprised to find Margaret still in his car, her profile softly blurred against the rain-streaked glass, the pine-tree air freshener dangling between them.

'About what happened earlier,' she said.

He said curtly, 'What happened?'

They sat for several minutes listening to the rain tapping coldly on the roof of the car.

'Nothing. Never mind.' Her voice was shaking. 'Thank you for the ride.'

Then she got out of the car and slammed the door, hurrying up her shining driveway, lit up by his headlights, before vanishing around the side of the house in a pocket of darkness.

What an ass he'd been. Now whenever he thought of that evening, she seemed lovelier than he'd first realized. More perceptive and intelligent. There was something about her – a kind of awareness, a responsiveness – that might leap out, suddenly, right at you. And yet, there was something depressing about her, too. Nervous. That shriek in the car, for instance, had made him jump half out of his skin. She had kissed him. No denying that. But then he'd behaved like an ass, let her go running back to her house when she'd clearly wanted to talk.

We should talk.

And so he was standing outside the Forge Café on a cold afternoon, under the skeptical eye of a cardboard turkey.

But he was early, and in no hurry to sit at a table by himself, drinking bad coffee, waiting to be told probably that he was an ass, so when Emily said that she and Nicholas were on their way to the Dairy Barn for an ice-cream cone, he fell into step beside her. Boris shambled between them, tugging at his leash.

'Nicholas is getting a reward for earning five beads for his bead jar today,' said Emily.

Nicholas received one bead for each calm or polite act he performed when he would have liked to do the opposite. Ten beads equaled an ice-cream cone or a candy bar. Beads could also be lost. She smiled down at her little boy and took his hand.

'But you're not going to lose any today, right, buddy?'

Nicholas gave her a panicky look from under his cap.

Emily listed Nicholas's latest achievements: that morning he had put on his coat without crying, climbed into his car seat without being asked, allowed Emily to leave him at the door of his classroom without grabbing her skirt and crying, and eaten his snack even though it was not macaroni and cheese.

George congratulated Nicholas, feeling sorry for him, his difficulties exposed so starkly in front of a stranger. Why did women believe that other people would find the minutiae of their children's lives interesting? He found his own sons interesting, but they were in high school, and actually were interesting, if only because of the depravity and risks involved in being in high school, and when they were younger he had been conscientious about not talking about them too much. Having children was a privilege, as Tina used to say, and like most privileges should be enjoyed quietly and mostly at home. He pictured Tina in her nubby pink flannel nightgown, wearing her glasses at the breakfast table, the boys beside her in matching pajamas patterned with trains, their thick hair sticky from sleep, sharing a plate of brown-edged apple slices.

He realized Emily had asked a question. 'I'm sorry?'

'How's the new book?'

'Oh, coming along.'

Meaning: how could you not realize that it's a disaster, a dull joke?

Emily gave him another understanding smile. 'I hear you're going to visit our book club in March. I'm really looking forward to it.'

He grimaced in a way that he hoped looked self-deprecating. They walked on for a few more paces and then Nicholas stopped in front of the Dairy Barn, a storefront painted black and white, designed to look like cowhide.

'Well, here we are,' said Emily. 'You've probably got a million things to do – but, if you don't, would you like to help us celebrate?'

From past mornings at the park with Feldman, George had perceived that Emily was not on steady ground with the other Ladies, as he used to call them. Maybe it was because she was a little younger than the rest of them, or because she was always talking about Gulags and peasant uprisings, but he got the sense that she was tolerated rather than embraced. And Boris was considered the most obstreperous dog in the park, barking and splashing into the creek, trying to hump other people's dogs, digging holes under the chicken-wire fence of the collective gardens and chewing holes in their hoses.

That dog, people always said when referring to Boris.

He felt a gust of sympathy.

'Okay,' he said.

Boris had begun barking at a bug-eyed Pomeranian sitting inside a parked Subaru. Emily tried to subdue him by grabbing his muzzle and holding it shut. 'Hush,' she said, then tied Boris's leash to a parking meter on the sidewalk outside the Dairy Barn while the Pomeranian scrabbled at the car window with its tiny paws and Nicholas looked on seriously under his fireman's hat.

Piano music began to emanate from within Emily's black leather bag, reminding him again of Margaret. He asked her what it was.

'Rachmaninoff.' Emily had opened her bag and was dredging up pens, books, tea bags, lipstick, tissues. 'Piano Concerto No. 2. It always makes me think of the years just before the Revolution. The unrest. Can't you hear it?'

Nicholas turned to look up at his mother in the doorway of the Dairy Barn. He was a small child, smaller than most six-year-olds, and yet there was something about his thin bluish face that was almost elderly.

Rachmaninoff continued to play, but she closed her bag. She had promised Nicholas not to answer her phone, she confided to George, unless for an emergency.

'Isn't that right, Nicky?'

Still her phone continued to ring as two teenage girls wearing long sweaters, tight jeans and tall brown sheepskin boots walked around them and opened the door to the ice-cream parlor. The smell of sugar surged into the cold air. Nicholas's chin trembled. His fingers twitched.

'See all the people who are *ahead* of us!' he cried out suddenly in real anguish. 'Mommy! There won't be any *ice cream* left!'

'Don't whine, Nicky.'

'But you're going to answer your *phone*. You're going to answer it *first*.'

'No, I'm not.' Emily gave George an apologetic look, then put a hand on Nicholas's back, opened the door and propelled him into the store. George followed, reluctantly. The door closed with a firm click. From outside on the sidewalk, Boris started barking.

They joined a line of seven or eight people at the counter, including a black woman George recognized from the town hall hearing a few weeks ago; she was wearing a white rabbit fur hat and a full-length white down parka that made her look like a snowman. She turned to smile at Nicholas, who stared back at her tearfully.

Emily's cell phone had mercifully gone silent. The call might have been from her husband, Jonathan, she told George, closing her bag. Jonathan was in New York, presenting a paper at a three-day economics conference. Accompanied by one of his graduate students. Willa Clamage.

'Rhymes with *fromage*.' Emily made a grim face.

Outside Boris was still barking. 'Whose poor doggie is this?' a woman's voice could be heard saying. 'All tied up alone on the street!'

Emily made another face, but did not turn around to look through the plate-glass window at Boris and whoever was fussing over him.

Willa Clamage, she went on to explain, lowering her voice, was the sort of young woman who wore ballet flats and short filmy dresses, even in November. Otherwise she was very smart.

'Most prized of all virtues in a graduate student,' Emily said moodily, resting her hand on Nicholas's shoulder. 'Second only to being impressed with your faculty advisor.

'I don't know why I'm telling you this,' she added.

It was clear to George that she was trying to distract his attention from Nicholas, who was clutching at her black coat, his face twisted with anxiety under his fireman's hat; but remembering Tina's accusation that he didn't listen to people so much as wait for his turn to say something, George decided to stay silent. He smiled sympathetically and, to his surprise, Emily went on with her story.

Three weeks ago, Jonathan had invited Willa Clamage to dinner. She arrived at the front door in a black slip of a dress. No coat. 'Oh, hi,' she said, as if surprised to find Emily in the doorway, and handed her a chilly narrow palm to shake.

'Welcome, friend,' Emily heard herself say. This was not a greeting she had ever offered to anyone else in her life. It made her sound Amish. What had possessed her? Again she made a wry face and George laughed. Emily's tale began to unreel before him. Willa Clamage in her black dress, white, severe, bird-like collarbones on display, facing off against pink-nosed, bespectacled Emily in an apron, wiping her hands on a dishrag.

Willa had not offered to help Emily in the kitchen, which Emily would never have allowed her to do – 'Still, it's nice to be asked.' Once dinner was served, Willa hardly acknowledged the meal, an intricate Provençal beef stew, served with home-made bread, followed by a pear tart. She had brought a bottle of chianti, which though reasonably good was not what Emily would have chosen to serve with her stew. Chianti was a thin wine. A big, full-bodied malbec would have been better. As he pictured Emily drinking Willa's thin chianti, George heard Willa's low nasal voice asking Jonathan complicated questions about the GDP that Emily could not follow. Whenever Jonathan spoke, Willa looked into his eyes, occasionally arching her back and lifting her slender white arms to bunch her black hair between her hands.

As soon as they had finished eating, Emily got up and bustled around the table, stacking bowls and gathering plates, briskly telling Jonathan to sit down when he offered to help. Poor overburdened Emily. Stews and home-made bread must be rarities, events to be celebrated and not something simply expected of her. But instead of celebrating his wife, and loading the dishwasher, and then giving her a back rub while listening to her analysis of fluctuations in the Russian ruble before 1917, weak-chinned Jonathan had volunteered to drive the coatless (very smart) Willa home.

Willa Cla<u>mage</u>, rhymes with damage. The schmuck.

'It really was a cold night,' said Emily, pallid in the fluorescent light of the Dairy Barn, a chalkboard listing ice-cream flavors hanging behind her head. Dark Cherry Delight. Double Chocolate Fantasy. Jonathan had returned home late, explaining that he and Willa continued to discuss his paper on aggregate expenditure curves; the very paper, in fact, being presented at the conference in New York that Willa and Jonathan were both now attending.

Emily's eyes widened. 'Why am I telling you all this?'

Once more her cell phone began to play Rachmaninoff. The black woman with the turban and the girls left with their ice-cream cones and the line moved forward.

'Maybe,' said George, 'you should answer it.'

But by the time she located her phone in the complicated depths of her enormous black leather bag the ring tone had stopped. She peered at the phone's little screen and then said she did not recognize the number.

Nicholas was gripping her arm. With a flourish, Emily dropped the phone back into her bag. 'See.' She kissed the top of his head. 'I'm not answering it.'

'What if it was something important?' he said, with a worried frown.

George saw that this must be one of Nicholas's more exasperating traits, his ability to fret over conflicting fears, a kind of ambidextrous anxiety that probably came on especially at night ('I want the closet door closed! But I want to see if something's in there!') and could quickly spiral into hysteria.

'Sweetie.' Emily bent down to look into his face. 'Don't.'

'What if it's an emergency?'

Outside on the sidewalk, Boris was barking again. Then he quit barking and began to howl. George offered to go out and check on him.

'I'm sure he's fine,' said Emily.

'But what if it's an *emergency*?' Nicholas was still fixated on the missed cell phone call.

Emily gave George another look of comic exasperation. 'Then the emergency will have to call someone else.'

He watched this exchange with disappointment. 'Performance parenting' is how Tina used to describe it. Seeking to charm listeners in public with one's patience and good humor, using one's child as a foil. Had George not been there, Emily would have told Nicholas to be quiet or no ice cream and that would be the end of it.

A bead for treating her kid to ice cream, a bead lost for treating him like a stage prop. Life in a bead jar. No wonder old Jonathan was banging Willa Clamage.

'Who's next?' called the teenage boy behind the counter, a pale gangly kid with a shaved head and a silver nose ring, a stud in one eyebrow and what looked to be a miniature spear piercing one ear, a menacing ensemble somewhat off-set by his cowhide-printed T-shirt, required of employees at the Dairy Barn. He reminded George of Aaron and Bradley, his own sons (still unpierced, thank God), who had scooped ice cream at the Dairy Barn for a month last summer. Where were they this minute? Probably stoned, riding in a car with-out seatbelts. Who was he to judge another parent? Kissing married women, following young mothers into ice-cream parlors, getting them to confide in him, like some kind of pervert.

Still, he had not once thought about what it would be like to sleep with gloomy Emily. ('That's all men think about', another Tina complaint.) A bead for him.

Nicholas blinked up at his mother, taking her hand with a grateful little shudder, and with something like composure the two of them moved toward the ice-cream counter.

'Do you want anything, George?' Emily asked, but when he glanced at his watch he realized that he was very late to meet Margaret, that she must be watching the door at the Forge, perhaps already gathering her coat and bag, face averted, paying for the cup of coffee she'd drunk alone. And he saw that he had now become, in fact, the ass he was afraid of being, a self-fulfilling prophecy he seemed powerless to escape.

As George was making his excuses, a dark bearded young man yanked open the glass door, calling out in a clipped Indian accent, 'Does someone in here own a dog?'

'Yes,' said Emily.

'You had better come. Something is wrong with it.'

Outside the streetlights had come on. Boris was sprawled by the parking meter, still tethered by his leash, paws jerking, breathing rapidly in shallow painful-sounding huffs as Emily crouched beside him, crooning his name.

Then she sat all the way down on the icy sidewalk in her big black coat and cradled his head in her lap, stroking his long tangled gray and white fur. A small crowd had gathered, several people asking at the same time what had happened.

It was a strangely beautiful sight. A woman sitting on the sidewalk in a monumental black coat, blonde hair streaming about her shoulders, passing cars illuminating her hair with their headlights, gilding the rims of her glasses as she bent over the big dog lying limp across her lap. George put an arm around Nicholas's small shoulders to hold him back; he wasn't sure why, maybe in case Boris turned violent, in the grip of some mysterious seizure. He could feel Nicholas trembling under his arm, as if Nicholas, too, were in the grip of something mysterious.

More people stopped to stare. It had started to snow.

Then Boris vomited onto Emily's black coat and stopped breathing. The young Indian man who had summoned them laid Boris out and tried to perform chest compressions, his heels rising out of the scuffed backs of his brown loafers; he had, George saw, a hole in one of his black socks. At last the young man straightened up, scowling, brushing at the knees of his thin gray trousers, on which two wet oblongs had appeared. No one remembered to thank him, and by the time George thought of it, the young man was gone.

Ashen-faced, Emily had once more gathered the limp dog into her lap and sat on the sidewalk smoothing his long tangled fur in the lightly falling snow, while Nicholas knelt beside her in his yellow boots and red fireman's hat, clinging to her black coat with his small white hands, his voice high and insistent, the words running together, as he asked, again and again, if this was an emergency.

II.

Snow was falling again and although it was mid-morning it looked like late afternoon. The sky was a muffled gray and tree trunks stood out darkly against the snow, patches of lichen glowing an unearthly green against the damp bark. Already the roofs of Littlefield wore snowy bonnets, fringed by icicles, and in the village berms of snow rose halfway up the poles of parking meters, and it was only the eighth of December.

Inside Duncklee Middle School, seventh-graders in Ms Manookian's social studies class watched the snow fall prettily outside their classroom windows and wondered if the buses would be late and whether school would be called off for tomorrow. The storm was expected to continue into the evening and through the night, with accumulations up to nine inches.

'It's always snowing these days,' said a child at the windows.

'Just like a snow globe,' said somebody else, for the second time.

The children enjoyed imagining another snow day, and thinking about the video games they would play and the possibility of sledding; yet even they began to worry about the roads, having heard their parents complain about dreadful conditions, and to wonder about the weight of snow on rooftops and how much more snow their own houses could hold before there was danger of collapse. For children the threat of peril is exciting, particularly when it comes to natural disasters; but the children of Littlefield had seen so much snow in the past few weeks that they had begun to fear something was out of balance in the universe. Then again, it was dark this time of year, the days getting shorter and shorter, which naturally made everyone a little uneasy.

Julia Downing was sitting in her newly assigned seat in the fourth row, looking over her homework in B Block. She liked to start every class by checking to make sure her homework was arranged neatly in her folders, which she had labeled with her label-maker. Each morning she woke up half an hour before her parents to arrange her folders, brush her hair and change her mind several times about the outfit she had laid out the night before. If there were a few minutes left before breakfast, she wrote in her journal, in which she kept a popularity record of the seventh grade. The top-ten list shifted every day. As of last night, Amelia Epstein was top girl and Anthony Rabb was top boy. Julia reckoned her own numerical placement at seventy-three out of the top one hundred.

While waiting for class to start, she took out her half-completed 'Survey of Littlefield', Ms Manookian's assignment for Friday. Writing a survey of Littlefield did not strike Julia as the kind of social studies project that would prepare her for high school and college. Shouldn't they be studying important places, like Philadelphia? Ms Manookian was new this year and probably didn't know she was supposed to be teaching them things that actually mattered. *If you were a historian surveying Littlefield today*, read the assignment sheet, *what would you notice and record for future generations?*

Julia frowned at the lined paper she had just taken out of her folder.

Littlefield: the Present

23 banks, 7 nail salons, 12 hair salons, 3 electrolysis salons, 4 test preparation services, 9 jewelry stores, 6 dog groomers, 3 drugstores, 17 dentists, 7 orthodontists, 1,146 psychotherapists, 679 psychiatrists, 1 bagel shop, 1 bakery, 6 coffee shops, 2 Chinese restaurants, 3 pizza parlors, 1 ice-cream parlor, 1 party-supplies shop, 4 liquor stores, 4 yoga studios, 1 Chinese-Baptist church, 1 Catholic church, 1 Episcopal church, 3 synagogues.

'I grant you poetic license,' Ms Manookian had said in class last week when she assigned the survey. 'Go wild!'

Hannah said that Ms Manookian was a man, poetic license or not, and that a couple of months ago she'd said something in D Block about having surgery that almost got her fired. Julia's mother, who overheard this remark while she was driving the soccer carpool right before Halloween, said that there was nothing wrong with being transgendered. Hannah said, 'I didn't say there *was*,' then stared out of the window for the rest of the car ride home while Julia's mother went on about the importance of recognizing the truth about yourself, and then started talking about a book she'd just read about a blind boy who wanted to be a professional baseball player. Julia rolled her eyes at Hannah and mouthed *what a loser*, but Hannah ignored her. Hannah was still mad that Julia's mother had nixed the skirt part of their supermodels costume, though Julia had secretly been relieved. Her legs looked too skinny in skirts.

Julia guessed she was doing the assignment incorrectly because she had not gone wild but instead looked through the business pages of the telephone book.

As she considered the problem of going wild she thought of Freckles the cat, now missing from Littlefield forever. '1 park,' she added to her list in pencil. '1 woods, with coyotes, skunks & bears'. She was fairly sure there weren't any bears in the woods, but her pencil eraser was almost gone, and made smudges when she used it, and anyway poetic license, she reminded herself.

A few nights ago she'd heard her parents talking in their bedroom after they thought she'd gone to bed. It wasn't that she was eavesdropping, just sometimes she liked to sit on the hall carpet with her back against their door when she couldn't sleep. She and Hannah once watched a scary movie about children who discovered their parents were dead and had been replaced by androids, programmed to say they weren't androids when questioned; but whenever the children weren't there, the android-parents went silent and stood around like statues. Feeling the vibrations of her parents' voices through their bedroom door was like an old lullaby, though one night she woke up on the hallway floor, face pressed against the carpet, and had to creep back to her bed in the dark.

Her mother said, 'I saw one in the Fischmans' backyard and again one night when –'

Julia's father said something. Then her mother said in a low voice, 'There's more and more of them.'

Now in class Julia added an insert sign before the word 'coyotes' and wrote 'a lot of' above it.

Standing at the blackboard, Ms Manookian began B Block by saying she was going to read aloud from the *Globe's* 'This Day in History' column, which she sometimes did to take up class time and give kids a chance to settle down and spit out their gum and hide their cell phones in their laps. She also sometimes read editorials from the *Gazette*; last week she read one about the dog that got poisoned right before Thanksgiving. 'Woof, woof,' said Albert Chang when Ms Manookian was done reading and half the boys started barking. 'It's not funny,' Hannah had yelled at them. 'What if it had been *your* dog?' Hannah was popular, so the boys stopped barking. If Julia had said the same thing they would have been howling.

Today she figured Ms Manookian was reading the *Globe* to impress Mr Anderman, the principal, who was observing the class along with the black lady who was living in the Fischmans' carriage house, whom Ms Manookian had introduced, embarrassingly, as 'the esteemed Dr Watkins from Chicago'. Dr Watkins smiled and waved from her chair at the back of the classroom. She was wearing a green turban and an orange dress. Mr Anderman sat beside her in his red bow tie and tweedy jacket, with his arms crossed under a world map and a poster of Gandhi tacked to the white cinderblock wall.

Parents must have been complaining again about Ms Manookian being disorganized. Last week they were supposed to be learning about taxation without representation. Instead Ms Manookian told a long story about when she was a child and her mother took quarters from her piggy bank to help pay for Sunday night ice cream, but Ms Manookian never got to choose the flavor. Then Brian Hobika raised his hand and wanted to know what flavor of ice cream Ms Manookian's mother chose, which led to a discussion about the best ice-cream flavors and why parents tend to like disgusting flavors like pistachio while kids like regular flavors like chocolate chip and cookie dough. It got kind of interesting, actually. But still, they were supposed to be talking about the American Revolution.

' "Today is December 8th," ' Ms Manookian read aloud from the front of the classroom. ' "The 342nd day of the year." '

Albert Chang began flipping a pen back and forth on his desk. Ms Manookian looked at him over the tops of her pink paisley reading glasses. Then she resumed reading.

' "On this day in 1776, General George Washington's army crossed the Delaware River from New Jersey into Pennsylvania, in retreat from the British.

' "In 1863, President Lincoln announced his plan for the reconstruction of the South.

' "In 1941, the United States entered World War II, as Congress declared war on Japan, a day after the attack on Pearl Harbor." '

She paused again, this time for dramatic effect.

' "In 1982, a man demanding an end to nuclear weapons held the Washington Monument hostage, threatening to blow it up with explosives he claimed were inside a van. After a ten-hour standoff, Norman D. Mayer was shot to death by police; it turned out there were no explosives." '

Ms Manookian flashed her big white teeth. Julia groaned silently. A teachable moment had appeared. Ms Manookian would now ask them a bunch of questions (showing off for Mr Anderman) to try to get them to connect George Washington crossing the Delaware in the wrong direction with Norman D. Mayer holding the Washington Monument hostage. Then a lesson plan would magically emerge. It would look as if Ms Manookian had known all along that George Washington and Norman D. Mayer had done something on the same day and had been waiting for Tuesday December 8th to present this coincidence to the class, when Julia would bet a hundred bucks that Ms Manookian hadn't thought of it until five minutes ago.

Outside the classroom window hung heavy swags of telephone wires, exposed-looking now that the leaves were gone.

'So, class,' said Ms Manookian in her gargly voice, 'what's interesting about this day in history?'

Nothing.

'Did anyone notice that *several* important Americans are listed today?' Ms Manookian looked fixedly out at the class. 'Can anyone tell me who they were?'

'Lincoln,' shouted Brian Hobika from his front-row desk.

Julia saw Mr Anderman uncross his arms and reach up to adjust his aviator glasses.

Brian had to sit in the front row because he had Issues. He was wearing his T-shirt inside out and backwards again, the tag in front. He had dark circles under his eyes. Hannah's mother had told Julia's mother that Brian's parents insisted that Brian did not need Ritalin, that he was only enthusiastic.

'Lincoln, Lincoln,' he chanted now, bouncing in his chair.

'Brian, please raise your hand and wait for me to call on

you. Yes, President Lincoln was one. Who else, can anybody tell me?'

Hannah raised her hand from two rows in front of Julia. Ms Manookian had moved their seats because they talked too much – or Hannah talked too much – when they sat together.

'George Washington. Our first president.'

'Very good. Thank you, Hannah.'

Hannah straightened the notebook on her desk. Julia wished she had a BB gun to shoot into the back of Hannah's ear. Hannah always thought she knew everything. Hannah was the one chosen to be in the geography bee last week. Hannah got to have a cell phone, while Julia's mother said cell phones for children were silly. Hannah was the star of the middle school chorus and got to have first pick of which boy in their grade was 'hers' and of course chose Anthony Rabb. Now she had decided to be a vegetarian and kept saying her lunch was more nutritious and better for the planet. Hannah was number seven on the top-ten list. Brian wasn't even in the top two hundred.

Mr Anderman was leaning forward, elbows on the desk of his desk chair, chin propped on his fists. Beside him, Dr Watkins was smiling at Ms Manookian and taking notes on a pad.

Ms Manookian smiled back. 'But there was one *more* American mentioned, right at the very end of the passage I just read.'

The class stared at her blankly.

'Norman D. Mayer? Who tried to hold the Washington Monument hostage? Can *anyone* think of a connection between George Washington and Norman D. Mayer?'

Hannah raised her hand again. Ms Manookian peered around the room to see if someone else might have an answer.

'Yes, Hannah?'

'The Washington Monument was built to honor George Washington.'

'Very good. And what did George Washington do that we honor him with a monument?'

'He's on the one-dollar bill!' shrieked Brian Hobika.

Under the poster of Gandhi, Mr Anderman adjusted his aviator glasses again.

Julia sighed. She almost never raised her hand, but now, for reasons she did not fully understand, but which involved a stirring of sympathy for Ms Manookian, because she had an Adam's apple and was new this year, and also involved the possibility that Ms Manookian might report something favorable about Julia to her mother next week during parent–teacher conferences – she slowly raised her hand.

'Julia?'

'George Washington led the American Army in the Revolution against the British.'

'*Yes*. Thank you.' Ms Manookian beamed.

'And Norman said he was going to blow up his monument.'

'That's right.' Ms Manookian looked at her encouragingly. 'And how else might they be connected?'

'They both tried to kill people,' said Albert Chang, flipping his pen excitedly.

'No,' said Julia, then stopped, realizing too late that she was in for it now because she'd have to correct stupid fat Albert Chang, and then lunch would be hell, Albert telling everyone she'd made him look dumb, breathing on her sand-wich, asking if she wanted to trade bites. *I gotta big bologna.*

Stupid class, stupid Ms Manookian, stupid entire universe.

'Yes, Julia?'

She took a breath. 'Norman threatened to blow up the monument because he *didn't* want people to be killed. He was against nuclear weapons.'

'Very good. So, Julia, do you see any other connection between George Washington and Norman D. Mayer?'

Outside the classroom the world looked absolutely still, except for the sky-colored snow falling again in great flakes. She was aware of the whole class watching her, especially Anthony Rabb, slouched in his seat by the windows, wear-ing his Red Sox jersey. Narrow green eyes, angelic blond curls, soft brutal mouth. Beautiful and ruthless, an expert sniper, picking off anyone who showed signs of intelligence.

'Norman was a loser freak who hated America,' said Albert Chang.

'And George Washington loved America!' Amelia Epstein swished her ponytail.

'Class!' Ms Manookian patted the air with her palms. 'I'm glad that you're so interested in this subject, but people must raise their hands if they want to speak. This is a democracy.' She gave Mr Anderman and Dr Watkins an aren't-kids-something look. 'Now, *Julia* was in the middle of answering my question. *Julia*, what were you going to say?'

Julia was staring at her desk, trying to decide if it would be better to cut her losses and not answer at all, when from the windows came a sibilant whisper:

'*Julia's* a loser freak.'

Several girls giggled.

107

'Downer Downing.'

'Quiet!' Ms Manookian glared toward the windows. 'Julia?'

But Julia was not there.

Millions of microscopic fragments of Julia now lay, invisibly, on the speckled beige linoleum tiles of the classroom floor. What was left in her chair was a phantom Julia, which she had learned to project at these moments, by sheer force of will, until she could reassemble herself, a process that would take days, even weeks, and was never entirely successful. Atomic particles of Julia could be found in many classrooms, in fact, on the playground, on the soccer field, in her oboe teacher's studio, even on the kitchen floor of her own home. They made a faint gritty sound when trodden upon, almost imperceptible except in moments when there was no other ambient noise.

The classroom wall clock was very loud. *Tick tick tick*. Like the imaginary explosives inside Norman D. Mayer's van as he faced a battalion of police cars beneath the Washington Monument. Outside the second-floor classroom windows the snow had stopped, revealing a bulging gray sky impaled on black twigs.

'So does anyone see any *other* connection between George Washington and Norman D. Mayer?' Ms Manookian's voice was unnaturally fluty. 'Nobody?'

Nobody.

'Well, all right. They were both in their own way revolutionaries. *Quite* interesting when you think about it. Okay, class. Let's open our textbooks to page 243, and look at the section on early drafts of the Declaration of Independence.'

Julia peered through her hair to see that Albert had raised his hand.

'Albert?'

Albert winched himself around in his seat to face the back of the classroom. He was wearing a green T-shirt printed with a skull surrounded by flowers. 'I was just wondering. I mean, if Norman and George Washington were both, like, revolutionaries, do you think they were both right?'

'Explain what you're getting at?' said Ms Manookian.

'I mean –' Albert was frowning at the back wall – 'was Norman more kind of like someone like Gandhi? Or more kind of like that person who poisoned that dog?'

Ms Manookian clasped her large hands and knuckled them against her lips, gazing for a long time over the tops of her reading glasses. 'What a good question, Albert,' she said at last, her voice reluctant, unsteady, the sound of a teacher who didn't have an answer ready and was stalling for time. Julia shivered.

But the very next instant a deafening clamor filled the room, a sound like ten thousand marbles shaken inside a huge tin drum. A sound that had become all too familiar in Duncklee Middle School over the last few months. Mr Anderman sprang to his feet. The children clapped their hands to their ears. Someone had pulled the fire alarm again.

12.

It was Bill's idea to host a Christmas dinner this year instead of going to the Number One Noodle House as they usually did. His idea to invite anyone they knew who did not have Christmas plans, which really meant anyone who was Jewish. For years Margaret had offered exactly this suggestion – probably to make up for neither of them having much family, Margaret's parents both gone and now his mother in Arizona with his brother – but Bill had always demurred. Christmas day was tiring enough as it was, with Julia overexcited in the morning and then dejected all afternoon, sloping about the house with a long face, fingering her stocking to see if she'd missed something in the toe. The whole commercial thing was toxic. Then let's volunteer at a soup kitchen, Margaret always said, and he always agreed that was a great idea, and every year they had dinner at the Number One Noodle House.

This year looked to be no different, starting with Christmas cards shuffling through the mail slot, most of them picturing kids and a golden retriever all wearing red Santa hats, posed in a snowy front yard. *Season's Greetings from the Schmidlapps! Greetings from the Wu Family!*

Greetings from the Necropolis. That would have been their Christmas card. With a photo of Julia's animal graveyard under skeletal hydrangeas in the snow.

A week ago, Margaret had said, 'Why don't you just *act*

like you love me? Sometimes if people act the way they want to feel, then they start to feel the way they want to feel.'

Dr Vogel said, 'Say more about that,' but Margaret said it was Bill's turn to say something. They both sat staring at the pink lotus blossoms of Dr Vogel's Oriental rug. Finally, he said, 'So you want me to pretend to feel something? Like some kind of robot?' When she didn't answer, he said, 'Why don't you tell Dr Vogel what you told me, about seeing dead dogs everywhere?'

Margaret looked as stunned as if one of them had just jumped in her lap.

Dr Vogel had of course wanted to hear more about that, but it was almost the end of the session and Margaret said she'd rather talk about it next time. On the way to the car she wouldn't look at him.

'Okay,' he said that same evening at dinner. 'Let's invite people over on Christmas. Let's really do it this time.'

It was the stress of what they were going through – it was infecting her, doing something to her brain. He'd read about this kind of projection stuff in a copy of *Psychology Today* in Dr Vogel's waiting room. Neurotic obsession. Common for people going through a bad time. The same thing was happening to him. For the last several weeks he'd woken every morning convinced the bed was full of bedbugs; his whole body itched. When he told Margaret they might have a bedbug infestation, she said he was just allergic to the new laundry detergent. Yet as soon as she used the word 'allergic' he understood what it was: he was allergic to her, to sharing a bed with her, and then the whole phantom dog thing made sense.

But it was starting to infect Julia, too. She stayed shut up in her room, coming downstairs only for meals, sitting hunched over her plate, hair hanging in her face, the pale nape of her neck exposed. Whenever he asked her questions about school, she answered in monosyllables, like a prisoner refusing to confess. Maybe having a party would help. Maybe Margaret was right: if they acted like a regular family, and people saw them looking like a regular family, maybe they could trick themselves into feeling like a regular family. The more he thought about it, the more the idea took hold of him. He pictured polishing the dining-room table himself, the way his father used to do it, with a rag and linseed oil, making the old wood shine. He pictured people standing around Margaret at the piano, everyone holding plastic cups of eggnog and singing 'Jingle Bells' and 'The Twelve Days of Christmas', 'Silent Night, Holy Night'. A kind of exorcism, maybe.

'Invite anyone you want to invite,' he told Margaret, mentioning the subject again the next evening. 'Tell Julia to invite Hannah. Invite her folks. The more the merrier.'

He'd figured Margaret would be glad he was finally in favor of a holiday dinner, would interpret it as a sign of commitment. But she only looked at him in a drained, hopeless way and said, 'No thanks.'

He should have been more sympathetic. It was practically obliterating her, what they were going through, and it was his fault, or mostly his fault. But he couldn't stand the thought of spending Christmas dinner alone in a restaurant with Margaret and Julia, the three of them sitting wordlessly over spring rolls and shrimp lo mein. So he brought it up again later as they were getting ready for bed, finally asking, 'Is this how you want Julia to remember her childhood, Christmas in a noodle house?'

'How do you want her to remember it?' she'd said.

Plenty of people had midlife crises and came out all right. Three-quarters of the couples in town were in counseling and the ones who weren't probably should be. And yet Bill couldn't bring himself to say to Margaret, 'We'll be all right.' Not only because he didn't believe they would be all right – which he didn't, but at this point he was prepared to pretend if it would make her feel better – but because it wasn't just their marriage that wasn't all right.

Three weeks ago he and the rest of the management at Roche Capital had been informed by the Securities and Exchange Commission that the company was being investigated. Allegations of insider trading. Everyone was going to be questioned.

He hadn't seen it coming. Who had made these allegations? What kind of insider trading? No one had told him anything and he himself had mentioned nothing to anyone. Not even Margaret. All he knew, and this from Passano, was that when the office computers crashed that afternoon in September, it wasn't a problem with their network server: while he'd looked out of his window at the river below, a remote-monitoring device was being installed in their system.

Now the green banks of the river were covered in snow, the feathery trees gone bare. As he sat at his desk, as he drove home, as he brushed his teeth before bed, he pictured SEC investigators rising up out of the gray water, as impassive as frogmen, flat-footing up those banks, across the bridges, filing into his office in black suits, carrying black briefcases, their dark gelled hair gleaming.

Could we speak with you for a few minutes, sir? We'd like to ask you a few questions.

But I don't know anything, he'd have to tell them. You may not believe me, but I really don't know how things got this way.

'It's got to be one of the gardeners,' Margaret was saying.

'There's no evidence pointing to a gardener.' Bill patted his red and green striped tie, a present from Margaret that morning. He'd given her pearls, forgetting that he'd given her pearls last year. He glanced around the living room at their guests. 'Let's not make wild accusations.'

'I'm not making a wild accusation,' said Margaret querulously. She was already on her second glass of wine. 'Look at all that graffiti.'

Since the death of Boris the sheepdog, graffiti had been appearing all over the village: *Leash Your Beast*.

'I'm just saying,' said Bill, 'accusations can get out of hand.'

Perched on the two sofas like a flock of owls were the four Melmans, Hedy Fischman and their new neighbor, Dr Clarice Watkins. He'd got a nice fire going in the fireplace. The Christmas tree was twinkling cheerfully. He checked again to make sure. Yes, there it was, a very nice Frasier fir, decorated with ornaments and glass icicles and frosted white orb-shaped lights that blinked on and off, reflected in the dark glass of the French doors. Below spread a skirt of fake snow, insisted upon every year by Julia. Very nice. But when he'd glanced at the Christmas tree a few minutes ago it looked as if it were covered with eyeballs and finger bones.

'Well, the gardeners *do* have a motive,' Naomi Melman was saying. 'My theory is they feel possessive about the park and resentful because they can't own it. Like neurotic tenant farmers.'

'Enough motive to poison dogs?' said Bill. 'Who has that kind of motive?'

'A sociopath,' croaked old Hedy Fischman. Dr Doom.

'A sociopath?' echoed Stan Melman.

'Someone reliving a frightening childhood experience of being attacked by a dog and now, in the grip of a narcissistic ideation, he is trying to control all his fears by killing what he believes to be the source of them.'

'Looks like the fire could use a little attention.' Bill put his hands on his knees to stand up.

He smiled apologetically at the Melmans: Naomi and Stan; Julia's friend, Hannah; and the son, Matthew, a thin, dark boy with protuberant brown eyes and the beginnings of a mustache, sitting beside his mother. Naomi was a good friend of Margaret's, but Bill knew the Melmans mostly from the girls' soccer games. Stan and Naomi were both psychologists. Stan was as usual wearing a black yarmulke; he had a thick graying mustache and beard and a benign-looking pink wart beside his nose. Mother and daughter had both dressed up in skirts and velvet tops – Hannah's skirt was very short; she was also in fishnet stockings – but Matthew was wearing a striped rugby shirt and torn blue jeans. For the past twenty minutes, while everyone else was chatting, Matthew had sat silent on the sofa contorting his face, apparently in the grip of private torments that Bill imagined must be hormonal. Several times this fall he'd seen the boy flash through town on his bicycle, squinting against the wind, pumping wrathfully. *Hell on wheels*, was the thought that had come to him. Along with an unexpected sting of envy.

Both Fischmans had been invited, but Marv wasn't feeling well, so only Dr Doom had come, in a black pants suit, a long black scarf wrapped around her neck, accompanied by Clarice Watkins in a golden turban and a leopard-print outfit that reminded Bill of bedspreads from the seventies. They'd all arrived in a rush of cold fresh air, awkwardly bunched together. He'd taken their coats and poured each of the adults a glass of wine, urged them to sit by the fire, grateful when the living room began to seem convivial.

As he was stirring up the fire with the poker, the doorbell rang again and Binx started barking. 'I'll get it,' he said.

Margaret threw him an unfocused look. 'Who could that be?'

A week before he'd gone to Walgreens to buy light bulbs for the front hall chandelier, though really just to get out of the house; as he was walking up and down the aisles, he'd passed a man in jeans and a windbreaker reading a magazine next to the family planning section – a man who looked familiar, but he couldn't place him. Until he realized it was the guy from the dust-jacket photo of a book on Margaret's nightstand. That novelist she kept mentioning.

The next thing he knew, Bill was introducing himself and saying, 'My wife's a big fan of yours. Margaret? You've met her, I think.' He held out his hand and, after a moment's hesitation, the other guy took it.

'George Wechsler.'

George was holding *Iron Man Magazine*, Bill noticed, so he asked if he lifted weights. George said he belonged to a gym and worked out twice a week.

'You know, I should be doing that.'

'Too busy?'

'Bad back,' Bill said mildly, noting the edge in George's voice. Probably figured out that Bill hadn't read his novel, or hadn't liked it. Shouldn't have said, My *wife's* a fan. Implying that he himself was not. Recalling that the novel had something to do with baseball, Bill said it was too bad the Red Sox hadn't traded for an ace and together they bemoaned the farcical performance of the Red Sox last season, agreeing that the bull pen should be beefed up and that the outfield still needed a slugger and predicting they'd be in the basement all spring. George kept looking up at him oddly, with a kind of truculent apology, the unconscious posture a short man takes with a tall man, Bill recognized, though George was built like a bag full of soccer balls. It struck Bill that this was cosmically unfair, that he should have been born to be tall, to enjoy the benefits of stature whether or not he earned them, while George had to work out to make up for being so short, and was forced to assert himself in a way that must feel exhausting and sometimes humiliating.

He asked George what he was doing for the holidays. When George admitted that he had recently separated from his wife and hadn't planned much besides watching football, Bill felt a flush of comradeship and heard himself say, 'Well, we're having kind of a catch-as-catch-can thing at our house on Christmas night. You're welcome to join us.'

As he said it, he wanted it to be true; he wanted to be the kind of spontaneous guy who hosted catch-as-catch-can dinners. A pot of chili on Sundays. Neighbors over for cookouts. Tag football in the yard. It had been years since he'd played football. He really should work out. Exercise improves your mood, everybody said, makes you feel more alive, and it would be another excuse to get out of the house.

117

'A bunch of people will be there.' He smiled down at George. 'We'd love to have you.'

Predictably George had protested: no, no. Thanks, but couldn't possibly. Not the Christmas type.

'Well, we're only inviting people who don't celebrate Christmas.'

'Members of the tribe?'

'Sikhs. Buddhists. We're still looking for a couple of Druids. Maybe a Wiccan.'

George smiled and thanked him again, then repeated that he couldn't possibly; yet the more he protested the more Bill felt determined to get him to say yes. Dr Vogel had suggested that he try seeking out the company of other men. Not colleagues, not the guys he worked with, but friends. Margaret had friends. She went out to dinner with them, celebrated their birthdays, asked after their ailing parents. Became friends with the mothers of Julia's friends, with people she'd met walking the dog. But not him. Not for years. He'd had friends in college, frat brothers. What had become of his friends?

He thought of his father's occasional phone calls, just to shoot the breeze, talk about the box scores and how he'd fixed the lawnmower motor with a fly wheel he found at the dump. Bill always had to cut the calls short and his father would say, 'Okay, pal. Catch you next time.'

Several times he'd thought about talking to Stan Melman. They often stood together at soccer games, arms crossed high on their chests, chatting about the weather, the stock market, the craziness in Europe and when it was all going to blow. On a really bad night a few weeks ago he'd walked over to Stan's house when he was out with Binx; but it was late, and he didn't know what to say if Stan came to the door. Instead he'd stood in the street for a long time, looking at the windows of the Melmans' house.

'Really, no.' George was replacing his magazine in the rack, edging toward the feminine hygiene section. 'But thank you.'

George had almost reached the end of the aisle when Bill had an inspiration. 'About my wife,' he said, following George.

'Look, I'm sorry, man,' said George, holding up both palms.

Bill held up a hand, too. 'I just wanted to say, she really did love your book.'

George seemed as taken aback as if Bill had just said Margaret was an astrophysicist and had won a Nobel Prize. Why should it be surprising that Margaret had liked George's book? Did he think she wasn't intelligent enough to appreciate it?

'She's reading it again, in fact. I keep finding it all over the house.'

'I think I'm visiting her book club,' muttered George.

'Well, she said yours is the best book they've read all year and she was just saying the other day how much she wants to talk to you about it.'

Untrue, but suddenly Bill felt he would do almost anything to try to persuade George to come to dinner. It would show Margaret that he cared about what she cared about. Or at least that he could act like it.

He took a step forward, not meaning to block the aisle but noticing that he had done so, also noticing that George's fists were bunched in his windbreaker pockets, the ridge of his knuckles outlined through the fabric.

Bill moved back a pace. 'Listen, it really would be great if you could join us. Margaret would be too shy to ask you herself, but she'd be so glad. It would be something for her, having you come to dinner. I know it's a big favor to ask, but really it would be great.'

George said he'd think about it. Bill gave him the address and said they'd be starting with drinks around six. He asked George again for the name of his gym, having already forgotten. He might want to join himself. Might be good for his back.

'Catch you later,' he said as George lifted two fingers in salute.

He figured there was a fifty-fifty chance George would show up. Margaret kept telling him to read George's novel, saying it might give them something to talk about – well, he'd gone one better: here was George himself, coming to Christmas dinner.

That would give them something to talk about.

'Goodness,' Margaret was saying coldly, hands clasped against her chest. 'Look who's here.'

George Wechsler was still standing in the foyer in his parka, holding a bottle of cabernet, snow capping the toes of his cowboy boots. He'd just introduced the two identical angular curly-haired teenage boys looming behind him. His sons, Aaron and Bradley.

She hadn't offered to take his coat, just stood in the hall looking at him under the too-bright chandelier. Bill couldn't understand it. Margaret was always so gracious to visitors, especially when she felt put out by them.

'Bill will take your coat.' And then she disappeared.

'Hope this is really okay.' George handed him the wine with a contrite grimace. 'Bringing the boys last minute.'

'Absolutely.' Bill clapped him on the shoulder. 'The more the merrier.'

He took their coats and led George and the two boys into the living room, where everyone blinked up at them from the sofas near the fireplace, as if until that moment they'd been sitting in the dark. George seemed to know some of the adults and Matthew Melman, and he introduced his sons. There were cries of *Please don't get up* and *No, no, you sit here.* Hedy Fischman moved to an armchair, as did Clarice Watkins; George and his boys commandeered one of the sofas, while Hannah and Julia fluttered onto the carpet to sit at their feet. Outside it was snowing again, snow tapping lightly against the windowpanes.

Snowiest December on record, Bill heard someone say. Someone else began talking about five skiers in the Alps who had just been buried in an avalanche. Even specially trained dogs couldn't find them. Everyone looked appreciatively at the fireplace, where the crackling and hissing of burning logs provided a cheerful counterpoint to the storm outside, though every so often a gust of wind blew down the chimney with a hollow shriek.

'More wine?' Bill was walking around with George's bottle of cabernet.

George's twins, Aaron and Bradley, were wearing matching khaki pants and blue Oxford shirts, as if to make what was already difficult even harder. Julia and Hannah huddled together on the floor, clutching their cell phones, pretending not to look at the boys, while George explained the whereabouts of the twins' mother, Tina, who usually spent

Christmas day with her mother, her brother, Fred, and his husband. But the man Tina was dating had invited her to spend Christmas with him at an inn in Dorset, Vermont, while for the first time the grandmother had elected to go to Fred's house, in the South End. Wanted something smaller this year, she said. The boys had chosen to stay with George.

'In Animal House,' he said, smiling, and the boys guffawed obligingly.

He was sitting back on the sofa as he explained all this, in his brown corduroy jacket and navy turtleneck, one arm stretched along the top of the cushions, a cowboy boot propped on one knee. Leaning over to pour wine into George's glass, Bill felt fussy and butlerish in his striped Christmas tie. I look like a stiff, he thought.

'Uncle Fred is macrobiotic.' Bradley Wechsler was scooping a handful of Goldfish from a bowl on the coffee table. He stretched out his legs, disturbing Binx, who had finally settled under the coffee table after running around the room, barking maniacally every time the doorbell rang. Bill had offered to put Binx in his crate, but everyone said to let him stay.

'And his husband is allergic to wheat,' added Aaron. 'They're making quinoa for Christmas dinner. And stewed pumpkin.'

Matthew Melman rolled his popped eyes and pretended to be choking to death.

'Excuse me,' said Bill, reminded that he should be assisting Margaret in the kitchen. 'No, no, we're fine,' he added, as several people asked if they could help.

Margaret was a good but anxious cook, never able to hide the labor involved when she made dinner for company. She was determined to do it 'right', spending hours in the kitchen stirring gravy and pinching pie crusts made from scratch, tensely consulting her recipe books. He'd been surprised when she bought most of tonight's dinner from Whole Foods, already prepared, down to the pre-cut slices of roast turkey; except for the mashed potatoes, which she was making from a box of organic potato flakes. 'I don't have the energy,' she'd said. But then yesterday she'd gone back and bought a fresh organic ham, saying that if they were going to do Christmas they might as well really *do* Christmas and that meant ham. It put her in an even worse mood when he reminded her that almost everyone they were inviting to dinner was Jewish.

'Oh, for God's sake,' she said.

'Are you *sure* you don't need any help?' Naomi asked, touching his sleeve as he passed her chair on his way to the kitchen. 'Please just let me know if I can help.'

In the kitchen, Margaret's back was to him; she was hovering by the stove, a dishtowel in her hands. The savory fragrance of baked ham lit the air, reminding Bill of Christmases when he was a child: the bustle and anticipation in the days before, the almost painful joy when he awoke that morning, then the sight of his father in his plaid flannel bathrobe, his wide pink face smiling at the bottom of the stairs, calling out, 'Looks like we've had a visitor!'

'How could you,' Margaret said, turning around, her face livid above her black dress and pearls. 'How could you invite *him*?'

'I thought you'd be glad.'

'Glad! Are you crazy? He's a complete ass.'

'Sorry.' He held up both palms. 'I thought you liked his

book. I was *trying*,' he added in a hurt voice that he realized sounded self-pitying, 'to do something nice for you. You always say I don't think about you. Well, I was thinking about you.'

She shook her head and reached for her glass of wine on the counter. When she put it back down, she said grimly, 'How do you know him, anyway?'

'I met him in Walgreens. We started talking about baseball and then got on to gyms. I've got to do something about my back. It's been killing me.'

She looked at him for a long moment as if she were having trouble believing what she was seeing. 'You know what, I am so incredibly tired.' She turned back to the stove. 'Tonight has pushed me right over the edge.'

'I'm sorry,' he said.

'No, you're not.'

'Of course I'm sorry you're tired.'

'Something's burning,' she said to the stove.

When Bill returned to the living room the conversation was once again revolving around dogs and recent editorials in the *Gazette*. He added another log to the fire. The wind had picked up outside; everyone could hear it sob and moan as it rushed around the house.

'Very unfortunate, Hedy,' Stan Melman was saying in a lenient voice. 'But a poisoned dog is not an example of general inhumanity.'

'Five dogs,' said Dr Doom.

'What we need,' said Naomi, 'is a real clue.'

'A *clue*, Mom?' sneered Matthew. 'What are you, Sherlock Holmes?'

Bill saw Stan put a hand on Naomi's knee.

Three weeks ago, a Littlefield police officer discovered Matthew passed out behind the wheel of his mother's mini-van on Brooks Street at two in the morning, an empty bottle of peppermint schnapps on the seat beside him; the officer also discovered Matthew had only a Learner's Permit. This incident had been written up in the 'Crime Watch' column of the *Gazette* and was therefore known to everyone in the room. Naomi had told Margaret he was having separation issues.

'A *clue*,' repeated Matthew sulkily.

'I just think it's so sad,' sighed Hannah Melman, smoothing her dark ponytail.

She was keeping her chin low and her eyes very wide as she sat on the carpet, gazing up at Aaron and Bradley Wechsler with her lips parted. 'The glare', Bill had overheard Hannah and Julia call this pose last weekend when Hannah was sleeping over. They were discussing 'the glare' in Julia's bathroom as they hung over the sink to peer into the mirror when he happened to pass by. Something to do with super-models. He tried to imagine Hannah as a supermodel. More likely than Julia, but too much nose. What he knew of supermodels came from leafing through *Victoria's Secret* catalogues that arrived at the house. Lately he'd been monitoring himself for a reaction. Legs, breasts. Nothing. Like looking at wax fruit.

Nice kid, though. At least she kept her hair out of her face.

When he glanced away from Hannah, he realized that Clarice Watkins was looking at him. He gave her a tentative smile.

'Hannah,' said Naomi, 'are your braces bothering you?'

'No,' said Hannah glacially.

'Then close your mouth, please.'

'What about the Middle Easterners?' Dr Doom spoke up from her armchair by the fire. 'Don't forget about the Middle Easterners.'

'What *about* the Middle Easterners?' Stan Melman was stroking his beard.

'Marv always says you cannot discount the Middle East. Do you know, there is a young Muslim man I see sometimes on Brooks Street when I take my early walk. Very angry-looking and never says hello. Looks like he'd like to blow something up.'

'Ahmed.' Clarice Watkins startled everyone; it sounded as if she had just said 'amen'. But it was a Pakistani law student to whom she was referring, an employee at the Forge Café who came in to bake doughnuts every morning. She explained that she frequently breakfasted at the Forge, where they had become acquainted. He was interested in torts. Ahmed Bhopali.

'I believe he's Hindu,' she added, smiling.

'Towel heads.' Smirking, Matthew took a handful of Goldfish and began tossing them into his mouth, one by one, missing several times. Behind him an icicle slipped from the tree and tinkled onto the floor. In her armchair Clarice Watkins stirred, her smile widening.

'Is Pakistan part of the Middle East?' asked Hannah.

Last week, after Bill had asked twice at dinner about her day at school, Julia revealed that Hannah had been a contestant in the middle school geography bee, but was eliminated when she did not know that the Wabash River divided Indiana from Illinois.

'I wouldn't have known that, either,' Bill said, to show Julia he was paying attention, but she'd looked at him like he'd admitted to shaving with a carrot peeler.

Why was no gesture he made the right gesture? Lately everything he did seemed clumsy, ungainly, as if he were trying to play the piano wearing oven mitts or sprint in a lead apron. The wrong presents, the wrong invitations, the wrong comments. He'd been convinced his problem was Margaret, that she was depressing, that he didn't feel anything for her, except guilt, and that he'd feel more with someone else, someone younger, sexier; but he was starting to wonder if the problem was something else, something inert and insensible about him.

I feel like a stiff, he repeated to himself.

'Why would Middle Easterners want to poison Boris?' George was asking.

'Religious differences.' Dr Doom was now gazing at the fire. Her wizened face held the ancient look of someone who has not slept through the night in decades and her dark little eyes glittered in the firelight. 'You think the world is secular because that is how we are in this town. As Marv says, we are living in a bubble.' Her accent made it sound as if she'd said bauble.

Could I actually be dead, thought Bill, and not know it? Wasn't there a movie about a guy like that? Just how wrong about life was it possible to be?

Once more the chimney moaned. Aaron and Bradley Wechsler went back to staring at their iPhones as the Melmans began asking George about his days teaching high school. Did he miss it? (No.) Had he found the kids to be unusually cynical? (Yes.) In Naomi's opinion, cynicism was an appropriate deflective technique among adolescents in a culture that sexualized childhood. Little girls dressing like *Victoria's Secret* models. What did Dr Watkins think? Dr Watkins said something about the idiographic character of a sociocultural reality.

'Childhood today,' said Naomi, 'is being blitzed.'

'We're all being blitzed,' said George.

The Christmas tree had become pungent with the warmth of the fire, filling the room with a deep clean forest scent, but now as Bill breathed it in he noticed another smell, slipped in underneath, something foul, a smell he recognized, though he could not say what it was. He shuddered, his whole body gone cold.

A log broke on the fire, erupting sparks. Under the coffee table, Binx thumped his tail.

Dr Doom raised her wine glass. 'I say limit the computer time and make them all play outside.'

'Like that would work,' said Matthew, rolling his eyes again.

'Such children,' she said.

13.

'Dinner is served,' called Margaret, emerging from the kitchen into the hallway, feeling wan and overheated in her black dress, her apron dotted with wet potato flakes. Everyone stood up at once and crowded toward the dining room, exclaiming at the table, laid with a white linen cloth, white linen napkins, her wedding china and her mother's silver. White tapers burned in four silver candlesticks, shining against the merlot-colored walls.

On the table sat wide bowls of green beans and Brussels sprouts and mashed potatoes, a tureen of gravy for the turkey slices, and a heaping plate of roasted red beets. Every few places she'd set a bottle of red or white wine, in a ring of green holly. Bill disappeared into the kitchen and came out holding the ham aloft on a white china platter, making an awkward show of staggering under it, pretending to collapse, though he was very pale and for a moment Margaret wondered if he might not be kidding. As a festive gesture, harkening back to her grandmother's holiday recipes from *Betty Crocker*, she had decked the ham with pineapple rings and maraschino cherries, secured by toothpicks, which she saw now had the effect of making the ham look as if it were covered in tiny archery targets. But Stan Melman clapped and said it was a work of art.

Bill began carving the ham at the head of the table, asking people to pass up their plates; for some minutes everyone became absorbed in handing around bowls and baskets of rolls and the butter dish, while under the table skulked Binx, sniffing at their ankles. Everyone asked for a slice of ham except Hannah Melman, who said that she did not eat 'flesh'.

'A toast to the cook!' called out George, raising his glass to Margaret.

She would not look at him.

'And a toast to the holidays,' said Bill in a hesitant voice, still very pale as he hung over the pink ham at his end of the table. He kept his glass raised. 'I'd also like to take this moment to toast my father. First Christmas without him.' They all murmured and raised their glasses again. Bill coughed. 'And here's to goodwill and fellowship.' Margaret noticed he was perspiring above his red and green tie. There was something cadaverous about him tonight; his collar looked too big for him. He'd lost weight in the last months, she saw with a pang.

'I don't know that I feel much goodwill these days,' Naomi said when the toast was concluded. 'Not with someone out there carrying around a bag of poisoned hamburger meat.'

'*Poor* Boris,' said Hannah.

'How is Emily?' asked Margaret. George kept looking at her, under cover of passing plates and bowls; deliberately she avoided glancing in his direction. 'I haven't seen her since it happened.' Last night when she'd taken Binx for a walk she'd swung her flashlight and caught a shaggy mat of long trailing fur by the syringa in the front yard. Binx had growled at the bush but nothing was there. That was often how it was. They were most visible when she knew they were there but was afraid to look.

Naomi said, 'Apparently her little boy is a mess.'

How is it, thought Margaret, that our afflictions become other people's dinner table conversations? 'I'm so sorry to hear it,' she said. 'Julia is a mother's helper for him sometimes. Aren't you, Julia? Have you noticed anything?'

'No,' said Julia.

'I've thought he was troubled before this, frankly.' Naomi paused again. 'Well, I don't like to talk about other people's children.'

'You've already said he was a mess,' noted Hedy.

Julia volunteered that Nicholas did scream a lot.

'Everything bothers him. Sensory Integration Disorder, that's my opinion.' Naomi leaned back in her chair. 'But Emily won't get him tested. Doesn't believe in slapping diagnoses on a child.'

'I must have Sensory Integration Disorder,' Margaret told Stan as he refilled her wine glass. 'Everything bothers me, too.'

'Any thinking person –' George smiled at her before she could look away – 'has Sensory Integration Disorder these days.'

She had not spoken to him since that night in her driveway. They had emailed back and forth, but then he'd stood her up when they arranged to meet at the Forge for coffee, where she had decided to tell him what she had seen that night in his car. Of all the people she knew, she figured George was the most likely to take her seriously, if only because it was his dog she had seen, and kept seeing, along now with the rest of them. She'd tried to tell Bill, but he thought he knew what she was talking about, which was worse than not being understood at all. But George might understand. Even now she was aware of wanting to ask him to look outside, just beyond the dining-room windows, at a massing by the hedge that could easily be mistaken for shadows on the snow. Sometimes she saw just one, but there were hundreds of them now, gray legions, small and large, some of them mangy and thin, patches of fur hanging loose, hides crawling with fleas and worms; some with ropes around their necks; some with legs crushed and trailing behind them; some still just puppies, fat bellies dragging along the ground. All of them with enormous baleful eyes. It was all the dogs of Littlefield, she had started to think, every dog that had ever been starved or beaten, run over, abandoned by the road, tied to a tree and stoned, torn apart in staged dog fights, drowned as a puppy in a sack. They'd crept back, crossing the years like miles, scenting their way home across an impossible distance, one by one, to gather under the oak trees in her backyard, in the softly falling snow, to stare up at her windows and wait for her to look out and see them.

George might not believe her, but he would be interested. That's what she had thought, at least, when she emailed him and asked him to meet her at the Forge. For him it would be a story, it would make that kind of sense. He would want details, what they looked like and what it felt like whenever she saw them – like a tremendous *irritation*, she would tell him, like the air is filled with bees, a repulsive feeling, intolerable and yet she found she could bear it.

In fact, she had started to crave it. Often now she got up in the middle of the night and went down to the living room to look out of the window. Sometimes she opened the kitchen door and stepped out onto the patio in her nightgown, shivering in the frigid glassy air. It was shocking, exhilarating, to be so afraid – and yet it was not quite fear, either, what she felt, more like a brightly polished dread, black and cold, fitted exactly for the base of her belly. For whole minutes she stood looking out at her stone waterfall, silhouetted against the night sky. *I know you're there. I haven't forgotten about you.*

She wasn't afraid of them; but she was afraid she was going mad.

George's interest would be consoling, no matter what he thought of her; if she could tell it as a story, the dogs she was seeing, a ghost story, then it might be contained. That's what she told herself as she sat waiting for him in a booth at the back of the café that afternoon, sipping a glass of ice water; she also relived, for the countless time, the few minutes when his mouth was against hers, tongue probing, stubbly chin scouring her face. She played with packets of sugar, stacking them like miniature sandbags, trying not to watch the café door.

The next morning she received an email message: *Sorry to miss you yesterday. Something came up. Could we try again?* She had not answered.

'Okay, everyone,' called Bill, finally sitting down. 'Don't let your food get cold.'

'But wouldn't you want to *know* if something's wrong?' Naomi was persisting with her analysis of Nicholas. 'What's the good of denying a problem that's right in front of you?'

'I was there,' George said testily. He rolled the stem of his wine glass between his fingers. 'I was there when the dog died. The kid was pretty calm, all things considered.'

'Why were you there?' asked Hedy.

'On my way to meet someone. But I got held up.'

Finally Margaret looked at him. *Oh, really?*

George looked back at her. *Yes, really.*

'Will he be all right?' Clarice Watkins was asking about Emily's little boy, Nicholas. She had been quiet all evening, apparently content to listen to the conversation; now at the sound of her voice everyone turned toward her, impassive and exotic in her gold turban and leopard skins, facing candles and baskets of rolls, the wall behind her like a stage curtain.

Naomi set down her wine glass and gave it a small deliberative turn. 'I certainly hope so. Kids are resilient.'

'*Some* kids,' said Hedy.

Binx was groaning beneath the table.

Resilient, thought Margaret, or just good at disguising that they weren't, which maybe added up to the same thing. Look at her this evening, hosting Christmas dinner at her lovely table with family and friends; she seemed not just normal but enviable. No one thought she was crazy. Her marriage was not over, her husband had not left. She had not had an affair. But she was balanced on the blade edge of disaster.

When she'd come home the night of the town hall hearing, Bill had been waiting for her in the kitchen. As she took off her coat, he commented on the two empty wine glasses and the empty wine bottle sitting by the sink. 'A friend stopped by, she said. She stood holding her coat, waiting for him to ask, 'Who?' Prepared to tell him about George, wanting and not wanting to see the expression on his face when she said, 'I had a glass of wine with George Wechsler. The guy whose book I've told you about.' Here, in our kitchen. We talked about adultery. George loves olives; he ate almost all of them. Look, here are the pits. Then I kissed him in his car. 'Fun night?' said Bill. He put his hands in his pockets and leaned against the refrigerator. 'Oh, you know,' she'd said, moving toward the door, 'how these things go.'

134

Poor Bill. Pasty and drawn, his tie askew, leaning on one elbow at the head of the table, smiling at Hannah Melman, who was talking about the middle school chorus. Stupid Bill. With that cataleptic smile. She could, this instant, lay down her fork, tuck her napkin under her plate and announce to her guests at the table that she was seeing ghosts, that Bill did not love her, that she had kissed George Wechsler in his car. She could say all that and the evening would slip from before to after, like an eel gliding into a pond. Everyone would be shocked. But then they would go home, and after a little while they would not be shocked anymore and would eventually forget about what she had said, and remember this evening only vaguely, and she would be as alone with her problems as she was now.

What *happened* to me? she thought. How could my life have ended up this way?

But yes, she thought, renewing her effort to focus on the dinner table conversation instead of the one inside her head, children are resilient. Julia, she hoped, was resilient. (Yet so hard to talk to these days.) That little boy would probably grow out of whatever was making him so unhappy and become a sensible adult. Unless he really did need a diagnosis?

'Do you ever wake up at night,' she asked Stan in an undertone, 'and find yourself asking, "Where are the parents?"'

Stan smiled attentively, as if waiting for the punchline, and then said he supposed occasionally he did. She smiled back and asked him to pass the wine bottle, topping off his glass before she refilled her own. Margaret had been aware of Hedy watching her with shrewd crinkle-eyed attention since the beginning of dinner; but now Hedy and Clarice

Watkins were discussing Marv Fischman's healthcare coverage. At the other end of the table, Aaron and Bradley Wechsler had started complaining about the SAT exam to Hannah, while Julia fed scraps of ham to Binx under the tablecloth and Matthew kept interrupting to say what was the point of going to college when you'd never get a job anyway. The wind was racketing against the windowpanes. She listened to the chink of silverware against china, wishing people would talk about something entertaining and sophisticated, something distracting. Books, or art, or movies. Naomi was wagging her finger at Bill, trying to persuade him, with the help of George, that free-market economies were incapable of self-regulation.

The roasted red beets on her plate seemed to be doing a lazy backstroke in a little white pool. When she looked up again George was pouring her some water.

She glanced at George. Briefly said thank you, then turned back to Stan.

Someone asked for the red wine and, before the bottle was passed down the table, Margaret splashed a little more into her glass and tried to listen to Stan, who had joined in the free-market conversation. Instead she found herself staring at Matthew, two seats down to her left. Matthew, in his striped rugby shirt, saturnine and faintly whiskered. Attacking his slice of ham as if he had not been properly taught how to handle a fork and knife. Naomi had told her about Matthew's run-in with the Littlefield police. Acting out, she'd said. Also, he wouldn't let her read his college application essay. Separation anxiety. Trying to show he didn't need her because he depended on her so much.

But, thought Margaret, by all logic it should be George's twins acting out – their parents actually were separated, mother taking up with a massage therapist, father writing about zombie baseball players – it should be *those* boys getting drunk and having run-ins with the police. Instead it was Matthew, whose parents were not only married but both psychologists. Or could that be why? In any case, poor Matthew, who looked like Raskolnikov.

She watched Matthew wolf down a bite of ham. Beside him sat small grave Julia, both of them listening to Aaron and Bradley Wechsler describe their summer backpacking trip in Wyoming. Matthew had probably spent last summer sprawled on his bed, playing violent video games and downloading pornography. Selling his Adderall pills online.

Julia caught her eye and scowled.

When Julia was a baby, a bib round her neck, she'd banged her tiny hands against the high-chair tray at dinner, crowing as Margaret spooned apple sauce into her mouth. It had been so gratifying to feed her, to see her quickly satisfied. Matthew had once been a baby, and here he was now, in a shirt like a convict's coverall, sneering as he asked Hedy for the bread basket. Two weeks ago he was slumped in the front seat of his mother's van, lit up by the glare of a policeman's flashlight, slack-jawed, pimply neck showing above the collar of his black leather jacket, reeking of peppermint schnapps. What was next for him? College rejections, crack addiction, car theft, venereal disease, the degradations of isolation and fear, a dusty back room that smelled of old cigarette butts overlooking a parking lot in some distant city, where he lay weeping on a filthy mattress, streetlights shining through broken slatted blinds, barred shadows across his

face, and as she followed Matthew to this desolate conclu-
sion everyone at the table looked up at her.

'Did you say something, Margaret?'

'Are you all right?'

'Fine,' she coughed. 'Something in my throat.' Blindly,
she reached for her wine glass, but again it was empty. She
picked up her water glass instead.

Anything could happen to any of us, she thought as everyone else resumed talking. To me and Bill, to Julia. And who
among the people at this table would truly care? They might
be *interested*, but would they spend even one sleepless night?
She put down her water glass, feeling suddenly chilled. Was
it possible that the dogs were a sign, a portent of something
bad about to happen? It seemed so obvious a possibility and
yet she had not until now considered it. They had seemed
only about her, not about anything else. But now she looked
down the table at her guests in their holiday clothes, laughing, eating, drinking red wine, talking about money and
doctors' appointments and the SATs. What if the dogs were
for all of them?

Silence fell over the table.

'The economy,' she stammered, realizing that once again
she'd made a sound. 'So awful. It's affected everyone. Bill's
firm is being investigated by the SEC.'

'*Margaret*,' she heard Bill gasp.

'Oh, God.' She tried to focus on him. 'I'm so sorry. Was I
not supposed to say anything?'

'It's probably nothing,' Bill was already explaining. 'Just
allegations.'

'Allegations?' echoed Stan.

Now everyone was peering across the candles at Bill,

tallow-faced above his buttoned-down shirt and striped Christmas tie. Margaret put a hand to her pearls. What had she done? He had mentioned the investigation a couple of weeks ago while they were discussing a phone call she'd received that afternoon from Julia's social studies teacher. A bullying incident, not serious. Julia called a name in class. 'Allegations' had sounded dry and unthreatening, and Bill had waved away her questions. 'Probably nothing,' he'd said then, too. She realized now she should have pressed him, but she'd been worrying about the phone call. In addition to the bullying incident, Julia was not participating enough in class. *Not achieving to her potential. Any concerns at home? Perhaps she is overscheduled?* 'Well, I hope everything will be all right,' she'd said to Bill. When he didn't mention the investigation again, she assumed that whatever it was had been resolved.

'I'm so sorry,' she said again.

And she really was sorry. Sorry for blurting out this news and catching Bill off guard, sorry for kissing George Wechsler, sorry for inviting people to dinner while out in the cold whirling darkness thousands of dogs slunk just beyond her lit windows, ears laid back, hackles raised, circling and circling her house, leaving not a single paw print in the snow.

Bill picked up his napkin and patted his mouth. Once he'd been hit in the head by a Frisbee as they sat on a blanket in the park with Julia; he wore the same dazed, abject expression now.

She tried to smile at him, but already her thoughts were rushing away in a different direction. Could Bill's unhappiness, his depression over the past months, have been less about their marriage than about what was going on at the office? He had withheld his worries about work, probably not wanting to trouble her, not mentioning them during their sessions with Dr Vogel. But could it be that Bill didn't know himself how much those worries could explain?

A new orderly matrix began to emerge from the turmoil and anguish of the past months. Bill was depressed about work. And she had only kissed George out of loneliness and pity, because his book was not selling well and his wife had left him, and because he was smart and funny and that wasn't enough to guarantee him anything. Bill would understand. After everyone left tonight, they would talk. She would ask him questions about the investigation; she would apologize for getting angry earlier in the kitchen. They would get into bed and turn out the lights. Binx was the only dog in their house. Even now, everything could be all right.

'Bill,' she murmured. 'Oh, Bill.'

But he was so far away at the other end of the table, explaining something to Naomi, who had asked about SEC investigative procedures. His face looked strangely small and boyish above his striped tie, his thin nose fragile and outsized, as if it belonged to someone else. If only he would look at her. But he was still talking to Naomi. She lifted a hand to wave to him, an encouraging signal, to let him know that everything would be all right – and knocked over Stan's wine glass.

'Ah!' said Hedy.

Margaret apologized repeatedly to Stan as he began mopping his shirt front with his napkin.

'Fuck me, Dad,' snickered Matthew. 'You look like you've been shot.'

'Matthew,' barked his mother.

'I'll get a sponge,' said Margaret.

'Let me.' George was already standing. 'Just point me to the kitchen.'

'But everything's such a mess,' cried Margaret.

Naomi called out to George to go left, and then launched into a long description of the best way to organize kitchen drawers and get rid of clutter.

Margaret wasn't listening. Because as she offered her own napkin to Stan she caught sight of something sharp and plain, bright as the flat side of the blade that had been lying beneath the confusion of her thoughts all evening. It was all just trouble. She might be going mad, she might be about to get divorced, she might be alone for the rest of her life, with no job and no money, but that's all it was. Just as the wine on Stan's shirt was only wine, it was only trouble. She was not the first to be in such a state, nor would she be the last. Whatever happened to her had happened to other people, who'd either survived or not, as she would survive or not, and the world would continue on, implacable and absorbing.

Life is interesting, Dr Vogel had said a few sessions ago.

If only, Margaret thought, I could see it all as interesting, then that's what it would be.

A capacious sadness filled her, and with it a great relief. At last she understood. At last it had come to her: she was just like everyone else who had troubles and if she was interested in her own troubles, she was also interested in theirs, and therefore she was not alone, would never be alone, even if Bill left her, even if she spent the rest of her life weeping in her bedroom with the door closed. The world and its troubles would be with her.

'Here we are.' George had reappeared with a sponge.

Under the table, Binx could be heard sighing and snuffling.

The Wechsler boys were talking to Matthew about a biology project coming up – dissecting a sheep brain, which they said was the same size as a human brain – while Hannah and Julia giggled and made disgusted faces. Stan Melman finished sponging himself off. Naomi was now offering advice about removing red wine stains: salt, she said, while George contradicted her and said seltzer. Naomi stopped advising about red wine stains and, perhaps to get everyone at the table talking about the same thing, began condemning a recent vandalized holiday display. Two days ago someone stole a seven-foot gingerbread man from the lawn in front of the town hall, snapped off the gingerbread man's legs and dumped his body on the steps.

'I mean, why kill a cookie? Who'd have thought to worry about that?'

Outside the dining-room windows it continued to snow. All that was out there was snow. Margaret breathed in deeply, feeling her lungs expand for the first time in months. She was so glad to be in her house, at her beautiful table, with candles and shining silverware, the red walls glowing behind the heads of these lovely people. She liked them all, she liked them so much, her guests, her family and the bright muddle of their mingled conversations, she loved that, too, all the marvelous, ordinary, perishable noise.

Smiling, she pushed back her chair, getting to her feet like someone standing up on a tightrope.

'I would like to make a toast,' she called out, conscious again of Hedy's small dark eyes upon her. 'A toast to my husband, Bill.'

Everyone else stopped talking and turned to look up at her.

'To Bill,' prompted Naomi, after a moment.

'To Bill.' Margaret raised her glass. 'And to all of our troubles.'

Something was not quite right about her toast, but she could not figure out what it was; only that no one seemed to be joining in. She tried to sit down again but miscalculated the position of her chair and fell to the floor. Binx shot out from under the table, barking madly, as everyone began pushing back their chairs, moving around the table to see if they could help.

Bill, she thought. Where is Bill?

But everyone was getting in Bill's way, so that he was the last to reach her. Margaret struggled to her knees, then fell over again, and lay on the floor calling out, 'I'm fine, I'm fine,' as George hoisted her upright by her armpits and then, with Stan Melman's help, lifted her into his arms. Swept with embarrassment at finding herself in George's short, powerful arms, Margaret shut her eyes and pretended to pass out.

'Where's your bedroom?' George was asking Bill in a gruff voice, holding her tightly. One of her black patent leather pumps had slipped off; the other was hanging from her toes.

'I'll take her.' Bill was next to them now; she felt him put a hand on her leg. 'It was hot in the kitchen,' he was saying. 'She's just tired, after being in there all day. I'll take her,' he repeated to George.

'I've got her.'

The side of her face was pressed against George's chest;

his heart beat against her temple, a succession of steady tender mallets.

'Just tell me where to go.'

'I'll take her,' said Bill, his arms now around her thighs.

He pulled slightly and George pulled.

'You've got a bad back,' said George. 'Let me have her.'

For another moment they both held her, like two dogs fighting over a stick.

At last Bill loosened his hold; he gave her thigh a lingering, almost friendly pat, then she felt the warmth of his hand withdraw. Then she heard Julia's voice – Julia's voice, so much higher and younger, as it was when she heard her speak on the phone – offering to lead the way upstairs. Next Naomi, saying she would come along as well. Someone else said, 'Here's the other shoe.'

George shifted his grip and heaved her higher onto his chest. She could not think now of what she would say to Bill. She could not think of anything. Her heart felt huge and full of blood. George was grunting with effort as he began carrying her up the stairs, gripping her more securely, his biceps tensing around her waist and under her knees. And from somewhere close by or far away, she heard the howling begin – it was only the wind, battering the north side of the house; of course it was only the wind, the wind, the howling wind.

14.

During her evening walks with Aggie through the snowy village, Clarice Watkins continued her practice of gazing into lit windows of kitchens and living rooms. Often she saw people sitting around a table under a hanging lamp, plates and glasses spread out before them like a deck of cards; or she saw the silhouettes of people watching wide-screen television sets on which one bright silent image swiftly replaced another, even battles or conflagrations cheerful-looking in their brevity. She could not, of course, see into upstairs windows, but she imagined children in their baths, mothers taking a washcloth to the seashell curve of an ear; parents later washing their own faces at matching pedestal sinks in bathrooms, discussing plans for the weekend: a movie, or dinner out, something simple, that new Italian place by the river?

A peculiar wretchedness had begun to hound her on these evenings. She missed her mother. She missed Dr Awolowo. No one knocked on the door of her borrowed office at Warren College, where she sat surrounded by another professor's books, his prayer rug on the wall and his framed photographs of Kathmandu. A silvery bloom had attacked the leaves of her rubber plant. Aggie was limping – Lyme disease, said the vet – and slept most of the day in her plaid dog bed, twitching and moaning.

Often lately she found herself staring out of her window

at a twiggy bush in the Downings' backyard, strung with berries, crimson against the snow, or forgetting to drink her coffee while watching a red cardinal perch on a green pine branch. Every evening she passed the Downings' house when she headed out on her walk with Aggie; through the windows she frequently saw Julia Downing lying on one of the living-room sofas, mouth ajar, reading a paperback book with a lurid purple cover that featured a pair of fangs. Opposite Julia sat her mother in an armchair, by a lamp, looking at an iPad. Behind her hung the gilt-framed corner of a seascape.

Glimpsed night after night, this pleasant scene had worsened the jittery, abraded feeling in her chest, as if a small sharp-clawed animal were scratching at her breastbone. Her uneasiness was more endemic, more oppressive than anything she felt during her fieldwork in Detroit, even in Azcapotzalco. Every evening she looked in at dining-room tables and television sets, at kitchens with shelves of imitation Fiestaware plates and coffee mugs, and whimsical wall clocks shaped like teapots and cats, and her throat tightened.

None of it was what she had expected. The tables, clocks, televisions. None of it was what, without realizing, she had hoped for. Why weren't these people happier? She had counted on them to be happier. To be insular, complacent, self-absorbed. And they were – yet also restless, anguished. And strangely infatuated with the idea of menace.

It was that girl, Julia, who disturbed her most. The house was locked against the dark, the room was warm; a beautiful painting hung on the wall. Still the girl read her purple book, desiring to be elsewhere, kidnapped by warlocks, trussed and gagged, headed for a stone tablet, a virgin sacrifice. She would trade it all – lamp, painting, her own mother – for a bleak adventure, never doubting that everything would be there when she returned, would always be there, that she did not have to do more than lift her eyes from the page and it would all still be there.

Had that child not noticed the way her father looked at her friend? Did she not see her mother collapse drunkenly at dinner, then disappear upstairs in the arms of another man? Did she really believe disorder and tragedy happened in books?

Out on the icy sidewalk, Clarice Watkins pressed a gloved hand to her forehead. Aggie grumbled, tugging at her leash, wanting to return to her plaid dog bed. They walked away quickly, Clarice no longer stopping to peer into the lit windows she passed, except to note how many lights had been left on in rooms that were empty.

Back in her own small, spare living room, brightened by her throw pillows and a rag rug she bought at the Harvest Fair craft show, she sipped a cup of chamomile tea with honey and considered writing an email to Dr Awolowo, just for the comfort of typing his name.

Her head hurt. The Downings' dog had got sprayed by a skunk in the yard two nights ago and a dark greasy miasma still hovered outside, clinging to Aggie's coat whenever they came back in from a walk. A noxious film had settled on the furniture, her plates, even infiltrating whatever she made for dinner. No amount of air freshener seemed to get rid of it.

I want to go home, she thought.

Yet, paradoxically, her fieldwork was going well. In the

past few months, she had received many invitations from local residents. In addition to Christmas dinner at the Downings' house, she had been invited to the Fischmans' New Year's party, a small gathering of psychoanalysts, where she met the Epsteins, who sent her an invitation to their daughter Amelia's bat mitzvah in February, and she'd been invited by Naomi Melman to a book club meeting in March, at which they would be discussing George Wechsler's novel. Yesterday Sharon Saltonstall telephoned to ask her to attend a coffee meeting with members of the Off-Leash Advisory Group and the chief of police.

'We can't just sit around and do nothing,' Sharon said hoarsely on the phone.

Two weeks ago, Sharon's old basset hound, Lucky, was standing near the driveway in a shoveled patch of Sharon's front yard when he began to stagger on his short, thickset legs; by the time Sharon got to him, it was too late. People no longer let their dogs out in their yards alone. Some dog owners drove to other towns to walk their dogs. More than a few were considering moving altogether. Task forces had been organized. A Take Back the Park march was planned for when the weather warmed. 'Our Dogs and What Next?' read an editorial headline in last week's *Gazette*. *What have been unleashed in this town are the forces of hatred and intolerance. A place bitten by fear is never the same place again . . .*

And yet Clarice Watkins thought she detected a waning of interest: since the dog problem had left the bounds of anything anyone could have expected, it had become fantastical, and as a result people in Littlefield were beginning to stop thinking about it. During her morning coffees at the Forge, she continued to hear customers express disbelief that 'this sort of thing' could happen in Littlefield, but more idly now, more out of habit. One morning she eavesdropped on an elderly couple who had arrived at the café wearing matching tartan wool hats. They shared a plate of scrambled eggs and an English muffin, briefly discussed 'all those dogs', then the old lady went on to talk about her canaries; that morning she'd found one lying on the floor of its cage. The old man asked for the salt. He said the eggs were hard. They left two dimes for a tip.

The young Pakistani, Ahmed Bhopali, was wiping down their table.

'What do you make of that?' Clarice asked him, but he only frowned, like someone picking up a dead bird, and shook his head.

Tonight she was attending a dinner in honor of a Warren College alumnus, an economist whose recent book, a reinterpretation of Keynesian equilibrium models, had been getting a lot of press. The dinner was held in the college art museum, tables set up in the marble-floored rotunda amid contemporary sculpture, all alumni gifts: a two-story tower of plastic detergent bottles, a 1968 VW Bug covered with black rubber beetles, three life-size human figures constructed out of paperclips.

In a black dinner jacket and chartreuse bow tie, the economist stood beside the tower of detergent bottles, shaking hands with guests. He was a youngish man with a small chin and glossy brown hair that curled behind his ears and fell over the back of his white collar. 'Thank you for coming. *So* pleased to meet you,' he said, gazing over her head as Clarice Watkins introduced herself.

Halfway through the dinner, a pinched, tired-looking woman sat down in an empty chair next to Clarice. After gazing restlessly around the cavernous room through her gold-rimmed spectacles, the woman introduced herself as Emily Orlov and said she taught Russian studies; then she remarked that *Samsa's Wheels*, the VW Bug sculpture, had cost almost a million dollars. 'Meanwhile the endowment is in the toilet and tuition is going through the roof.' She took off her spectacles and peered at them for a moment before putting them back on.

It was her husband who was being honored tonight. People began to clap as he walked past the human paper-clips to stand behind a wooden lectern. Clarice clapped, too, and leaned over to tell his wife she looked forward to reading his book.

'Here.' Emily Orlov reached wearily into her large leather purse and pulled out a book. 'I have an extra copy.' On the cover, red, white and blue dollar signs bounced on a green dollar-bill trampoline. *Up and Down: The Rise and Fall of American Prosperity and Why It Pays NOT to Learn from Our Mistakes.*

The answer, as best Clarice could glean from the economist's speech, was that market-driven stupidity was good for the economy. Cycles of imprudent investment periodically ruined swathes of small investors, creating room for cannier, more vigorous and adaptive investors.

'Rather like a controlled burn,' he explained, to laughter and applause.

. She noted this observation down on her steno pad.

After his speech was over, dinner guests lined up to meet the economist, who sat at a table furnished with two stacks of his books. Clarice was glad to have a copy to add to her archive of primary documents, which included Naomi Melman's book, weekly issues of the *Gazette*, the engraved invitation for Amelia Epstein's bat mitzvah, several homework assignments from Ms Manookian's social studies class and online minutes from all the town hall meetings she had attended. Also a flyer that she'd found rolled up and fixed to her doorknob with a rubber band: *Wayne's Happy Paws Snow-Shoveling Service: Call Wayne! First shoveling free! Also minor household repairs! Gutter cleaning! No job too small!*

Document everything, Dr Awolowo repeatedly reminded her. No embellishments.

Beside the economist hovered a skinny black-haired girl wearing ballet slippers, a tight black sequined jacket and a short gauzy black dress. Whenever he signaled for another copy of his book, the girl took one from the stacks, opened it and bent gracefully forward from the waist, as if preparing to curtsy.

After quietly watching the girl for a few minutes, Emily Orlov said, 'Doesn't do to pass judgment on people, does it?' Then she added, 'But that outfit took looking for. A lot of consideration of effect.' Emily was wearing a long-sleeved cotton dress covered with the sort of sprig found on dust ruffles. 'It's very hard not to be judgmental.'

Clarice agreed this was true.

Emily repeated that it was hard not to be judgmental. Almost impossible these days when the world was such a mess, and she began talking about the village, the aldermen and their poor decisions when it came to school budget cuts, the graffiti, what had happened to the dogs. 'Obviously, the dogs are a symptom of a more systemic problem, but we all take it personally.'

Her little round glasses flashed. At the table beside the lectern, her husband caught hold of the girl's wrist for an instant as she handed him another copy of his book.

A page from Clarice Watkins's steno pad that evening:

One can view the village of Littlefield as a carefully constructed refuge, an achievement that, these days, seems as admirable as it is fragile, and perhaps deserving of whatever protections, social and otherwise, that can be afforded. What is surprising to the outsider is that Littlefield does not consider itself to be a refuge. The citizens here believe they are no different from citizens anywhere. Although they stay apprised of current events it appears they believe that what happens in their village is equally serious, that their personal burdens are equivalent to any suffered elsewhere . . . Or perhaps their recognition of the world's great problems, which they feel powerless to remedy, amid their own relative comfort, is driving their preoccupation with problems of their own, which they (protectively) view as enormous, baffling, inimical . . . ?

These notes did not strike her as especially useful.

15.

Hedy Fischman was reading the regional news to Marv, in bed for the third day with flu-like symptoms. According to iTriage, a new app on Hedy's iPad, the flu should be treated with fluids and rest, unless a high fever and a cough develop and progress to shallow breathing, delirium and pneumonia-like symptoms, in which case a medical professional should be consulted. Currently Marv was in a stable condition in his blue striped pajamas, eyes closed, two pillows behind his head, petting Kismet curled on the bed beside him with his good hand. By the window, Hedy reclined in the chaise longue in her black velour tracksuit and sheepskin slippers; she had already read aloud much of the *Globe*'s online national news and was now only summarizing articles she found noteworthy, peering through the bottoms of her bifocals, the jet-beaded chain swinging gently whenever she turned her head.

'Municipalities have run out of money for snow removal. Snowplow operators across Middlesex County are on strike.' She scrolled down further. 'Let's see what else we have to worry about.'

A school bus driver in Haverhill was arrested for drunk driving. Three hikers had been stranded on Mount Greylock, believing their cell phones would rescue them. In Pepperell, hundreds of blackbirds had fallen from the sky for no apparent reason and lay dead on the sidewalks. A young man in Leominster had just been arraigned on charges of kidnapping his estranged girlfriend, stripping her naked, tying her to a park bench early in the morning and smearing her with peanut butter, leaving her to be attacked by squirrels. The girlfriend had survived and was being treated for hypothermia and was expected to make a full recovery.

'Now *that's* a story.' Hedy looked over the tops of her glasses at Marv.

She tapped open the business section and noted that FBI agents had appeared at the office of Roche Capital Management with a search warrant. The FBI's Boston office had issued the following statement:

> Per FBI guidelines, we cannot confirm what investigation this is for or why it is being conducted. We cannot confirm what evidence was collected or if further evidence will be needed and as this matter is sealed we have no additional comment.

A spokesman for the US Attorney's office in Boston also declined to comment. Officials at the Securities and Exchange Commission also declined to comment. It was left to Hedy to comment.

'Poor Margaret!' she said. 'Poor Bill! The world is going crazy. What's next?'

Marv said that was the million-dollar question.

'What do you think, sweetie?' Hedy leaned forward to ask Kismet. The little dog had rolled onto her back so that Marv could scratch her belly. 'Hey, you.' She snapped her fingers. 'Give us an opinion.'

Kismet stood up and pranced about on the bed, lifting up her dainty black paws. Then she fell over and played dead.

'What a comedienne.' Hedy hoisted herself slowly from the chaise longue. 'Oof, oof.' She arrived at the bed and bent over to pat Marv's hand, then straightened his blanket and tucked it more securely around his middle. 'Enough news. Should I fix us some soup or a pastrami sandwich for lunch?'

It was decided they would have both. Why not?

'Live a little,' said Hedy, and snapped her fingers again at Kismet.

After a mild spell and a bit of snowmelt, arctic weather returned; once more rhododendron leaves furled tight, icicles hung from every roof, and as February dragged on drifts of snow hardened along the streets of Littlefield and turned a cinereous gray, encrusted with dirt and black flecks of leaf mold, looking less and less like snow and more and more like rubble.

On the first of March Julia Downing awoke before dawn, as she had almost every morning since Christmas, and ran through the multiplication tables in her head, waiting for the enormous fish that lay on her chest to slide off and flop onto the floor. Often lately she'd had to name all the US capitals to persuade the fish to budge – once she even had to list the original signers of the Declaration of Independence – but this morning the fish was more yielding than usual and by the time she reached the seven times table she was out of bed and hunting for the clothes she'd laid out the night before. After dressing in the dark, she slipped into the hall and went downstairs to toast a bagel.

Enough light reflected into the kitchen from the snow

outside that she could make out the muffled shapes of the stove and the refrigerator as she felt her way to the light switch. Binx was asleep in his crate in the mudroom; he woke up long enough to thump his tail. He was too destructive, her mother said, to leave unattended in the house, but Julia hated to see him cooped up, like an animal in a zoo. While she waited for her bagel to toast, she stood at the kitchen sink, watching the new goldfish, Mike II, glide back and forth above the ceramic castle in the bowl on the windowsill. Mike I had died the day before Christmas and been flushed down the toilet, a replacement companion for Ike bought from Pet Mart the same afternoon. She hadn't noticed until her mother mentioned it almost a week later.

'I'm sorry I didn't tell you.' Her mother pressed her wrist against her temple. She was having one of her headaches. Lately she was having headaches two or three times a week. 'I didn't want to spoil the holidays.'

It was then Julia understood that Mike I had been lying on her chest in the mornings.

After Freckles disappeared, she'd buried his favorite cat-nip mouse and read aloud a poem by Carl Sandburg; when Elvis the guinea pig, Kiki the parakeet and all the other gold-fish died, plus whatever drowned in the pool filters, she'd held funerals by the stone waterfall and then buried them under the hydrangeas. For Mike I, the toilet. The conse-quences were clear: denied a proper burial, Mike I had grown monstrous with outrage. Into her dreams swam his swollen scaly abdomen, his immense yellow eye, his horseshoe-shaped mouth from which sprouted tentacle-like feelers. Her room had taken on the algaenous reek of a neg-lected fishbowl.

Yet Julia had not acted right away, distracted by not being invited to Amelia Epstein's bat mitzvah – Hannah was going – and haunted by memories of Christmas dinner, when her mother had fallen off her chair and had to be carried upstairs by Aaron and Bradley Wechsler's father, her slip showing, a run at the heel of her nylon stockings. An event so humiliating that Julia had at first mistaken the fish on her chest for the weight of shame. Her mother spent the rest of Christmas vacation playing gloomy rhapsodies on the piano, while her father staggered about the house grimacing like someone trying to swallow a spider. Then Lily and Maya Saltonstall's dog was poisoned. It was drawing closer, some sort of disaster. Despite these signs, Julia still had done nothing and then it happened: right after Valentine's Day, old Dr Fischman died.

Fish-man.

'What's wrong?' her mother asked when Julia clapped her hands over her mouth at this news during dinner. 'Honey, you hardly knew Dr Fischman. What is it, Julia. Are you sick?'

That evening Julia lit a votive candle beside the goldfish bowl and sprinkled in flakes of fish food while reciting the Lord's Prayer. Three days later she tried eating a few flakes of fish food herself, then saying the Lord's Prayer. After googling 'Mourning' on her mother's iPad, she found websites for How to Deal with Loss, Stages of Mourning, Rites and Rituals, as well as directories of local funeral homes offering discounts and promotions.

Grief is a guest, read the opening statement of one website. *It deserves accommodation.*

For the past three days Julia had covered her bedroom

mirror with a towel and started wearing an old blue soccer T-shirt torn at the shoulder, though her mother made her change into a different shirt before going to school.

Acknowledge guilt, advised the same website. *It needs a room, too. Usually the best one in the house.*

'I'm sorry, I'm sorry,' Julia whispered every evening, standing for a few minutes by the kitchen sink watching the goldfish swim around their ceramic castle.

Then a few days ago Binx started sneezing. Probably a dust allergy, said the vet, when Julia's mother called for a phone consultation, but he suggested running some tests just in case.

Yesterday at school, Julia realized that she had never asked about the results of Binx's tests. At home, she found her mother asleep on one of the living-room sofas, a gray wool shawl flung over her legs; her mother looked old, waxy, cheeks fallen in, hair stringy, the corners of her mouth turned down. Julia put a hand on her shoulder to wake her up.

'What about Binx's tests?' she asked.

'What tests?' her mother said groggily.

As Julia buttered her bagel now in the dark kitchen, her fingertips went cold.

Something more active must be required to appease Mike I, some sort of penance. A test. Because things were getting worse, she realized, leaving the knife by the sink and forgetting to put the butter back in the refrigerator. She had been careless, she had not been respectful of the dead, and now things were getting worse.

Maybe she could start by taking Binx for a walk in the mornings, which her mother was always asking her to do. Usually whenever her mother asked her to walk Binx a powerful lassitude seized Julia, turning her legs to tree trunks. Her reluctance had nothing to do with her love for Binx, but with the conviction that anything her mother requested somehow violated her most vital liberties. These, then, were the tasks she must perform. *Without being asked*.

Instead of eating her bagel, she wrapped it in a paper towel and carried it with her into the mudroom, where she took her puffy pink down coat and pink fleece hat from the peg by the back door and pulled them on, followed by her snow boots. She stuck the wrapped bagel in a pocket, found the leash and then opened the door to Binx's crate. 'Shh, shh,' she said as he scrambled to his feet and shook himself, dog tags tinkling like bells.

Outside it was still dark, but from the trees came the sweet uncanny sound of a few birds calling singly to each other above the deep blue snow of the neighbors' yards. Next door lights were on in the Fischmans' carriage house. Binx stopped to sniff the sidewalk, then lifted his leg on a snowdrift.

As Julia stood shivering and hugging herself, listening to the birds, something ran under the streetlight and across the Fischmans' driveway, something dark, the size of a big dog. At the end of the Fischmans' driveway it stopped and looked back at her, black eyes shiny and uninvolved; the next instant it was gone.

A coyote. Her mother saw them all the time, but Julia had never seen one before. Her heart began to pound. Why had she seen it now? Could it be a message of some kind, a warning? Perhaps from one of her dead grandparents, or from Dr Fischman himself? Julia had been visiting websites on reincarnation over Christmas break; she had also, one afternoon, looked up Norman D. Mayer on Wikipedia. He'd worn a blue snowsuit and a black motorcycle helmet that December day on the National Mall; his van was white. Last spring she had visited the National Mall with her parents, stood looking at the Washington Monument, perhaps on the very spot where Norman D. Mayer had once parked his van.

She kept a lookout for the coyote as she walked down the driveway to the sidewalk, Binx capering at the end of his leash. Coyotes were fearful creatures, she'd read in the *Gazette*. Nocturnal. More afraid of people than people were afraid of them. Maybe that was the coyote's message: something brave had to be done, a brave act like Norman D. Mayer's, to keep anything else bad from happening. She would take Binx all the way to the end of the block instead of just to the end of the driveway, even though it was dark and a coyote was out there. Her cheeks tingled in the clear frosty air.

She began walking to the end of the block and then, when nothing happened, she walked to the end of the next block; she crossed Ballard Street, where Hannah lived. Two more blocks and she and Binx were at the village. All the shop windows along Brooks Street were dark; only a mail truck and a few cars rolled by, the salted road crackling under their tires. Walking faster, she passed the post office, the Bake Shoppe, then the Dairy Barn and Walgreens. In another block she was passing the snow-covered elementary school, three buses like enormous gray loaves in the parking lot, and then the entrance to the park. Beyond stretched the meadow, pale blue and luminous.

She stayed on the sidewalk. In another minute she was

passing Avalon Towers, which overlooked the park on one side and Silsbee Pond on the other.

She stopped on the sidewalk and looked down at the pond, a hundred feet beyond the parking lot for Avalon Towers and a chain-link fence with a gate. A perfect frozen oval, like a hole punched out of the sky, halfway rimmed by trees. At the far end of the pond squatted a dark crenellated building, the bathhouse, where she had often changed into and out of her bathing suit when her mother took her to the pond for swimming lessons. Inside, the bathhouse smelled like wet diapers; the walls were streaked with mildew and plaster was falling off the ceiling. But in the milky blue light of dawn thin vapors rose from the ice and in the distance the bathhouse looked like a fairy-tale castle, swathed in mist.

How lovely, Julia thought, surprising herself by using one of her mother's words. She usually felt peevish when she heard her mother describe something as lovely: a flowering tree, an autumn leaf, a sunset. 'Oh, look,' her mother would say. 'Quick, look at how lovely this is.' Her urgency at these moments always seemed overdone. But now Julia understood that the vision before her was indeed lovely: shimmery and vanishing and slightly unbelievable.

She had been looking down at the pond for several moments when the breeze shifted; it lifted her bangs and with it came a yelping sound that arose from out on the ice. A goose was flying overhead, honking. The sky was turning lavender, brightest across the pond where it met the trees, almost red through the bare branches. And then she saw something she had not noticed at first: a shadow that materialized into a small white shape, yards off shore.

Binx began barking, standing on his hind legs at the end of his leash. Julia squinted. Then she pulled Binx into the parking lot, all the way to the fence, to get a better look. It seemed to be moving on the ice, wobbling a little back and forth. A puppy, she thought. A puppy that was lost. A fat white bulldog puppy.

The coyote she'd seen earlier crept into her mind; how easy it would be for the coyote to run across the ice and snap the puppy's neck with its jaws. She put a hand on the gate and rattled it. Padlocked and looped with a chain.

Out on the ice the puppy sat down and began to whimper.

As he cycled down Brooks Street, preoccupied by the narrowness of the bike lane and by the frigid air needling through his black watch cap and the red knitted scarf wrapped around the lower part of his face, Ahmed tried to concentrate on constitutional law. He had been too tired last night to finish studying for this morning's exam. He was always tired. Yesterday the professor had called on him: 'Mr Bhopali, explain to the class, please, the "Dormant" Commerce Clause.' He could not answer. He did not know. It was too hard, getting up at four o'clock in the morning six days a week to be at the café by five to put the first trays of doughnuts in the oven, bussing tables until nine. Except today, when he asked to leave before seven to study for his constitutional law exam, which was to be administered at ten. Ugh, another pothole. He had not been raised for such a hard life. It was bad for his *constitution*. Ha! That was a good one. Ugh, ugh. Instead of riding on this treacherous roadway he should be at home sitting on a yellow cushion wearing a clean linen kurta, having breakfast brought to him on a tray. Sunlight filtered through the tall louvered shutters, glowing in the red glass vase on the high wooden shelf by the door. 'Yes, Mother. I will have more tea.'

The taste of bad coffee lingered in his mouth; the smell of fried dough clung to the scarf wrapped over his nose. As he jolted along, too hot and too cold in his woolen pea jacket, he passed large brick houses where he would not be welcome; large cars drove too close to him, spraying his loafers and pant legs with slush; and into his mind stepped a small round black woman in a turban, who visited the café several times a week for an early breakfast and spoke to him pleasantly, asking attentive questions. She was not young but she had an attractive smile. Last week she had inquired about his father's computer repair service in Karachi and whether the Forge Café gave him paid sick leave. But when he asked if she would like to go out to a movie, maybe to his room afterward for a glass of wine, she shook her head. Why did she regard him with such interest if she did not want to sleep with him?

Women were foreign and incomprehensible, Massachusetts was foreign and incomprehensible, and now, after hitting that pothole, his bicycle was making a metallic clicking sound, followed by the hard bumpity, bumpity, bumpity of a flat tire.

Carla Manookian was driving too fast on Brooks Street, late for an early meeting at school with Mr Anderman, checking her lipstick in the rearview mirror. She'd slept through her alarm, set to wake her at five thirty so she could grade last Thursday's pop quizzes (Who were the Minutemen? Were there more British casualties at Lexington or at Concord?), and also have time to put on her make-up. Three parents had sent complaining emails to Mr Anderman in the last month, accusing her of not returning schoolwork 'in a timely fashion', wrote Mr Anderman in an email of his own, attaching the parents' emails and requesting 'a consultation'. He'd had it in for her since he'd visited her B Block class in December.

Her lipstick looked orange. The idea with make-up was to wear it so that it didn't look as if you were wearing it. She always looked like she was wearing it. Why wasn't she returning schoolwork in a timely fashion? Because every time she looked at a pop quiz she wanted to garrote herself, that's why.

It hadn't been very hard to climb over the gate, especially because of all the snow that had been plowed up against it. She left Binx on the other side, though, tied to the fence. Her plan was to stand at the edge of the pond and call to the puppy. Speak to it in a soothing tone and see if she could coax it to crawl to her.

The day was brightening, everything becoming distinct.

Binx was barking from the parking lot, but at the sight of Julia coming down the bank the white puppy had stopped whimpering. No collar. Maybe it was a stray. Maybe she could keep it. It looked like it was shivering. Remembering the bagel in her pocket, Julia crouched down in the snow by the pond's edge to take a closer look at the ice. Maybe she could hold out the bagel and get the puppy to come to her that way.

'Julia?' her mother would be calling up the stairs by now. 'Julia? Are you awake?'

The ice was the whitish-gray of old cotton underwear,

pitted and rucked, interrupted in places by a mottled bruised color. Where the ice met the bank she could make out ghosts of leaves and sticks below. If she walked out just a little way onto the ice she could toss the bagel to the puppy. So it would know that she was friendly. Just a few yards. Four or five yards. Maybe seven. Not far at all. Still she hesitated, kicking the ice with the heel of her snow boot.

Light shone glassily around the pond. High above the turreted bathhouse floated a cloud. It had, she saw, a fin and a tail.

Dragging his bicycle onto the snowy verge of the road, he tried to figure out what to do about his flat tire. He was not far from the entrance to that old people's home; he could leave his bicycle chained up there and walk the rest of the way to the college. Already the gods had sent him a bad day and it had barely started. As if they had decided he was complaining, a terrible barking started up as he wheeled his bicycle into the parking lot. A big black dog was leaping back and forth, tied by its leash to a chain-link fence. 'Shut up,' he yelled to the dog, thinking it was barking at him. But then he saw what was making the dog bark. On the other side of the fence, below a snowy bank, stretched the pond and standing on the ice five or six yards from the bank was what looked to be a young girl in a pink coat and hat.

He cried out, dropping his bicycle with a clang, and ran across the parking lot.

The black dog barked and barked, jumping about on the end of its leash. He glared at the dog, keeping a careful distance from it as he ran at the chain-link fence; he was up and over it in a moment, and the next descending the steep frozen bank toward the pond, crab-like, slipping and sliding in his loafers.

'Stop!' he called, holding out his arms. 'Miss! Please! Stay where you are!'

Her face was white and small under her pink tasseled hat; he could see that she was frightened, though it could be that she was frightened of him, a man shouting at her in heavily accented English. What was she doing out there? Merciful gods.

'Stop, please!' he cried.

She had got lipstick on her teeth – how did that happen? She peered at her mouth in the rearview mirror, trying to dab at her teeth with a Kleenex. Oh, God. Now she had lipstick on her chin. And her hair was a mess. She would have to pull over. Right ahead of her was the entrance to Avalon Towers. Pull in there and get out her purse. No way was she getting out of her car at the middle school and having Mr Anderman see her looking like a ghoul –

Followed the next instant by a percussive jolt and a heavy clang.

'Come back!' shouted the man on the bank. 'Miss! You will fall through the ice!'

'I can't come back,' said Julia. She wished he would stop shouting.

'Please! Come back! What are you doing?'

I'm rescuing a puppy, she thought. What does it look like I'm doing?

A deep crack had appeared in the ice between her and the shore.

The man was wearing loafers in the snow and a dark blue jacket over gray pants. He had unwound his long red scarf from around his neck and was now trying to throw the end of it to her, but he was standing too far away and the scarf was too short. He looked cold and unhappy. On the snowy bank above him, Binx was leaping about like a dervish behind the chain-link fence, barking and whining. Thin cracks webbed the cloudy ice at her feet. She took another step backward.

Five steps on to the ice and it broke under him; now he was standing in water to his knees. He kept calling to the girl to stop but she was retreating across the ice. Did she want to die? Anger flashed through him and momentarily he stopped shaking.

'Come back!' he shouted. 'Have you no sense?'

From far behind him came the rubbery shriek of skidding tires followed by a tinny crash.

Without looking, he knew his bicycle had just been run over. Two hundred and fifty dollars. Used. His Droid razor phone had been in his satchel. Two hundred and ninety-nine dollars on eBay. And his lunch: chicken salad on rye, free because he made it for himself in the kitchen at the Forge Café – but not totally free because labor had been involved – plus an apple and an orange.

Now he could explain the 'Dormant' Commerce Clause: what you lose, you don't have.

'Come back!' he shouted as his legs went numb.

High, thin voices, the chorus singing something sad, a song from *Rent*, teachers weeping audibly and students holding battery-powered votive candles as Mr Anderman welcomed Hannah on to the auditorium stage. Hannah, wearing a new black dress from Urban Outfitters, holding a single white rose. *Julia was my best friend. I knew her better than anyone . . .*

Another figure had appeared on the banks, a tall woman in a brown hooded parka, stumbling along behind the fence in short, high-heeled black boots.

'One of my students!' Ms Manookian was shouting into a cell phone, her voice clear and certain like someone answering a simple multiple-choice question. 'It's one of *my* students!'

Julia was so grateful to be claimed unequivocally that she forgot to be surprised at the sight of Ms Manookian on the banks above the pond; she was also relieved to be no longer alone with the strange bearded man. He had stepped onto the ice, which broke beneath him; now he was standing in water up to his knees, cursing in a language she did not understand, still trying to throw her his red scarf. Ms Manookian continued to shout into her cell phone, giving what sounded like directions. It was fully light now. Cars had pulled into the Avalon Towers parking lot; people were getting out of them to stand by the chain-link fence. In the distance Julia heard the wailing of coyotes.

'Help!' she finally cried, looking toward Ms Manookian. 'Help!'

As if in response a fire truck and two police cars pulled up to the fence above the pond, red sirens revolving. Several firemen in black boots and fluorescent green overcoats jumped from the fire truck as two policemen in dark blue padded jackets began climbing over the fence. The first policeman across slid down the snowy slope, motioning with a hand to the man with the red scarf, while another policeman walked slowly toward Binx, holding out his fist. Binx stopped barking and sniffed the policeman's fist, then wagged his tail. Now the firemen were wrestling what appeared to be an inflated yellow sled out of the back of the fire truck. It had long metal runners; they were hoisting it over the fence.

A third policeman held a gray bullhorn. He stood behind the fence looking out at Julia, his head tilted toward Ms Manookian beside him, who was telling him something and gesturing with her long bare hands. A moment later he raised the bullhorn to his mouth.

'JULIA. STAY CALM.'

At the clear, definite sound of her name booming across the ice, she shuddered. Cold air was seeping up through her jacket and her whole body felt numb. She looked at Ms Manookian standing beside a policeman, firemen now climbing past them over the fence, and forgot about the puppy and thought instead of the National Mall, as wide and flat as an airplane runway. Lined with enormous stone buildings built like tombs, filled with the most important things in the world. Natural History. Air and Space. And in the middle of it all, caught in the gravitational field between the white-domed Capitol and the granite obelisk of the Washington Monument, had stood Norman D. Mayer in his snowsuit and helmet, as lonely as an astronaut.

What had he felt as the police called his name and ordered him to surrender? Had it been like this, a strange feeling of lightness? He must have viewed the tiny swarming scene before him with a kind of pity, realizing that laws no longer applied to him, even gravity no longer applied to him, he was held by nothing in the world but himself.

She turned her head to glance back at the puppy, but it

wasn't there. When she looked around again, another crack had appeared in the ice in front of her.

She took one more step backward.

'JULIA. DO NOT MOVE.'

The ice is cracking around my feet, she wanted to say, but she had lost her voice.

Ms Manookian was speaking to the policeman with the bullhorn; he listened and nodded, holding the bullhorn away from his mouth. The man with the red scarf had thrown his scarf to the policeman on the bank, who was hauling him out of the water. Another policeman was inching down the slope carrying a blue blanket; in a few moments the two policemen had wrapped the fierce-looking bearded man in the blanket. Even from a distance Julia could see him shivering; his teeth were bared and his face had turned the color of clay. Both policemen stayed close to him, one with a hand on his shoulder. At the fence, people were calling out suggestions and comments, taking photos with their iPhones.

Julia shuddered again. The bumpy ice around her feet looked like a smashed windshield.

'JULIA. REMAIN CALM. WE HAVE CALLED YOUR PARENTS AND THEY WILL BE HERE SOON.'

Ms Manookian waved. She cupped her hands around her mouth, crying out in a voice that sounded thin and unreliable after the bullhorn, 'Don't worry! Don't worry, Julia!'

One fireman had dragged the yellow sled down the slope and was nosing it onto the ice. The other fireman was pulling on a black rubber suit.

'Don't worry!' cried Ms Manookian.

The fireman in the black rubber suit was lying on the sled, propelling it toward her by pushing against the ice with his black gloved hands while the other fireman played out a length of rope. From far away came the steady throb of a helicopter.

Julia looked up at the sky to see that the cloud with the fin was still there.

I hope you're satisfied, she addressed it tiredly. Then the ice cracked again.

16.

For weeks Margaret had hardly left the house. She sent Bill to the grocery store, the drug store, on whatever errand must be run; Binx had to be walked, but she kept those walks as short as possible, heading away from the village, hurrying home again, keeping her head down, and especially in the evening doing her best not to look at anything but the sidewalk. They were there, they were always there, but it was her job now not to see them.

It was her job to stay home. In the days immediately after she fell through the ice on Silsbee Pond, Julia had not wanted to be alone. It was like having her again as a young child, when she wanted to be with Margaret everywhere, followed her from room to room, clung to her hand at bedtime and begged her to stay until she fell asleep. For a while, when Julia was six or seven, she used to ask the same questions, every night: *What's the saddest thing that ever happened to you? What's your worst memory?* Margaret worried Julia must have overheard something about the years before she was born – though Margaret couldn't imagine how, since she and Bill never discussed it – but unwilling to explain what she was sure Julia could not understand, she had talked about her parents, who had died within a few months of each other several years earlier. They had been elderly, both in poor health. Julia had seemed satisfied with this information; she had scarcely known her grandparents but their deaths were logical sources of sorrow, and eventually she stopped asking her unsettling questions. But now she had started again, more probingly: *Was that really the saddest you've ever been?* Yes, Margaret told her. That was the saddest I've ever been. *Are you still sad about them?* Night after night, Margaret sat at the end of Julia's bed, leaning against a bolster, listening to her breathe, Julia's body so slight beneath her quilt she seemed hardly to be there.

Don't you dare, Margaret said silently to the dark windows. *Filthy beasts.*

She told Bill that Julia needed to stay home for a week or two, as long as she wanted. To rest, she said. To recover, though it was true, Julia seemed fine. An ambulance had been waiting when she was brought off the ice; in five minutes she was at the hospital emergency room, where Margaret and Bill rushed in to find her sitting on a gurney behind a curtain, swaddled to her nose in a quilted white electric blanket, a tuft of soft brown hair sticking up on top of her head, like a damp chick hatching from an egg.

The doctors all said she was fine. *Kids are resilient.* A little shaken up, but fine.

'I want her home with me,' Margaret told Bill.

He thought Julia should go back to school after a day or two. Get back to normal. 'She's fine,' he said. 'You're going to make her think this was something more than it was.' But in the end he gave in.

She'd spent those days in the house with Julia listening, waiting to hear her footsteps on the stairs, the sound of her moving about in her bedroom. When Julia was a baby, Margaret had been terrified she would stop breathing in her sleep and during Julia's naps would hurry to her room, sometimes two or three times, to peer in at her from the doorway; in the middle of the night she would wake even out of a deep exhausted sleep and run down the hallway to Julia's room to check on her. Now she invented excuses to knock on Julia's door for the simple relief of seeing her cross-legged on her bed, reading a book or hanging over the laptop. '*What?*' Julia would look up. 'Why do you keep coming in here?' And they would have their usual arguments, about Julia's tone of voice, about whether she spent too much time on the computer, until Julia said something spiteful, which was the real relief, because then Margaret could retreat, flushed, angry, buoyed by hurt feelings, until the old dread seized her again.

But soon Julia wanted to go back to school. She really was fine. Her fall through the ice had become a story to be told again and again to Hannah and in answer to questions posted on her Facebook page, every day more exaggerated, less serious, requiring more exclamation points, emoticons and double question marks.

Her explanations sounded so reasonable: she thought she'd seen a puppy. A white puppy. But it was just a lump of snow. It was early morning, the time of day when the light plays tricks on you. Why was she walking by the pond in the first place? She wanted to take Binx for a walk. He was getting fat because he didn't get long walks anymore. Of course it was an incredibly irresponsible thing to do, all Margaret's friends agreed, but kids are so impulsive; at least now she'll never make a mistake like that again, at least she's learned a lesson about being careful. Although it was hard to tell what Julia had learned, once she went back to her iPod, to her monosyllabic replies at dinner and to keeping her door closed.

'What did you see?' Margaret asked, again and again. 'Tell me. You can tell me.'

'Nothing, okay? I thought I saw something but it was nothing. Leave me alone.'

Julia had gone back to school last week. Kids had put up signs, decorated her locker. 'Welcome Back, Julia!' was displayed on a computer monitor mounted on the wall in the foyer. Julia had not disclosed any of this herself; Hannah had told Naomi, who reported it to Margaret. Someone had captured her fall through the ice with an iPhone and posted it on YouTube; Julia had become a minor celebrity.

Margaret had to resist the urge to text her four or five times a day (Bill had bought Julia a cell phone, for 'emergencies'), just to ask how she was doing; she had to limit herself to two or three questions when Julia finally walked up the front steps in the afternoon. How was school? Anything interesting happen today? Really, *nothing*?

It had been weeks since Margaret slept more than an hour or two, and when she did sleep her dreams were thin and restless. She kept having one dream over and over: of herself riding on a bus and looking out the window. The bus passed a grassy triangle where three roads met, with the river beyond, and on the grass stood a dark-haired man in a bright blue suit. As he turned to look at her, staring at him from the bus window, she saw he had the face of a vicious dog. But she was not surprised – or she was surprised, but only in the way one is surprised to see an old acquaintance in an unexpected place. The dog-faced man seemed to recognize her, too, and lifted a hand as the bus passed by.

Finally Naomi gave her a vial of Ambien. 'You've got to get some sleep.'

Naomi kept saying Margaret needed a break. A change of scene. Margaret herself had started to wonder if this might be true. Just yesterday morning as she walked Binx down Rutherford Road, the sun had come out for the first time in days and she had felt a little better. The air seemed milder than usual. Errant warm currents flowed up from the sidewalk, escaping from beneath melting banks of snow, and she had been seized by a desire to keep walking. Somewhere in the world people were sitting outside at round café tables with iron tops perforated like lace, sipping wine and wearing sunglasses. What if she drove to the airport with Julia, got them both on a plane and flew to – Florida, the Bahamas? Just got up and *went*? She heard a clatter of palmetto fronds; a balmy sea wind wafted from the east. But then the temperature dropped and once more it began to snow.

Yesterday morning Naomi had called to ask if Margaret would drive Clarice Watkins and Hedy Fischman to tonight's book club meeting. George Wechsler was at last coming to talk about his novel. Clarice's car had a broken headlight and Hedy never drove at night anymore. Margaret said she wasn't sure she was going; she would have to think about it. Hedy called next: neither she nor Clarice had read George's novel, but Hedy wanted to see what all the fuss was about and Clarice had never visited a book club; she was curious to see what one was like.

Margaret figured Naomi had engineered all this, so she would feel obligated to go to the book club meeting and wouldn't be able to back out at the last minute. She said as much to Bill when he came home from work that evening, adding, 'I don't really want to go.'

'For God's sake,' he said, turning away. 'Get out of the house.'

Now Hedy and Clarice were sitting in her warming car while Margaret cleared off the windshield and the back windows with a scraper, snow squeaking under her boots, brushing off the headlights, which glowed through lids of ice. Snow sifted down the back of her coat collar and settled into her hair. By the rhododendrons she saw something move, but it was only the shadow of a branch in the headlights.

'Well,' she said a few minutes later, inching out of her driveway. 'Here we go. Wish me luck.' Beyond the windshield wipers, the world was filled with static.

'Bill's home,' she said a moment later, though no one in the car had asked about Bill. 'And Julia can always call if she needs me.' She thought of her bathrobe, the lamp by her bed. Her nightstand, on which waited a glass of water, her book, the vial of tablets.

She bent over the steering wheel as they reached the street. Clarice said that she was doing fine and that the road looked pretty clear.

'I'm a little nervous,' Margaret confessed. 'It's been a while since I've been out. And to be honest, I don't know how I'll face George again, after what happened at Christmas.'

'Don't be silly,' said Hedy, mummified by scarves in the front passenger seat. 'It was a nice evening. Wasn't it, Dr Watkins? We all had a very nice time.'

George, to his credit, had been a gentleman. Emailed her the next day to say thank you for dinner and to say he hoped she was feeling better. Margaret gave a little laugh. For weeks she hadn't been able to think of that night without slight vertigo, and yet now it seemed hardly worth remembering.

They had left Rutherford Road and were heading toward the village. The streets looked so different at night, muffled by snow, bushes turned into small hills, dark houses into mountains. A white mailbox stood on four legs by the curb, watching her drive by.

The three of them were squeezed onto a couch, amid an assortment of kilim pillows, each holding a glass of wine, Hedy still wrapped in her big black coat because she said she was chilled to the bone. Margaret was playing with the silver ostrich charm hanging around the stem of her wine glass. Naomi had given everyone an animal charm, to protect against mixing wine glasses and spreading germs. Flu season.

Yes, Julia is doing much better, thank you. Back to normal. It was very scary but we think she's learned a lesson. You know kids: act first, think later.

She'd listened to herself repeat this short litany four or five times since their arrival as women she knew came up to inquire after Julia. Too much homework, everyone murmured. Too many reality shows on TV, making kids believe they can do anything. Look at the way they cross the street without looking. But clearly all of them thinking: screwed-up parents. She stared at the plate of cheese and crackers on the coffee table.

When she looked up again Sharon Saltonstall was standing over her in a green cable-knit sweater, her wide face a cauliflower of concern. Margaret repeated that Julia was doing much better. Then she said she was sorry to hear about Sharon's dog.

Sharon said it had been hard, but Lucky went quickly and didn't suffer, and it turned out to be an aneurysm, natural causes after all. In any case, compared to what Margaret was going through, she couldn't complain.

'Boy, you guys have had a tough time.' She was leaning down, hands braced on her thighs. 'What a scare with Julia. I don't know how you let her out of your sight. I'd be home with her every minute. Really sorry to hear about your husband's firm, too. Boy, that's rough.'

Margaret agreed it had been a hard time.

'That story in the *Globe* was awful.'

'Yes, it was.'

'Gosh, hope he'll be able to find another job.'

From across the room, Margaret saw herself sitting on the sofa, a slim blonde-haired woman in a blue silk blouse, holding a wine glass and smiling, a small piece of barbed wire in her mouth.

'Excuse me,' she said. 'I think I'll get some more wine.'

When Margaret sat down again, Sharon had vanished.

'Odious woman.' Hedy leaned forward among the scratchy pillows. 'Poof! I got rid of her. Piece of cheese?' she said, lifting a cracker toward Margaret.

Hedy had at last taken off her coat to reveal a hairy brown cardigan that looked like coconut matting. In the living room's low light, her small dark face might have been a carven mask, cheeks sunken, nose beaky, heavy pouches under half-closed eyes.

'She will be fine. Isn't that right, Dr Watkins?' Hedy ate the cracker herself, then reached out to pat Margaret's arm. 'Your Julia. She is very young. She will be okay. And Bill,' she added. 'Him too. You will see. In the end, it will be okay.'

Margaret saw herself turn her barbed smile on Hedy.

'You will see,' said Hedy, subsiding back into the pillows.

She had gone to sit shiva with Hedy after Marv died. Hedy had worn the hairy brown cardigan then, too. The house had been airless and overheated, full of the odor of damp wool coats and the nutty stale smell of rewarmed coffee. People sat in twos and threes in the darkened rooms, eating poppy seed cookies and talking in soft voices, while Hedy's little gray dog ran in circles, yip-yapping.

'It needs to be fed,' Margaret heard someone murmur.

'That thing always needs to be fed,' said someone else.

Margaret went into Hedy's pantry and found a bag of kibble in a cabinet; she poured a cupful into the dog's dish with a sound like hail on a tin roof. As soon as she put the dish on the floor the dog began gobbling, little black eyes bulging. Finally it looked up from its bowl and she thought she heard it say thank you.

In the Melmans' living room women clustered in the soft lamplight, holding wine glasses, admiring Naomi's collection of Kokopelli figures playing pan pipes on the mantelpiece, everyone dressed in silk and light wool, their animal charms winking. Naomi's children had been banished upstairs, along with Stan and Skittles the dog. Every now and then screeches of TV laughter came from above and the sound of Skittles's tail thumping the floor.

George arrived a few minutes late and was surrounded by a pack of women, led by Naomi. Hedy was in the middle of telling a story about a Viennese uncle of Marv's, a medical student studying to be a psychiatrist who had known Freud and had once been allowed to photograph Freud lying on his famous couch. When Marv's uncle fled Vienna, he gave the photograph to his landlady. What that photograph would be worth now! George turned around and caught Margaret's eye; he smiled at her. Hedy was still talking about Marv's uncle, who became a hat salesman in Newark because no American medical school would accept his Viennese degrees. 'And he could have been another Freud.' Hedy raised both palms.

'What a shame,' said Margaret, watching George turn back to Naomi. Naomi was wearing a brick-colored raw-silk blouse and a necklace of what looked to Margaret like bent nails.

'So this is a book group.' Hedy sounded unimpressed. 'So what have you been reading?'

'Well, George's book, of course.' Margaret nodded at the copy Naomi had placed on the coffee table, next to the cheese plate. 'Before that we read *Bleak House*.'

'Eh?' Hedy struggled to sit up again among the pillows, the beaded chain on her glasses swinging. 'Do you know, I'm going to tell you something. I want you to listen. Children do not think like adults. What makes no sense to you made sense to her. That is how it is. But I am sure you are worried.'

'All I do these days is worry.' Margaret lowered her voice. 'About everything.'

Hedy gave a twitch to her hairy cardigan. 'Yes? Well? As Marv says, worry is part of the language of love. You worry about what you love.'

'You also worry,' said Margaret, 'about things you're afraid of.'

'Yes, well,' said Hedy.

She seemed about to say something else when Naomi called out, 'Find a seat, everyone!'

Naomi had pulled a straight-backed chair in from the kitchen and set it for herself in front of the fireplace. Installed next to her, in a throne-like bamboo Papa-san chair, was the author, smiling gamely above his blue denim shirt, unsnapped to reveal a few curls of graying chest hair, the stem of a wine glass in his fist.

'More chairs in the dining room if anyone needs one.' Naomi sat gripping the seat of her straight-backed chair, beaming impatiently. 'Okay! As you all know, we have a special guest tonight, and we're going to begin by saying hello to George Wechsler, who has agreed to talk to us about his novel.'

'Hello, George!' chorused everyone.

Naomi began by asking George to give a brief history of how he got his start as a novelist. George revealed that his father, a high school math teacher in Brooklyn, had told him there were two ways to get ahead: the stock market or a trust fund.

'But since I wasn't interested in the first and wasn't getting the other, I focused on girls.'

Dutiful laughter.

'And pretty soon I noticed the best way to get girls' attention was by being a basketball star or playing football.' In his Papa-san chair, George leaned forward, smiling adamantly. 'Unfortunately, I dribbled like a guy playing football and played football like a guy dribbling.'

More dutiful laughter.

'So I started writing poetry. Figured it worked for Lord Byron. Had some success with the editor of the school literary magazine. Went on to major in English in college, dooming myself to a future of low-paying jobs, a requirement for all serious writers.'

Several women were now looking at the floor. But George was launched into his story, familiar to anyone who, like Margaret, had read his website biography: years of rejections from publishers, mornings of waking at five a.m. to write at the cold kitchen table, the struggle over whether he should just 'chuck it' and go to law school; then the precious month alone in a friend's cabin in Maine when he took the six hundred and fifty-page manuscript on which he had labored for ten years 'and turned it like an ocean liner', pointing it in a new direction and throwing three hundred pages overboard.

Expressions of astonishment.

'So that's my story.' George sat back and drank half of the wine in his glass, then set the glass on the floor.

A regretful sigh seemed to run through the room. Hedy had dozed off among the pillows. Clarice was staring fixedly at a Kokopelli figure. Margaret was thinking about George's harsh voice: tonight there was something almost tender in it – something greedy and youthful, and also unwary. She winced and then wondered where George's wife had been while he was in that cabin in Maine.

'Any questions?' asked Naomi.

After a few long moments of silence, Naomi said, 'Well, *I've* got a question. George, I've been dying to ask. Is any of this book autobiographical?'

With a grateful smile, he began explaining that everything a writer writes is autobiographical, since it all comes from his own interests and observations, his own fears and obsessions. 'We all sing the same note,' he concluded, scowling apologetically. 'Me, me, me.'

The laughter was genuine this time. Then Naomi asked

George if he would mind reading aloud a passage from his book. They all waited as he leafed through the copy that had been lying on the coffee table, announcing finally that he'd like to read a scene toward the end.

He cleared his throat. In a slow, resonant voice he began reading one of Margaret's favorite passages, the moment when the young hero's rabbi father, sitting on the temple dais at his son's bar mitzvah, listens as the boy interrupts his Haftorah reading, in Braille, from Judges 13:10–14, to tell the congregation that in a world of confusion and false gods it's important to listen to yourself and believe in your dreams – and that if his father, Rabbi Pinchas, would only have faith in him, and send him to baseball camp in Fort Lauderdale, then he, Danny Pinchas, might someday be drafted by the Yankees.

After a stunned moment, Rabbi Pinchas rises slowly from his chair. In front of an aghast congregation, he falls to his knees. Shaking a fist at the empty ark, he cries out, *Isn't it enough? Haven't I suffered enough?*, repeating this question for nearly a quarter of a page until at last, from the very back of the temple, he is interrupted by the tired old voice of Krasnick the janitor.

So, rabbi, tell us. What is enough?

George stopped reading, allowing the final word to vibrate in the air.

There was a lull, a sense of emotional percipience, followed by a smattered ovation that grew stronger.

'Thank you, George.' Naomi was grasping the armrest on George's Papa-san chair. 'What a powerful moment.'

George thanked her and leaned down to pick up his wine glass.

Now women began raising their hands with questions for George. Do you write on a computer? How did you find your agent? Someone inquired into his literary influences.

Twain, Melville, Hemingway. 'And Poe, of course.'

Margaret had been playing again with her ostrich charm, but she looked up as George began talking about Poe's haunted characters. He said the living dead were manifestations of 'unappeasable longing' as well as fear and grief, and that the unseen were always with us, something Poe understood better than anyone, which was why he was a psychological genius.

She could feel everyone in the room listening to him differently now, attentive and thoughtful, until he introduced the psychology of Moses Finkle, the zombie hero of his new novel – 'because who's deader than a ball player who never hit above 180?' – when Naomi interrupted.

'Do you read any women writers?'

After thinking for a few moments, he mentioned George Eliot and a young Senegalese poet-activist whose name he had trouble pronouncing. 'There are others,' he added uncertainly, an elbow propped on the armrest of the Papa-san chair, one hand loosely cradling his empty wine glass. But before he could list them, Emily Orlov, sitting across from Clarice in a bentwood rocker, announced that she thought his novel was about 'the recognition of human isolation' and said Krasnick the janitor reminded her of a character in a short story who tells all his troubles to his horse because no one else will listen to him.

'It's hard to find real companionship in this world,' she said, rocking back and forth.

Murmurs of assent rippled around the room.

Someone asked about the novel George was working on now, while someone else refilled his wine glass. Margaret watched him lean back in the Papa-san chair, cowboy boots crossed at the ankles. Once more he began talking about Moses Finkle, when from the back of the room came a husky, imperious voice.

'I have a question.'

George's mother-in-law, Mrs Beale, was standing in the doorway wearing a trench coat and a Liberty scarf, with a small elderly woman hunched in an old fur beside her. Margaret hadn't seen her come in; she must have arrived while George was reading.

'Yes?' George sat up.

The room hushed instantly.

'It seems to me,' continued Mrs Beale, 'that when Sybil here and I were girls, a lot of novels were about people giving up things for love. And *doing* things for love.'

'I'm not sure I understand the question,' said George.

'That *is* my question. Love does not seem to be in novels nowadays.'

'Are you talking about romance novels?'

'I am *talking* about the job of the novelist. *Your* job as a novelist.'

'Are you asking,' said Naomi, wearing a strained, hostessy expression, 'if writers should love their characters?'

'No,' said Mrs Beale scornfully. 'I am saying that novelists are doing a bad job, in my opinion. It is lonely being a person, very lonely, as *that* young woman pointed out.'

She gazed at Emily, who had taken off her spectacles and was polishing them on her blouse. Emily made a throaty noise and put her spectacles back on.

'I don't see how this relates to my book,' said George, with surprising gentleness.

'What we need in this world –' Mrs Beale gave him a severe look in return – 'are bravery and honor. Models of decency. Not more zombies and monsters and *strange* behavior.'

She stood very straight in the doorway, her expression militant above the epaulets on her trench coat; beside her, Sybil hunched into her fur collar, smiling with chipmunk panic.

'Just so I understand,' Naomi tried again, 'are you talking about –?'

'Husbands and wives who promised to love each other, for instance.' Mrs Beale pointed a bony finger at George. 'In sickness and in health. *That* is a good subject for a novel. Why don't you write a novel about a bad husband who apologizes to his wife and they get back together?'

A pause sheathed the room, like ice encasing a twig. Margaret closed her eyes. When she opened her eyes again, George was looking steadily at Mrs Beale.

'How about you write that book,' he said, 'and I write one about an old lady who puts up anonymous signs in the park, upsetting a lot of people?'

Two dull red patches appeared on Mrs Beale's flat cheeks.

'*Mine* were polite.'

'That's your story.'

'*Naturally* that's my story.' Her voice was sepulchral. 'Because it is the *true* story.'

Everyone had started to murmur. Beside Margaret on the sofa, Clarice Watkins was noting something on a steno pad.

'You want a true story?'

Once more the room hushed.

George had pushed himself out of the Papa-san chair and was on his feet by the fireplace. 'I'll tell you a true story.' His voice was dangerously subdued. 'Listen to this one. A man spends his goddamn life sitting in a goddamn chair trying to figure out the exact words for how a blade of grass looks in the morning, while everyone else is *out* there, *doing* things, because he loves the goddamn world so much he'd claw his eyes out to understand five minutes of it.'

His face was terrible, Margaret thought, the face of Rabbi Pinchas howling at the ark. On the mantelpiece behind him, two Kokopelli figures appeared to be blowing pan pipes into his ears.

'But guess what? It's not the world's business to explain itself. Your *job* is just to sit there until it finally hits you in the face.' His voice had dropped lower, so that everyone leaned forward to hear him. 'And maybe what hits you smells like roses or maybe it smells like dead fish, or maybe –' his voice sank to a snarl – 'it smells like a werewolf's asshole.'

Margaret pressed three fingers to her lips.

A few feet away, two women were whispering.

'Did he say –?'

'Yes, he did.'

'That's not very nice. Also, I don't get it.'

'Me neither. Too much sitting if you ask me.'

But George was not finished.

'And for your information –' he glared at Mrs Beale – 'telling people what to do isn't a very effective way of getting things to happen.'

Naomi was standing now, too. 'George, this has been such a fascinating evening –'

But George was already shouldering his way past Sybil and Mrs Beale, stiff as sentries in the doorway. A moment later the front door slammed.

How excruciating it had been, thought Margaret, watching him get angry – so crude, embarrassing, almost suffocating, like watching someone get sick on a plane, and yet for the first time in weeks she felt a flicker of hopefulness. She wanted to remember exactly what he'd said; it seemed crucial to remember, but already the words were drifting away and all she could recall was something about what hit you and that the world's business was not to explain itself.

Other women were beginning to stand up, tugging at their blouses, looking for where to set their wine glasses. Naomi was twisting her necklace.

'I suppose that's enough discussion for tonight. Anyone like more wine?'

'No need for him to get so huffy.' In the doorway, Mrs Beale's long face looked drawn and very old above her Liberty scarf. 'Sybil,' she said hoarsely, 'where are you? Could we go home, please. I am feeling rather tired.'

'Enough,' sighed Hedy, from the depths of the sofa, 'was tonight maybe too much.'

17.

It began in the grocery store with buckets of unopened daffodils, stems bound together with rubber bands like bunches
of asparagus. Carried home and placed in a vase of water,
the daffodils opened within two days, filling one's house
with a delicate, waxy scent.

Next snowdrops, here, there, so early, so tenuous, a clutch
of sunny delirium.

Then came weeks of cold rain that washed away even the
peak of snow in the library parking lot, followed by gray
days that made students at Warren College yawn through
afternoon classes and sleep through morning ones – sleeping, too, through Dr Clarice Watkins's series of noontime
seminars on theories of modern social structure and the
influence of global destabilization – while at night they kept
vampire hours, histrionic lyrics pulsing through ear buds
connected to their iPods, eating cold pizza that tasted of
cardboard and stalking each other on Facebook. Something
in them was stirring. They wandered further into the Web,
news passing before them on search-engine pages: war
criminals acquitted, movie stars arrested, rivers swelling,
dams breaking, the polar ice cap melting faster and faster.
Vaguely frightened, they began tracking down kindergarten
classmates, former camp counselors, teachers from middle
school. Photographs appeared, to be liked or not liked –
people smiling, people wearing silly hats, people naked – also

posted slogans, obscene song lyrics, snatches of quoted poetry:

> When the hounds of spring are on winter's traces,
>> The mother of months in meadow or plain
> Fills the shadows and windy places
>> With lisp of leaves and ripple of rain . . .

As night faded toward morning and the pizza boxes lay empty, the students were filled with a restless desire for even greater knowledge. Would they ever experience sex as something other than sordid and incidental? Ever be able to buy a house, lift their own children into their arms? Did life hold fierce secret joys they could not yet imagine?

They rubbed their eyes and readjusted their ear buds, then returned to Facebook. Only to find themselves glancing up every so often at their pale reflections in the dark rain-streaked windows, wondering what else was out there.

Rain, rain, rain.

Then at three o'clock one Tuesday afternoon the sun appeared.

Suddenly all the splendors of late April were on display: yellow forsythia, pink azaleas, tight purple clusters of grape hyacinths. Green mist hung about tree branches as the first buds appeared and everywhere the air was mild and smelled freshly of earth. 'Such *weather*,' people all over Littlefield kept exclaiming. Even people who prided themselves on being realists were moved at the arrival of spring, believing against their better judgment that whatever sadness and worry they carried were at last beginning to lift.

Redbud, dogwood, quince. Tulips, narcissus, violets in the

grass. Torrents of lilacs. In the collective gardens of Baldwin Park, gardeners in fleece jackets pulled up pallid soggy stalks from last year's planting, crumbled moist soil through gloved fingers. Deep in the woods, ferns were unfurling from tiny cocked fists under oak leaves so new they were salmon-colored. Everything sticky and furred and succulent, burgeoning, bursting, unrepentantly blooming.

On a bright cool gusty morning, as wind blew down the sidewalks and threatened tulip heads, knocking them first one way then another, George Wechsler faced his computer, working on a scene between Moses Finkle and his former agent, Sam Gruber. Moses had just spent three pages convincing Gruber that he had been brought back to life by a kid praying over his baseball card. Now they were discussing Moses' brief season with the Kansas City Royals, particularly the high point of his career, in 1962 when he'd saved a game against Cleveland by chasing down a line drive and diving, mid-air, to make a stunning bare-handed catch. The crowd had been on their feet! The next day Moses dropped an easy pop fly; two days later he was sent back down to the minor leagues. Gruber had just said to Moses: *You had your chance at the brass ring, buddy, and you didn't grab it*. And Moses had replied: *The brass ring was brass, Sam. I'm ready for something in gold*. George was trying to decide whether he meant this conversation to be read ironically and wondering, in general, how to make his novel less about baseball and zombies and more about the dark laboratory of the soul, when the doorbell rang.

Looking down from his study window, he saw Margaret Downing in a beige raincoat standing on the front steps with her black dog, clutching the leash with both hands. Her face was turned toward the budding magnolia tree in his front yard.

She'd been walking the dog –

That was the first thing she said when he opened the door. She'd been walking the dog and realized – it must be – that she was by his house, and thought – his magnolia! – had just thought to stop by – not stay long – had just wanted to say – hoped she wasn't bothering him – his magnolia was so beautiful that she –

All while he was repeating please, please, come in. Hoping that none of his neighbors had seen her standing on his front steps.

They were still talking over each other as he conducted her and her dog past the dank stew of boots, sneakers and cleats piled in the front hall. He ushered Margaret into the living room, into the red velveteen armchair by the window, then gathered up limp *New Yorkers* and old *Playboys* from the coffee table – whisking away also a roll of duct tape and a plastic tube which looked to be the beginnings of a bong – before hurrying into the kitchen to give himself a moment to think.

Why was she here? What did she want?

Should he offer her something? He found a canister of stale macaroons, left over from Passover. He put three or four macaroons on a clean plate and carried the plate out to the living room.

Her black Lab was lying across her feet. An uglier beast than George remembered, and no longer a puppy but a big fat brute with a wet-looking coat like a seal's and a hoggish snout. Just then a sulfurous smell floated up. Flatulent, too.

The dog growled as George laid the plate on the coffee table.

'Hush, Binx. *Down*,' she said. 'He's gotten impossible,' she said apologetically.

George hovered on the other side of the coffee table, offering Margaret coffee, then iced tea and finally a beer, though it was not yet ten o'clock. She said no to everything and sat up straight in the red armchair with the expression of someone who has seen a mouse but is determined not to mention it. Finally he sat down on the sofa opposite, keeping his distance from the dog.

He'd heard about her daughter falling through the ice. It had been in the papers and even the boys had talked about it, an edge of awe in their voices he hadn't heard in years. She could have *died*, they kept saying. He'd wanted to send Margaret a note at the time, an email, but he couldn't think of what to say, and in the end had done nothing; even when he saw her at that book club meeting, he'd said nothing, shocked at the sight of her, huddled on a sofa, looking like she'd nearly died herself. Even now her skin looked sallow against the musty red upholstery of the chair, especially compared to the creamy flesh of the magnolia blossoms just opening outside the windows. She had removed her raincoat to reveal a pale pink blouse with pink cloth-covered buttons, darker pink lace at the collar. A thin gold necklace glinted at her neck and from her ears dangled jade beads set in gold filigree caps. Judging by the earrings and the lace on her blouse, her fair hair pulled back in a clip, George saw that she had arrayed herself scrupulously this morning. He did not know from whence the words 'arrayed' and 'scrupulously' had come – they seemed to have blown in through the door when he opened it for Margaret, along with *whence* and a few yellow catkins that now lay like caterpillars on the braided rug in the hall. But there they were, like Margaret herself, mysteriously presenting themselves to him.

Taking a macaroon between her thumb and forefinger, Margaret gazed at it intently; a moment later she dropped it on the floor and with a sharp exclamation bent over to look for it. Her dog was too quick and, rooting around on the carpet, snapped up the macaroon while she scolded him. Next she announced she had lost her house keys somewhere in the chair and began to hunt for them, crouching down to reach under the cushion.

'I'm sorry,' she said, in a high artificial voice. 'I don't know what's wrong with me. I feel like I've been losing everything lately.'

George stood up to help her look and a moment later realized she was kneeling, flushed and trembling, eye level with his belt buckle.

'Yes!' She held up a small silver ring of house keys.

Staring down at the parting in her hair, he noticed that she needed to touch up her roots. Faint lines etched around her mouth; a dusty halo of fine dry hairs outlined her face; below her eyes, bluish shadows. It was not kind, or fair, he realized, to examine people so closely, and yet he could not make himself look away.

She lowered her gaze and began playing with the keys in her hand, shaking them and saying, 'I don't know how – I don't know –'

'Here,' he said brusquely, and reached down to help her to her feet.

Her dog growled again.

'I just meant to stop by. I've wanted to talk about –'

They were both standing now; he still had hold of her arm. She gave a convulsive jerk, as if startling awake.

'Bill's whole firm has been shut down. We may have to sell our house.'

George took hold of both her elbows.

'I think he's seeing things.'

She described hallucinations Bill had been having: imagining their bed was full of bedbugs. The Christmas tree ornaments had looked to him like eyeballs. Twice he thought he'd seen his dead father, holding a bottle of beer.

'What do *you* think?' she asked. 'Could they be manifestations of –?'

'Sounds like regular nuts to me.'

Her eyes looked bright, as if she were on the point of tears. But in a determined voice she went on, 'What you said a few weeks ago, at the book club meeting –'

'Don't remind me.'

'No, no. That's not what I meant. I haven't been able to stop thinking, what you told us about Poe and the unseen being with us, and fear and grief, and being hit with –'

'Crap,' he said, dropping her elbows, 'all crap, the minute you start talking about it.'

'You don't understand.' She stared at him. 'Oh, what am I doing here?' She pressed her hands to either side of her face. 'What am I doing?' Looking so distraught that his exasperation vanished.

Quickly he gathered her into his arms and kissed her, breathing in a floral perfume that emanated from the pink lace at her collar. At that instant, her dog launched itself from the rug, snarling, teeth bared.

'Jesus!'

'Oh, my God.' She'd grabbed the dog's red collar with both hands, jerking it backwards. 'Did he bite you? I'm so sorry. Binx! Bad dog! I hope he didn't bite you. We haven't had him fixed yet and he's gotten so aggressive. I'm so sorry. I'll get him out of here.'

'No,' he said. 'Wait.'

While Margaret held the dog by its collar, George snatched up the end of its leash and tied it to a leg of the coffee table. Hanging half in the air, the dog scrabbled helplessly with its forepaws, making a strange low grizzling noise deep in its throat that sounded almost sorrowful.

'You can let him go,' he told her, stepping back.

Immediately, the dog sank down on the rug beside the coffee table. Margaret spoke to it sternly, put her hand on its big black head and told it to stay, while it rolled its muddy eyes up to look at her. When she saw that the dog was secured and would not follow them, she let George lead her across the room, holding her once more by the elbow, but now as if she were a convalescent or someone elderly. Yet when they reached the bottom of the stairs, she went up first, rapidly, easily, her black clogs almost noiseless on the worn plum-colored carpeting of the stairs, so that she was waiting for him when he reached the landing.

Once he might have found her awkwardness exciting, even touching; but the truth was they were both at an age where it was upsetting to be clumsy and inept. She had stepped on his foot when they were maneuvering onto the bed; she'd failed to understand that he wanted her to take off her blouse herself – not wanting to hazard those cloth-covered buttons, which might be only decorative. And yet something like ardor swept through him, something that felt like urgency as he pressed his mouth to hers and pulled, finally, at the pink buttons on her blouse; they proved to be real and gave way with surprising ease. Whenever he stopped kissing her she began apologizing and saying that she did not know why she was there. Several times her dog howled from downstairs and she apologized for that, too. He kissed her harder, realizing with some disappointment that she expected him to overmaster her. Eventually she stopped talking and there she was – hair loose on the pillow, eyes deep blue, the skin of her throat pulsing.

'I want – I want –'

'Hush,' he said, and went back to kissing her.

A little while later he asked, 'Do I need –?'

By then they both had most of their clothes off and she was making encouraging noises. He managed to locate a condom in the top drawer of his bedside table without too much fumbling.

Her breathing quickened.

Everything was – it was just as he liked to imagine –

But it was then that his old enemy slipped into bed with them: the third person.

He mounted her, he found himself reading, he hoped not aloud, from a continuous feed of pornographic bulletins that appeared to be running across the headboard. *His well-muscled buttocks heaving.*

'Oh,' she moaned. 'Yes.'

No, he thought, gritting his teeth. No.

With a tremendous thrust he –

A long stricken howl sounded in his ears.

Outside magnolia buds swelled and surged magnificently open in the sun.

Afterward they lay for a time, side by side, looking at the shifting gray and white leaf patterns thrown by sunlight on his bedroom wall, sharing a kind of collegial relief that their ordeal was over, as if they had delivered a joint lecture that was received with indifference and then had retired to a campus bar. He was surprised not to feel ashamed, but instead oddly proud of himself. It was not the end of the world. It was even pleasant, to be lying next to a woman who did not seem to mind that they had not achieved what they set out to do, but had instead been waylaid by other notions, other demands. She had not wept, either, which he'd expected given her earlier apologies.

The room was warm and mellow, fragrant with an apple core he'd left last night on his bedside table. The bedclothes were comfortably rumpled. They were talking about first memories. She had just said something about a blind knocking against a window sash in the summer breeze (had she been reading Virginia Woolf?), and was asking whether he thought people's lives rested, somehow, on a first memory (were all literate women possessed by Virginia Woolf?), when he heard himself say, 'I've never outgrown mine.'

Which wasn't what he meant to say; he didn't know what he meant and wasn't even sure his first memory *was* his first memory – something about touching a dog's rear end and having his hand swatted came back to him – but once more he felt her attention turn to him, and the heady sensation of having someone want to hear him talk about himself, mixed with the opulence of lying in bed in the middle of a sunny morning, made him keep talking.

His first memory was of carnival lights: the Ferris wheel's lit web of steel struts and stanchions, and below the treasure-box glow of lights against an indigo backdrop. Also the side of his father's head, the dark curl of an enormous ear. He was being carried away from the lights, home to bed, probably, but what he really recalled – and even now the memory smote him in the chest – was watching those magical lights recede, turning and turning, as he was borne off on his father's shoulder, his protests small and unheeded.

'Pretty Freudian, huh?'

She did not respond, but lay looking at the ceiling.

Finally she sighed. 'No. Not Freudian, I don't think.'

'The ear part.'

'Well,' she said, 'maybe just that part.'

This was kind of her. But now he wanted her to leave. His memory had depressed him. Now it seemed more about his father's ear than about the Ferris wheel, an image he had privately cherished. It was almost eleven. He could hear the postman clump up the front steps, arrive at the front door and stuff envelopes through the mail slot. Her dog began barking downstairs. Margaret was talking again about Bill. His job. Her worries about him. This, too, depressed George. Here he was with a woman in his bed, but all she could talk about was her poor deadbeat of a husband. He stopped listening and began thinking about his novel and the scene he had left off writing. Perhaps it was Margaret's earlier mention of Bill's father making ghostly appearances, but as he lay there thinking of Moses Finkle, it seemed to George that

Moses Finkle was standing at the end of the bed. Wearing old gray Kansas City Royals pinstripes, tight across the waist.

Margaret was still talking about Bill. 'He says he feels no desire for anything. We haven't had sex for a year. Even before that it was – for a while we tried –'

He had so many questions for Moses. What's it like to strike out with the bases loaded at the bottom of the ninth and hear twenty thousand fans groan in unison? What's it like to watch the next guy hit a triple, a rocket out to left field, and in that moment know, not just suspect but *know*, that you'll never be major, that you'll always be minor league in the thing you've given up everything to do? Would that be enough to pull a guy out of his grave, the chance to do it all over, be better, be *great*?

Moses shook his head. His blue batting helmet, scarred and blackened with pine tar, hid most of his face, but from the tilt of his chin George could read disapproval.

Margaret's voice had dimmed. 'It was all – too – complicated somehow.'

George made an effort to sound interested. 'Yeah?'

'Sort of – heavy. I kept feeling it was my fault –'

Sex in middle age is like making a matzo ball, he heard Moses Finkle say from the end of the bed. *It requires a sensitive touch. Too much handling and it turns to lead. You have to put everything together, lightly.*

George sat up halfway against his pillow. My God! What a line. Sex advice from a zombie! He had to write it down before he forgot it. His heart was racing. He'd been worrying that a zombie baseball player was too derivative – Shoeless Joe Jackson, the Malamud book – but a zombie Jewish sex therapist! That was new. That was all his. No more baseball player. The whole story would have to be revised, but it was falling into place. The boy wouldn't find a baseball card; he'd find a *business* card, an old faded business card, stuck to the sidewalk outside an adult movie theater in Albany. Or maybe Moses would be summoned from the dead by the boy's grandfather, a rabbi, with a congregation full of dysfunctional marriages, to deliver a series of miraculously effective sex education lectures ('Mazel Tov for Masturbation!', 'Why Make Putz a Four-Letter Word?'). The story would take place in the Catskills; Moses could come back to life in the Borscht Belt.

Beside him, Margaret was gazing at the ceiling and slowly twining a lock of hair around one finger. She looked like she could lie there all day. He had to get to work; his fingers were trembling with the need to start typing. But could he tell her to go home without ruining the fraternal feeling that had sprung up between them?

Already he saw her opening the door for herself and walking quickly down the front steps. In another moment she had gained the walkway, passing under the magnolia branches, and was onto the sidewalk, striding away toward the corner, the sun on her hair and the wind in her coat, that ugly black dog loping beside her. At least he should offer her coffee or a cup of tea. But then she might stay even longer. Also, he'd just noticed she had a mole on her neck she should really get looked at.

How impossible everything always turned out to be.

'Anyway, I think it *is* my fault –' her voice had sunk to a whisper – 'at least –'

For an instant Moses Finkle lifted his batting helmet; George glimpsed a dark, admonitory face that bore a strong resemblance to old Hedy Fischman's.

Margaret had stopped speaking. She seemed scarcely to be breathing, and George realized she was waiting for him to say that *he* found her desirable, in spite of his earlier performance, which must be confirming her worst fears about herself. He should reassure her. He should say something gallant, something complimentary.

'About what happened earlier,' he muttered.

For a long moment they looked hopelessly at each other.

'It's not Bill, it's me,' she whispered.

'What?'

'I'm the one seeing things.'

George sighed, 'You and me both, sister.'

'I see ghosts.'

'Who doesn't?'

'No, *really*.' Her eyes were huge and frightened. 'I'm trying to tell you something.'

'Listen, two minutes ago I had a ghost telling me how to make matzo balls.' He pointed. 'Right there by the footboard. I kid you not. Matzo balls. How's that for Freudian?'

For a moment she looked shocked, and then bewildered, followed by angry, then sad, and as he watched each expression flit across her face, changing her features from lovely to plain to something in between, he thought how extraordinary it was that so many selves could inhabit a single person. Why was anybody ever lonely?

As if she'd had the same thought, suddenly she began to laugh. It was an infectious sound, made up equally of despair and relief, and a moment later he began to laugh, too; it wasn't long before they couldn't seem to stop. They rocked on the bed, laughing and laughing, until their eyes leaked tears. *Whoo whoo*, they both cried as they tried to catch their breath. He was blotting his eyes with a corner of the bedsheet.

'Oh, I'm going to die,' she gasped.

'Me too,' he wheezed.

This set them off laughing once more, Margaret snorting in a way that was not becoming and George goatishly kicking his bare legs in the air. How absurd they looked, he thought. How absurd they *were*. But when they had quieted a little, enough to notice the leaf shadows moving on the wall and hear the birds calling back and forth in the trees outside, he turned to her again and what happened next was not absurd; in fact, it was unlike anything he could have imagined.

18.

It was Hedy Fischman's birthday. She was eighty-four. No party, she'd told Clarice. Too much fuss. As Marv always said, any fuss was too much fuss. Since Marv died, Clarice and Hedy had fallen into the habit of having dinner together once or twice a week. Maybe just a little dinner, said Hedy, when Clarice proposed a celebration. Clarice bought colored party hats and pink and yellow crêpe-paper streamers to decorate the carriage house kitchen, and roasted a pair of plump squabs, flavored with cumin and served with wild rice and a corn-and-red-pepper chutney. She downloaded a recording of Edith Piaf, Hedy's favorite chanteuse, as she called her, singing 'La Vie en Rose'. Two votive candles on the table, a bottle of white wine.

At exactly six thirty, Hedy appeared at the carriage house door in her black velour tracksuit, reading glasses swinging on their beaded chain; she was leaning on a walking stick, little gray Kismet at her heels. 'Ah, Edith,' she said, listening for a rapturous moment. 'That *miserable* woman!'

After tripping over the little dog in April, she'd started using the walking stick – not a cane, but a telescoping staff, the kind used by hikers and villains in spy movies. She made a humorous show of brandishing her stick now at Aggie.

Perhaps it was only the brightness of the kitchen, but as Hedy sat down at the table it seemed to Clarice that she had shrunk over the past few months and when she put on her glasses her dark eyes became huge in her sharp old face, as if she were staring at something astonishing.

Outside the kitchen windows it was broad daylight.

Hedy eyed the squab on her plate and said she felt like a cat under a bird feeder, but she ate with greater appetite than usual, greedily picking the little bones clean. They wore the party hats, silver with blue stars; each drank a glass of wine. They spoke of how no one went out walking after dark in the evenings anymore, people seemed afraid to leave their houses. The police were not doing enough. A new citizens' organization had been formed, an online group. Patrols, they were proposing. Video cameras posted on telephone poles and mailboxes.

'So much bad news,' said Hedy. 'Let's talk about something else.'

For a long time they talked of Hedy and Marv's life together – fifty-two years – their trips back to Israel, a trip to Poland 'to visit my demons', their practice, all the things they had done. Blueberry cobbler for dessert, served in a bright yellow dish. One pink birthday candle stuck in the middle. Even the dogs had a treat: organic milk bones.

Just enough fuss, was Hedy's opinion.

After they had eaten the cobbler, the two women removed their party hats gingerly, so as not to snap their chins with the elastic bands; then, leaving Edith Piaf singing and the votive candles still burning, carried their coffee through the living room, where Hedy spotted Naomi Melman's book, *The Bright Side*, on the coffee table, and said that Edith Piaf was proof that you could indeed feel good about bad things, and then out to the little back porch. They settled into the two wicker rocking chairs, which squeaked and crackled in mild protest, flakes of white paint drifting onto the porch floorboards. Aggie and Kismet lay down on the porch between them with companionable sighs and groans and soon began to snore. Hedy drank her coffee noisily, then set the mug on the floor. A few minutes later, she was snoring gently as well.

Clarice rocked back and forth, looking at the laurel bushes in their bed of pachysandra and listening to the evening around her, the *dee-dee-dee* of a little black-capped bird in the hedge, the rush of a car passing on Rutherford Road. At seven thirty the sky was still full of light, one of those soft spring evenings when the breeze smelled of honeysuckle and felt like silk, the air laden with promise and desire. She tried to imagine what it would be like to live with someone for fifty-two years and then, one day, to find that person gone.

Dr Awolowo's long, handsome, creased face appeared among the laurel leaves. His dark fingers stroked his gray beard, reaching up to adjust the heavy black frames of his glasses, the lenses catching the light of the setting sun. *Clarice, my dear.* She felt his beard brush her cheek.

A firefly bobbed in the laurel bushes, winking at her between the dark leaves.

She sighed and rocked for a while longer, looking at the gray fence at the end of the yard. Tomorrow she had a lecture to give; it was getting late. She was about to stand up, to wake Hedy and suggest they go back inside, when from the other side of the privet hedge came the twang of a screen door opening and then the sound of it snapping closed, followed by footsteps.

Wood scraped against stone, two people were settling

down in chairs. After a moment, voices began speaking, one male, one female, both pitched low, yet audible. It was Bill and Margaret Downing, but their voices sounded so concentrated, so reduced that they might have been speaking from inside a box.

'She can't hear us out here. She's watching a movie up in her room.'

'Well, let's keep it down. Now go on, tell me again what you said just now in the kitchen.'

'That I've been wanting to tell you. I've been waiting to tell you. That it just never seemed like the right time – you've been so depressed –'

'How long?'

Clarice could feel the pulse in her fingertips against her coffee mug.

'A few weeks. A month.'

'Every *day*?'

'No, of course not.'

In the blue sky hung a pale, round, pitted moon, looking strangely like the vaccination mark high on her mother's arm. She realized she was holding her breath.

Hedy was awake and had put on her glasses. She lifted a finger to her lips. From a distance came the rattle of the trolley, passing through the village, and the faraway sound of singing. The voices continued.

'Are you in love with him?'

'I don't know. I don't think so.'

'So why –?'

'Why am I telling you this now? Because I want to find out if it even matters to you.'

'Of course it matters to me.'

Another long pause. On the worn porch floorboards Aggie moaned in her sleep. Light was slowly draining out of the sky, absorbed into the leafy treetops as if they were great tender green sponges.

There came the soft sound of someone weeping.

Hedy was rocking in her rocking chair with a ruminative creak. The little bird had fallen silent but deep in the shadows by the fence was a dry rustling, like something small tunneling through old leaves buried in the pachysandra.

Finally one of the voices began again.

'We've been married for a long time. We've gone through a lot together. You and Julia are all I have in the world.'

The other voice said nothing.

'But I'm still young enough. It's not all over for me. I don't want it all to be over for me. I don't want to be with someone who says I make him feel dead.'

A breeze sighed raggedly through the laurel bushes. Once again the firefly blinked on and off, disappearing only to reappear again somewhere unexpected. Hedy's lower lip was pushed out. She was shaking her head.

This time the voices were silent for so long that it seemed as if the conversation must be over, but just as Clarice began to think of standing up they resumed.

'So I've had a little time to think. Tell me. Is it just about sex?'

'What?'

'Because, you know, if it's just about sex, I want you to know, I think it's okay with me.'

'It's *okay* with you?'

'If it's just about sex.'

Aggie moaned softly again, paws twitching.

'What do you mean, it's *okay* with you?'

The other voice did not answer.

'What are you saying to me?'

Again there was no answer.

Then out of the waiting silence came a low guttural cry, a cry so bereft and abandoned that it seemed hardly human; the hair stood up on the back of Clarice's neck and she felt her heart stumble. Still the moon sailed overhead, stony-white and more clearly outlined since the sky had darkened.

Hedy was leaning on her walking stick, the rocking chair rocking emptily behind her with a sound like knuckles on wood. The dogs hauled themselves up as well and stood with their noses pointing toward the back door of the carriage house. As she got to her feet, Clarice's legs were trembling as if they had gone to sleep.

She opened the door and then one after the other they walked inside and made their way silently back to the kitchen, back to the pink and yellow streamers and the toppled party hats on the table, the plates smeared with the purple remains of blueberry cobbler. The votive candles were still burning; Edith Piaf sang on in her tragic, scratchy voice. They sat down heavily.

In her black velour tracksuit, Hedy was as dark as a crow. Clarice watched her pick up a shard of pie crust and crumble it between her little claws.

'Very sad,' she said at last. 'They always seemed like such a nice couple. So attractive. Her especially. But as Marv always said, every house is haunted.'

Clarice nodded dumbly. Not for the first time, she wondered if Marv had actually said all the things Hedy said he said. And then she realized that in such a long marriage it probably did not matter, and also that she had the answer to what she had been wondering before.

They stared at the littered table. Edith Piaf was once more singing 'La Vie en Rose'.

'Well, there it is,' repeated Hedy. 'What can you do but feel sorry? Tomorrow I must go to the grocery store. I am out of eggs. With an egg, Marv always said, you can survive anything.' She sighed. 'Thank you very much for dinner. It was so nice. Come, my Kismet. Are you under my chair? Yes? Little beast? Little monster? Time to put you to bed.'

Clarice stood on the steps, watching Hedy and the little gray dog make their slow, careful passage along the shadowy driveway to the back steps of the big dark house. Hedy had left a light on above her back door and as she reached the door she turned to lift a hand.

Across the driveway, lights were on inside the Downings' house. It appeared they had gone in. Yes, there was Margaret, moving alone past the kitchen windows, pausing now at the sink, now opening the refrigerator, now returning to the sink.

'How I hate making dinner,' she had told Clarice a few days ago when they happened to meet in the driveway. Margaret was watering pots of red geraniums with a green garden hose. Emily Orlov had just dropped off Julia, who'd been babysitting for her little boy. Before going into the house, Julia had demanded to know what was for dinner.

'Chicken stew,' said Margaret.

Julia made a face like someone forced to eat sand and slunk off. After watching her go, Margaret went back to watering the geraniums, playing with the hose so that arcs of water flew like sparkling lassos into the air. That's when she said she hated making dinner.

'I have made dinner almost every night for fifteen years,' she added with a little laugh. 'And no one ever really likes what I make. Sometimes they don't even notice what it is.'

Inside the carriage house kitchen, Clarice closed her yellow curtains. She blew out the votive candles and turned off Edith Piaf. She ate the rest of the blueberry cobbler and drank what was left of the wine, and then washed the dishes and stacked them in the dish rack to dry, threw away the party hats and the crêpe-paper streamers. She went up to her bedroom and took two sleeping pills, though it was only nine o'clock. She washed her face, brushed her teeth, put on her nightgown. While she lay in bed, waiting to fall asleep, she did not think of Dr Awolowo, as she usually did at night, or of her notes, or even of the grant proposal she was writing, but of Margaret Downing standing with her hose, making lassos of water in the air.

19.

Her mother had agreed with the school guidance counselor that Julia should quit soccer and oboe lessons until the fall because it would be a good idea for her to have some unscheduled time. Julia saw the guidance counselor every Tuesday and Thursday during lunch. Mr Gluskin. Mr Gluskin had a huge jar of jellybeans on his desk and let her take as many as she wanted. He called them his 'magic pills' but otherwise he was okay. Mostly they ate their sandwiches and talked about soccer.

'Did you see Mr Gluskin today?' her mother would ask, when she got home. 'How was it?'

'Fine,' Julia always answered.

One night at the dinner table her mother suggested Julia might want to see an actual therapist, but Julia said only loser freaks went to therapists. It made her feel sick, that her mother wanted her to see a therapist.

At least she hadn't said 'the worry doctor', like some kids' parents.

Her mother was the one who should see a worry doctor. She walked around the house holding her hands out with her palms up, as if she were catching raindrops, or she stood looking out of the windows. Sometimes she could hear her mother in the hallway, breathing outside her bedroom door. If Julia wanted to walk into the village, her mother wanted to go with her. If she came down to the kitchen for a snack, her mother wanted to fix it. 'How are you?' she asked all the time. 'How are you feeling today?' 'I love you,' she said, every night at bedtime. 'No matter what happens I want you always to remember that. And anything you ever want to tell me, I want you to know that you can. I love you so much.' Then she would sit on the edge of Julia's bed, looking at her expectantly. Julia always shuddered. The thought of saying *I love you* filled her with a kind of marshy horror, similar to when she opened the pool filter and found dead frogs floating belly up, so fleshy and fragile, so hopelessly swollen. But her mother seemed to be waiting for her to say something, so she could ask questions and worry about it.

'You worry about me too much,' she said to her mother one night. And her mother said, 'It's my way of watching over you, even when I can't be there.'

Three or four times in the evenings, her mother had been in the kitchen, looking out of the window as she made dinner, and then suddenly she demanded, 'Do you see? I think you do.' But when Julia looked out of the window, nothing was there.

The house was too quiet. Binx had quit barking – ever since he'd had his operation, he lay on the floor whining. He'd stopped growling at people and trying to bite the mailman. Julia tried to make it up to him, patted him and brought him dog bones, but he only looked at her with his penny-brown eyes and then turned his nose to the wall. Lost his mojo, said her father. 'Just a little traumatized,' her mother said. But he was almost catatonic. Even waving toys at him, which usually made him growl and charge like a mad bull, didn't work.

She was only allowed on Facebook for an hour a day; also she'd dropped her cell phone in the girls' bathroom two weeks ago and someone stepped on it, so no texting, and now she'd read all the *Twilight* books twice. So when Nicholas Orlov's mother asked if she'd like to start coming over on Tuesday afternoons to watch Nicholas, Julia said she would.

Surprisingly, her mother had agreed to this plan.

'Tuesdays?' she repeated, standing in the kitchen holding a dishtowel.

'Until five.' Julia finished eating an apple and threw the core at the trash can but missed, then waited for her mother to yell at her to pick it up.

'I've been asked to accompany the middle school chorus on Tuesdays,' her mother said instead. 'Naomi recommended me. They lost their usual accompanist. It would be good for me to get out of the house. But I thought you might want me to be here.'

'No,' said Julia. 'Why would I?'

Sometimes nasty remarks like that could make her mother cry. But this time her mother kept twisting the dishtowel and staring abstractedly at the pie tin wall clock over the stove, as if she were using the clock to figure out a word problem in math.

Mrs Orlov had been looking for a regular nanny since Mr Orlov moved out, but so far hadn't found one because Nicholas screamed every time a nanny came to be interviewed. But he liked Julia. At least he didn't scream when she showed up at the front door, though often he screamed later on. Mrs Orlov paid her five dollars an hour. Hannah got eight dollars at the Saltonstalls' – but that was for two kids; also those girls got into fights and had to be separated, and insisted on doing dress up and face painting, which had to be cleaned up afterward. There was only one of Nicholas and he just played with Lego.

Julia had gone to the Orlovs' house for the past two Tuesdays. Her mother had insisted on driving her each time, though it was only three blocks, and Mrs Orlov dropped her back at home. But today her mother had to be at chorus rehearsal early, so Julia would have to walk.

Binx was lying in the middle of the kitchen floor like a gigantic ink blot, hardly moving. The vet had prescribed some sort of anxiety medication for him. The pills were pretty, bright blue; they reminded her of Mr Gluskin's jellybeans, but they hadn't done anything yet. To make up for leaving him alone, Julia decided to give Binx an extra one now, wrapped in a piece of roast beef. He seemed a little happier right away, so she gave him one more.

'He must be sad,' she said, stroking his big head, 'that he'll never have children.'

'He'll be all right.' Her mother was looking out of the kitchen window as usual. Above the sink the goldfish circled their ceramic castle as if hypnotized. 'He'll get over it.'

But she suggested Julia take Binx along to the Orlovs'. 'He could use getting out of the house, too. I'll call Emily right now and ask.'

Mrs Orlov thought a visit with Binx would be nice for Nicholas, who had been missing Boris.

'So what do you want to do today?' Julia asked after Nicholas's mother had left them in the living room with a pile of Lego. It was just after three. They were sitting cross-legged on the carpet while Nicholas worked on a Lego helicopter. He was wearing yellow shorts and a red T-shirt with a blue stego-saurus on it.

Binx lay next to them on the carpet, farting.

'Why don't you two take Binx into the yard?' his mother called from her study down the hall. 'It's so nice outside.'

From the living-room windows, Julia could see white sun-light on the slanting roof across the street, interrupted by the shadow of a chimney like a gigantic rectangular black Lego. Beyond were green treetops and the flat blue sky.

'No,' said Nicholas.

Binx farted again.

'Oh, come on,' said Julia. She leaned over and whispered, 'We'll go to Siberia.'

Nicholas sighed. 'Okay.'

Julia snapped Binx's leash to his collar, then let Nicholas hold the leash. They went into the kitchen, each pausing to grab a handful of chocolate-covered peanuts from a yellow plastic bag left open on the counter while Binx stood watch-ing them. They ate the chocolate-covered peanuts one at a time, trying to toss them into their mouths; Julia insisted they pick up the ones that fell onto the floor. 'Chocolate is bad for dogs,' she told Nicholas. 'It can give them a heart attack.' She was gratified to see him crouch down and pick up each chocolate-covered peanut. 'No fair,' Hannah had said when Julia told her Nicholas and his mother sometimes ate ice cream for dinner; at least, their kitchen sink was often full of white china bowls holding puddles of congealed pink ice cream. According to Hannah, Mrs Saltonstall's idea of junk food was home-made tapioca pudding.

'Looks like snot,' said Hannah. 'No wonder those kids act so deranged.'

When people asked Nicholas's mother how she was doing, she said, 'Life is fine in Siberia.' She had said this to Julia's mother two weeks ago after giving Julia a ride home, Nicholas sitting in his car seat in the back. Julia's mother had been in the driveway with Dr Watkins, chatting and watering pots of geraniums. She put down the garden hose and came to the car to talk through the driver's window.

'How are you, Emily? How are you holding up?'

'Life is fine in Siberia.'

'Well, it's been pretty cold here, too,' said Julia's mother, though this was not true. It was only May but twice they'd turned on the air conditioning.

Last week Nicholas had told Julia Siberia was in his backyard. He pointed it out now when they opened the kitchen door: between the birdbath and the swings sat a folding metal lawn chair surrounded by cigarette butts and two empty wine bottles; beneath the chair was splayed a swollen paperback book that had been left out in the rain.

Julia squatted down to look at the soggy cover. A picture of a horse, black and scribbly, like a drawing she could have done in elementary school, and beyond the horse a scribbly snow-covered stable. Stories. She leafed to the first one, careful not to tear the damp pages.

' "To whom shall I tell my grief?" ' she read aloud.

'Drop it!' cried Nicholas, yanking on Binx's leash. But he was only digging at an anthill.

'So what do you want to do?' Julia asked him, letting the book fall back onto the grass.

He shrugged. The downstairs windows were open and they could hear his mother talking in a low, clogged-sounding voice, though not what she was saying.

'She's speaking Russian,' said Nicholas. 'Probably to my grandmother.'

'Is your grandmother Russian?'

'No. She lives in New Jersey. Look at how fast I am.' Nicholas ran back and forth across the yard, yanking Binx along with him.

'Wow,' said Julia. 'That's fast.'

They decided to walk into the village with Binx. Julia wasn't sure she and Nicholas were allowed to walk to the village, but she didn't want to ask Mrs Orlov while she was on the phone. Anyway, it was only two blocks. 'Hey, what's up?' Julia would say if she saw someone she knew sitting on the bench in front of the Dairy Barn. 'This is Nicholas. I'm his babysitter.' She opened the latch on the gate.

Mica glittered in the pebbles at the edges of people's yards and for half a block a big orange butterfly floated above its own shadow down the sidewalk ahead of them. Julia insisted on taking Nicholas's hand when they crossed an intersection, and she held Binx's leash. It was kind of fun being out with Nicholas, pointing to the pebbles and the butterfly. But as soon as they reached the corner of Brooks Street and turned right at the post office to head into the village, Binx started pulling on his leash and making loud gagging noises. Two people coming out of the post office stepped back in alarm.

'Shhh,' said Julia. 'Cut it out.'

Binx lunged ahead, dragging them past the post office toward the Dairy Barn, hacking and gagging, toenails scratching the sidewalk; Julia no longer wanted to see anyone from school. She suggested that they go home and finish Nicholas's Lego helicopter.

'Naah,' said Nicholas, letting go of her hand. 'Naah, naaah.'

Something had gotten into Nicholas. Maybe it was the balmy breeze or the sun bouncing off passing car windshields to snatches of radio music. Maybe it was the smell of garlic and vinegar coming from the open door of the Number One Noodle House across the street. He began to run in zigzags on the sidewalk, flapping his hands and nearly colliding with people walking down Brooks Street. He ran past the Dairy Barn, past the Forge Café and the Bake Shoppe, while Julia yelled at him to come back, but he kept zigzagging and flapping. Fortunately, everyone on the sidewalk thought he was cute.

'Are you an airplane, little boy?' asked an old lady in a straw hat and wraparound sunglasses outside of Walgreens. She had long crowded teeth.

'Help! Help!' he shrieked.

Julia groaned aloud. Last week when Nicholas was having a tantrum after one of his Lego towers collapsed, she'd told him the story of thinking she saw a puppy out on the ice of the Silsbee Pond, and trying to save it and then falling through the ice and having to be saved herself by a fireman in a yellow rubber raft. The story seemed to get longer and more improbable the more often she told it. Nicholas made her repeat it three times. Finally, to avoid telling the story a fourth time, she found the YouTube video on his mother's computer while she was lying down in her bedroom. 'Help! Help!' she could be heard shouting, her voice like a wisp of smoke. Suddenly the camera view jostled up toward the sky; when it came back down there was a hole in the ice where she had been standing.

'Where'd you go?' Nicholas kept asking, eyes big and

deer-like. He wouldn't believe her when she said she didn't really remember, though this in fact was true.

'Someplace cold,' she said at last.

'But you came back.'

'Of course I did. You see me here, don't you?'

'Help! Help!' he kept repeating now. It was his new favorite saying.

'Help! Help!' Nicholas cried again at the old lady in front of Walgreens.

'Sorry,' Julia told her, just as Nicholas darted away down the sidewalk. At that same moment Binx wrapped his leash around a streetlight. By the time Julia had pulled the dog free, Nicholas was out of sight.

In the woods of Baldwin Park, five or six yards off the trail, Matthew Melman sat on a rock smoking a joint and swatting at a mosquito buzzing around his head. The mosquito was making it hard for him to concentrate on the rock. He was trying to figure out the rock's exact color. Recently he'd been trying to categorize things other people never noticed as part of his blog: *The Importance of Not Giving a Fuck about What's Important*.

The rock was full of other rocks, various colors of gray. Steel gray. Lead gray. Gunmetal gray? Could he *see* something as gunmetal gray if he had never seen a real gun? Trippy question.

He tried to imagine what his mother would say if he pointed a gun at her.

You're having separation issues.

After another toke he swatted at the mosquito again, wondering if the mosquito might *be* his actual buzz. Also a trippy question. Trippy questions, he'd decided, were the only questions worth asking. At the end of ninth-grade English, Mr Wechsler had given him an old copy of *On the Road* and a Xeroxed copy of 'Howl'.

'Time to start driving your brain, kid,' he'd said, 'before somebody else does it for you.'

Matthew was flattered at having been singled out by Mr Wechsler, whom he admired for occasionally using profanity in class, but also afraid he'd been insulted. He hadn't read either the book or the poem until last winter, when he'd seen Mr Wechsler at the Downings' freakish Christmas party, and went home and found them in a backpack stuffed under his bed.

Immediately he'd recognized himself as Sal Paradise with a touch of Ginsberg. Unshaven, untamed, a poet-blogger vagabond. Sort of like Mr Wechsler. That's when he'd started growing a beard. For a while he smoked in the icy garden shed behind his house, surrounded by bicycles, rakes, hoses, the lawnmower, a small plastic red tank of gasoline, also the Nautilus machine his mother never used and had finally banished from the house because it made her feel guilty. ('And God knows,' she'd said, 'I have enough of *that*.') But one afternoon when his mother was nagging him to clean up his room, he slammed out of the house and rode his bike to the park to uncork his head. After leaning his bike against a tree, he walked into the snowy woods, taking the trail to the left and then plunging off into the trees, looking for a good place to light up a joint. That's when he discovered the rock, rising up like a huge knee, in a little clearing by itself. The Philosopher's Stone, he decided to call it. For stoned philosophers.

After that he went to the woods as often as he could, reserving the garden shed for rainy afternoons. He kept matches, rolling papers and a lid of pot in the pocket of his denim jacket at all times, enjoying the outlaw thrill of sauntering through the halls at school with concealed narcotics. Getting high – even thinking about getting high – gave him a sense of raffish travel, of hasty departures and dusty sunset arrivals, which made up for the burnt taste in his mouth afterward and the irritable feeling that nothing good was ever going to happen to him.

It wasn't his fault he had not gotten into any of the colleges he'd applied to. It was even kind of a distinction. Unlike the douchebags in his class, he had not lied on his college applications about spending spring break building outhouses in Costa Rica; he hadn't claimed that being a camp counselor for two months at the Jewish Community Center had taught him the values of responsibility and caring for others. Under 'extracurricular activities', he'd listed 'Police interrogations' and 'Driver's Ed'.

I am a wastrel, he wrote in his application essay, which he had refused to allow his mother to proofread. *I believe in the value of blowing it, of fucking off, of rejecting the phantasmal capitalist scurry and 21st-century techno-cultural Moloch mind traps. I am awed by all that is out there that I don't want to do. The number of things I don't want to do is so huge that I don't have a clue of what I don't want to do.*

Secretly, he had believed his essay, lifted straight from his blog, would strike admissions panels as so brutally honest and profound that he would be accepted everywhere. It was a shock when rejections began to arrive. He felt betrayed and humiliated for trusting college websites, which had advised him to be himself and claimed that admissions officers valued originality over grades and SAT scores. Moronic colleges. Totally unserious. All people did in college was get drunk and fall out of dorm windows. But on a cold wet day in April, huddled on the Nautilus machine in the dark garden shed amid the smell of mildew and gasoline, he had wept over his final rejection, from the University of Chicago.

When at last he left the garden shed, his mother had been waiting at the kitchen door. At the sight of her long, anxious face, his eyes filled again. He wanted to run across the yard, throw his arms around her, bury his face in her shoulder, have her stroke his back and tell him again that there was a college for everyone and that somehow (she would call someone) it would all work out.

'Well, I guess you'll have to get a job and apply again next year,' his mother had said instead, when he handed her the rejection letter.

What kind of a mother *says* that?

This morning she told him Radio Shack was accepting job applications. Also that it was time to shave; he was starting to look like an Islamist militant.

'And honey,' she'd said, 'enough smoking dope. It's immature.'

Shooting was too good for her.

Dragging Binx away from a dropped ice-cream cone, Julia ran toward the Walgreens parking lot, calling and calling for Nicholas to come back, seeing his little red shirt bobbing far ahead of her on the sidewalk, vanishing, then reappearing. Twice Binx wound his leash around a parking meter. Something had gotten into him, too. He kept planting his feet mulishly on the sidewalk and growling; she had to jerk hard on the leash to make him move. Several people stopped her to ask if something was the matter, and because they were adults, she tried to explain, but it took too long, so she had to apologize and continue running, hauling Binx along with her.

Somewhere beyond Walgreens she lost sight of Nicholas's little red shirt. She ran down Brooks Street toward the elementary school. Maybe Nicholas had run to school to play in the playground. She ran past the elementary school. The playground was empty. Beyond the playground, the soccer field was empty. In another half a block she was running along the weedy sidewalk above the park's bowl-like meadow.

The joint had burned down to a roach and was singeing his fingertips. As he tossed it to the ground he felt his mind disconnect from his body and float with a gentle whine over his left shoulder. 'I have nothing to offer anybody,' he thought somberly, 'except my own confusion.'

Forgetting that this was not an original statement, and envying Sal Paradise, who probably didn't have a mother, he watched himself lie back on the rock, holding a last lungful of smoke. He watched himself gaze up at the shifting leaves and sky, his face going slack as a breeze lulled his cheek.

Hush, said the breeze.

Someone was crying. Slowly he exhaled the smoke from his lungs and watched it spiral into the sky. From a great distance, it came to him that what he was hearing was a real cry. High and hopeless, like air escaping a balloon. His own unuttered howl. Recorded by the universe and played back to him.

★

'Nicholas,' she screamed.

No one was in the park. Mothers didn't let children play on the grass anymore; most of them wouldn't even walk through with strollers. But Nicholas probably only remembered the park as fun. Where kids played games after school. Red Rover. Hide and Go Seek. That's what he was probably doing right now. Hiding behind a bush or behind that old tree in the meadow, waiting to pop out and yell, 'Help! Help!'

Nicholas was so clearly before her in his red T-shirt that she felt herself grab his small sweaty hand, heard herself say in a furious relieved voice like her mother's, *I was so worried. Don't make me worry like that*. But as she started to sprint down the slope into the meadow, she tripped over Binx's leash.

Down she went, Binx yelping with her. Julia banged her knee on a rock, got a grass stain on the elbow of her new shirt. By the time she looked up again, the meadow stretched emptily, vast, indifferent, sprinkled with white clover. In the collective gardens, chicken-wire fences sagged in the afternoon sun; the handle of a shovel gleamed silver, stuck in a heap of black compost.

'Mama,' she whimpered, holding her throbbing knee. Beside her on the grass, Binx whined, licking a paw. Then he sat up alertly and sniffed the breeze.

Nothing moved but the tops of trees at the dark mouth of the woods.

She staggered up, clutching the leash as if it were the end of a rope, and limped down the rest of the slope and past the collective gardens. When she reached the meadow she began to run in the direction of the creek and the footbridge, calling, 'Nicholas, Nicholas,' while Binx forged ahead, big shoulder muscles working, tugging and twisting on the leash, until the leash lifted, as if by its own accord, right out of Julia's hand. He streaked across the meadow. A moment later she saw him spring toward the creek, hang suspended in the air for a black split second, before he splashed, with an oozy gulp, into the mud; the next minute he was swarming up the bank on the other side and then, as if sucked into the woods, he was gone.

Matthew stared down at the figure before him. An elf or a troll in bright red and yellow. Some kind of Technicolor woodland creature. He understood that it was a vision, granted to him by a celestial force aligned with his brain waves, and also that it must be addressed.

'Hey, dude,' he said finally, 'what the fuck are you doing here?'

In response the creature opened its mouth and gave a piercing wail.

Instantly it morphed into a kid Matthew recognized from day camp last summer at the Jewish Community Center. A pale snively little kid, in saggy orange swim trunks, a kid who peed in the pool and kept announcing it, making all the other kids squeal and demand to get out.

'Dude,' he said, scrambling down off the rock. 'Dude. Shut up, okay?'

To his amazement, the kid closed his mouth and lifted his small tear-stained face to gaze up at him. Matthew tried to think of what he should say next; he was so thirsty his tongue felt like a gym sock.

'So, like, where's your mom?'

Mistake. The kid's peaky face crumpled; once again his mouth went square. For three full seconds there was an immense and absolute silence and then he howled again. A long, terrified, inconsolable howl that went on and on, getting higher and sharper, louder and more desperate, ululating like a siren. *The* howl, Matthew realized. Like something cosmic, it infused the whole woods, making branches sway and twigs snap.

'Whoa,' said Matthew, crouching down and grabbing the kid's shoulder. 'Whoa, whoa.'

He kept repeating *whoa*, *whoa*, squeezing the kid's shoulder until finally he stopped howling and began gulping instead, long shuddery gulps, dragging an arm across his leaky nose. Jesus Christ, Matthew thought, surprised to find himself shaking. What a lot of noise one little kid could make, and what an outrageous, unbearable noise – like shrapnel in his brain. Thank God he was just whining now, but as Matthew leaned against the rock to catch his breath, a shadow flickered through the trees. And from no more than twenty yards away came an answering growl.

Julia stumbled across the footbridge, half running, half limping toward the mouth of the woods, tall grass whipping her bare calves. Her throat ached from calling, 'Nicholas, Nicholas,' her breath coming in gasps; she had a stitch in her side and she couldn't stop picturing her mother staring at the clock that afternoon.

Two trails stretched before her. She hesitated and then plunged off to the right, running along the trail past a tree trunk split in half and a gray boulder that resembled a sleeping baby elephant. She had never been in the woods by herself before. Branches and leaves closed above her so that it was like running into a green tunnel. Left she turned, then right; she was running hard, covering a lot of ground – but there again was the tree with the split trunk and the elephant boulder. How had that happened? But she had no time to think; she kept running, taking a different path this time, one marked by a blue blaze on a tree. More trees, more branches overhead, the world a soft green blur. She heard the sound of someone else's footsteps and realized Nicholas must be just ahead; but no, it was only the drumming of her heart. How could she have run so far and not found him? After a few minutes she saw the split trunk once more and the elephant boulder, and now she no longer had any clear idea of where she was running to, or even why she was running, only that she must keep on, and as she was running a branch hit her in the face and once more the elephant and something she had refused to think about was suddenly, sickeningly right there. Her mother asleep on the sofa, face white and sunken. Her father's sad grimacing. 'I can't hold on much longer.' Her mother's voice, on the phone to Hannah's mother two nights ago. 'Dr Vogel says we'll have to tell Julia soon –' Then she broke off. 'Julia, is that you?'

Hardly eating dinner. Headaches. Collapsing at Christmas ('Just tired,' her father had said, looking away). *I love you. No matter what. I want you always to remember . . .*

Three children in the woods. No one knows where they are, and at this point neither do they, so perhaps their location should be clarified, if only for the inattentive universe. The meadow of Baldwin Park (now empty) leads to the wooden footbridge over the creek and then stops at the woods, where after a short distance two trails fork in opposite directions: Matthew and Nicholas both followed the one to the left and have wound up together in a small clearing fifty feet off the trail. The woods are full of brushy white pines and an understory of scrub oak. Matthew and Nicholas are quite hidden. Even loud sounds become muffled in such a dense place, though creaks and rustles seem amplified wherever one is standing. As for Julia, she took the other trail, which is really a loop, something she did not know, and she is running in circles.

But where is Binx?

Another growl, this time closer. A footfall in the dry leaves. 'Get up on the rock, dude.' Matthew seized the kid and boosted him up, a hand on the seat of his shorts, realizing too late that the kid's shorts were wet.

A shrill chorus started up: *icky Nicky, icky Nicky.*

'Hey, Nicky.' He tried to make his voice sound camp counselorish. 'Stay up there, okay?'

The kid crawled to the top of the rock and then turned to stare down at him, eyes dark and round in his little white face.

'Okay? Don't move.'

He wiped his damp hand on his jeans, heart beginning to hammer as he bent down to pick up a stick lying near his feet, but he was still stoned enough to think, *This is pretty cool. Like, there's something* OUT *there*, when another twig snapped.

Never, ever go into the woods alone, her mother used to say every time they visited the park when she was little. You could get lost and no one would hear you.

No farther than the bridge. Promise me.

Whenever they went to the park, Julia thought about the woods where you could get lost and no one would hear you. In fairy tales, you had to do the thing you were not supposed to do. Bite the apple. Drink from the well.

Once when her mother was talking to another mother, she had run across the little bridge. Stood at the mouth of the trail, looking in at the cool, imperturbable stones, the fan-like green ferns and dark tree trunks rising from quiet brown heaps of dead leaves. What a relief it would be to go into the woods and get it over with. To find out what happened when nobody could hear you. She'd imagined a cave, vines, a pool of black water. Rising from the pool, a white beckoning hand. But then her mother had snatched her up, scolding, and carried her back to the park.

Julia stopped running and slid her hands to her knees, gasping for breath. High above branches of leaves and pine needles the sky was still as blue as a circus balloon, but in the woods it was beginning to get dark.

Head hanging low, ears back, haunches rising and falling, the creature stepped darkly into the little clearing, drawing some of the shade of the woods with it. Matthew stared; all the stories he'd ever heard about coyotes in the woods sprang at him. But this was no coyote. It could not be categorized, even down to its color. Wet coal? It kept its tail down, its mouth gaped open. Foam collected at the corners of its wide jaws, dripping greenish slime.

And though Matthew realized he was stoned, and that he was seeing what he was seeing *because* he was stoned, he knew this only distantly, like something written on a blackboard for him to memorize.

The creature stopped and slowly began moving its heavy slick head back and forth, so that for a moment in the uncertain light of the woods it seemed to have three of them. And then he smelled it, rank and rotten, like waterlogged dead things at the bottom of a well.

Stoned or not, he knew what he was facing – something terrible, something old and terrible – and though Matthew also understood that he would never be able to defeat it, that it was too powerful, too basic, too faithful to its own dark instincts, he realized that it had been conferred upon him to try.

He waved the stick in his hand, *swish, swish*, like a sword.

The creature bared its teeth. Black gums. White fangs. Yellowish eyes.

Its big muscles quivered. And then it growled. Deep and low in its chest.

He waved the stick again.

'Scat?' he said.

And the thing leapt.

A child's faraway scream.

Then nothing.

Julia stayed where she was, standing on the trail in the middle of the woods. As long as she stood there, as long as she didn't move in any direction, she could stay just as she was, not knowing anything, not responsible for anything, just a girl lost in the woods.

Eventually she stepped off the trail and sat down on an old rotting log covered with bright green moss. She breathed in the soft, dry scent of decomposing leaves; the log, when she looked at it, was lively with charcoal-colored armored bugs crawling in and out of holes. Everywhere she heard cracklings, like a hidden fire, secret stirrings beneath old leaves, all the way into the clayey soil down to the roots, which she understood to be stirring, too, sending hair-like feelers toward the surface of the earth. The world was full of live and dead things. *What's the worst thing that ever happened to you?* she used to ask her mother. And then one day not long ago she asked her father and he told her.

'Did you bury them?' she'd asked.

Her father had looked confused for a moment and then said something about building the waterfall by the pool, a kind of memorial.

It came back to her now, this conversation, and as it did she knew at last what her mother was seeing when she stared out of the kitchen windows. This realization reached Julia numbly, as if she were standing on the ice once again, cold air rising up in drafts. She was not all that her mother had ever loved or worried about.

I will never forgive her, she thought, surprising herself because she knew this was true.

Voices called out. Shadows moved in and out of the trees. The sun shifted overhead and a patch of whiteness shone beside her, a kind of neutral blankness that was nevertheless calming. She had been shivering; now the coldness let her go. But for a long time Julia continued to stay as she was, sitting on the log, fingers of sunlight reaching toward her through silvery pine needles. And though she did not notice, when she got up at last and walked back to the trail, the patch of whiteness followed her, all the way out of the woods.

20.

It could have been a lot worse, Naomi told Clarice Watkins over a glass of wine at the Tavern, though it was bad enough. Matthew bitten three times on the arm and once on the leg. Eighteen stitches. The animal had to be destroyed, of course. Sent to a farm, they told the girl, to look after sheep, but she wasn't stupid. Kids always know when you're not telling them something. Better to be truthful, no matter how bad it is.

Clarice nodded as she listened. She had finally mastered the 'record' feature on her iPhone, which allowed her to relax during conversations and actually hear what people said.

'I mean I love dogs, I have one, too,' Naomi was saying. 'But that thing wasn't safe around children.'

The postman testified the dog tried to bite him every time he came to the house. Even Margaret admitted it wasn't the first time he'd gone after someone. They'd had him fixed, thinking that was why he was so aggressive, but it was just bad nature. Some dogs were like that. Out of control.

And poor Emily. Scared to death when she realized little Nicky was lost, though he'd been fine, of course, thanks to Matthew. Naomi had seen Emily last week at Clean Up Littlefield Day, picking up trash around the trolley tracks; she looked like someone who'd been walking barefoot for miles in the snow. That brute of a husband, running off with a student. What was wrong with people? Didn't they understand that actions had consequences? That little boy was a mess already and now –

Naomi ordered another glass of chardonnay and talked on in a way Clarice had come to recognize: a busy woman drinking wine on an evening out, freed from kitchen tyranny and from helping with homework, enjoying the brief luxury of feeling fortunate, moved to consider all the hard luck among her friends.

On and on she went:

Poor Margaret especially. A lovely woman, but an absolute wreck. This last episode with Julia has pushed her right over the edge. Now she thinks she's seeing things. One minute she's looking at a bush, the next it's a dog. Well, no surprise, given the monster she had right in her house. That's what I told her. I said, Margaret, you are projecting, and it may even be helpful, a defense mechanism, given all your stress. Because the woman is barely functioning. Marriage on life support. She's been having an affair, which I'm sure you've already guessed, so this isn't news: George Wechsler. I know. I don't see it, either. Anyway, Bill's firm shut down, the poor man out of work and on antidepressants. About time, frankly. I suggested that months ago.

And then Julia. One thing after another. First her stunt on the ice, then taking the boy and that crazy dog for a walk and losing them both in the woods. Comes home afterward and doesn't say a word, with half the village out looking for her. Just goes to her room and closes the door. Probably posted the whole thing on Facebook. That YouTube video of her received almost 800,000 hits. Can you believe it? Margaret's finally got the girl in therapy. I finagled an appointment with someone I know, a very good person. No easy thing these days, let me tell you – every child in town has some kind of anxiety disorder. I blame it on the dogs. Kids are resilient but there's a limit.

Sweet, though, how Matthew stuck up for little Nicky, saying *he* didn't think the dog should be put down. Wrote about it in his blog. Very political. Quotes poetry. I'll give you the link. Of course, I'm his mother, but I can't help feeling proud. Out for a walk in the woods, just to clear his head – high school these days! so much pressure! – when he finds little Nicky sitting on a rock, all alone, bawling like a lamb. Tries to calm him down and that creature *springs* out of nowhere. Had to fight it off with a stick. Frankly, if there were more kids like Matthew, sacrificing themselves for others, the world wouldn't be such an awful place. He's taking a gap year, by the way. 'Mom,' he said, 'when I go to college I want to go there to learn something.' Isn't that smart? But he's very interested in the University of Chicago. Oh, that's *right*, that's where you teach. How funny. I was just saying to Stan –

After listening to Naomi talk at the Tavern until almost eleven, Clarice was at her usual window table the next morning at the Forge Café, drinking a third cup of coffee and listening to Ahmed Bhopali in his stained white kitchen coat.

Ahmed's voice was wounded, intimate; he kept his mouth very small, like a man lodging a protest through a keyhole.

The Littlefield police had been harassing him for months. Ticketed him for chaining his bicycle to a parking meter in front of the post office; cited him for jay-walking across Brooks Street; given him a warning for sitting in Baldwin

Park after dusk. Treating him like a dog. All because a dark-haired man with facial hair was spotted spray-painting the front of a college test preparation office on April 16th. A person of interest.

Ever since then, the police had been stopping anyone who met that description, including Ahmed, twelve times.

LEASH YOUR BEAST was all over town, stenciled on banks, nail salons, the Dairy Barn, even across the front door of a yoga studio. No dogs had been poisoned since November and yet it was as if they were all going to be, at any minute. The whole village was hysterical. The Department of Public Works could no longer keep up with graffiti removal.

Last week Ahmed decided to shave off his beard in the hope of looking less interesting; but yesterday ('the final piece of straw'), a policeman threatened to arrest him for shoplifting as he left Walgreens with an electric razor he had tried to return. His beard was too thick for electric razor blades and had burned up the motor. Thirty-four dollars and ninety-nine cents.

'I did not poison any dog,' he said. 'Why would I? I do not care about any dogs.'

Clarice nodded. She had adopted her professional listening look: raised eyebrows, head tilted to the side. She had listened so much in the past nine months that her ears had become enormous. It was hard to fit them through doorways. When she lay down at night, she had to fold them, like wings, against her pillow.

'But no more,' Ahmed was saying.

His white coat looked like a painter's smock with its dabs of pink and brown icing, the yellow smears of batter.

Ahmed's fingers, too, looked like a painter's fingers: long and sensitive, not very clean under the nails. He also had something of a painter's way of looking critically around the room, displeased by its composition. At a nearby table sat a large, pale, bearded young man, wearing a green sweatshirt in spite of the heat, slumped over a cup of coffee. Ahmed glared, perhaps at the man's beard.

He had quit his job, he told her. Baked his final batch of doughnuts.

'I will be very happy to leave this place. It is too crazy.' Gingerly he patted his clean-shaven chin, pocked with bloody nicks.

Clarice put a hand to her eyes to see him more clearly in the glare from the windows. The sun had risen past the rooftops of the village since she first sat down; now sunlight blazed in at an angle that made it difficult to look at anything but what was directly in front of her.

'All people do here is complain about problems,' he was saying. 'They say they are scared about everything. But they do not realize what the real problem is. The problem is that everyone has problems. I have decided I do not want to be a lawyer and spend all my days solving people's problems.'

Good idea, she heard herself say.

He stared at her. 'I am going home to open a computer repair business with my cousin.' A moment later, with a small formal bow, he added, 'You are a sympathetic person. May you succeed with your endeavors.'

After Ahmed returned to the kitchen she went back to her laptop and her notes. She was typing up her grant proposal. Dr Awolowo had proposed her for a university fellowship.

It is my hope that this community, which might be declared by reason of its insularity, economic security and lack of significant cultural or manufacturing achievement to be of no interest, be reassessed as providing strategic research materials that may be applied generally to questions of . . .

The working title for her monograph on Littlefield was *Never Enough: Toward a Sociocultural Theory of Trained Incapacity and Discontent in an American Middle-Class Village and the Effects of Global Destabilization on Conceptualizations of Good Quality of Life*. She had planned the first chapter: a case study of Margaret Downing. Margaret would serve as the 'face' of Littlefield.

On her steno pad, open beside her laptop, were the following handwritten notes:

Overeducated and unemployed, M.D. is married to a latent pedophile whose investment firm is under investigation for insider trading, while she herself conducts an affair. Her adolescent daughter, J., has responded to the deviant behavior of both parents by deliberately walking onto the thin ice of a local pond – a YouTube video of which incident has been widely viewed. A few months later, she lost herself and another child in the woods, perhaps in a second attempt to gain widespread social media attention. J. is an example of today's technology-addicted but intellectually crippled middle-class youth, depressed, overscheduled, poorly served by the public education system and by so-called 'helicopter parents', simultaneously overprotective and neglectful.

M.D. herself responds to stress by turning to alcohol. At a holiday dinner party, she collapsed in front of guests and several children; over the objections of her husband, she was then carried up to her bedroom in the arms of the man who subsequently became her lover . . .

Like her once pleasant village, turned into a place of suspicion and fear by a spree of dog poisonings, M.D. seems menaced by forces beyond her control . . .

. . . her own dog turned from pet to vicious . . .

. . . she is the embodiment, therefore, of the phenomenon of . . .

Clarice frowned at her notes.

Often she reminded herself that Galileo had made his students repeat *I do not know*. 'A way of seeing is also a way of not seeing,' she told her own students, quoting Kenneth Burke. 'To focus on object A involves a neglect of object B.'

But the problems of Margaret Downing were all too obvious: the ennui of a loveless marriage, resulting in attempts to connect with external sources of emotional intensity: elaborate seasonal decorations; sentimental German music played endlessly on the piano; and, of course, the banal affair with a sexist male novelist, whose emphasis on sports culture epitomized the phallocentric world that simultaneously rejected and enslaved her, leading to the inevitable emphasis on youthful appearance amid the decline of middle age – blonde salon highlights, yoga classes, skin coddled daily with serums and moisturizers that cost as much as the yearly income of a bean farmer in Rajasthan – all adding up to the worst kind of social blight: the completely self-absorbed human being.

Like the lungs of frogs, Margaret Downing exhibited unusual simplicity and transparency. One could almost see her blood circulate. In the wilderness of life, she was a view of mown lawn. She was the famous sketch from Leonardo's notebooks, multiple arms and legs pointing in various directions, going nowhere.

But Margaret could not be simultaneously a frog, a view, a sketch by Leonardo. Or perhaps she could, which made her something else altogether. Clarice recalled Margaret's toast at Christmas: *To all of our troubles!* Margaret at the book club meeting, her pale strained face. *All I do these days is worry . . . about everything.* Margaret's desolate voice from the other side of the dark hedge, floating in the evening air. *What do you mean, it's okay?*

And then an incident from several weeks ago: Margaret in her silver station wagon, big black dog in the back seat, stopped at a red light on Brooks Street. Margaret staring straight ahead, holding the steering wheel, tears sliding down her face. Then the light changed and Margaret drove on. What had she been weeping over this time? Husband? Lover? Her sad skinny child? Perhaps she was not completely self-absorbed. She was weeping about everything. But did it matter? To notice and weep, to worry about everything and yet do nothing in particular.

Clarice discovered that she had spilled coffee on her steno pad. After blotting the spill with a napkin, she resumed typing. Behind her the bang and clatter of pots and dishes being washed in the kitchen grew louder, and the voices of men at the counter, grumbling about last night's Red Sox game, grew more insistent, and the gabbling of a woman at her left, speaking into a cell phone about spending a hundred dollars on a pair of sandals she didn't need but thought were cute but now wasn't sure she liked, became deafening. All that noise steeped in the acrid smell of coffee, which had left an ashy taste in her mouth. She stopped typing.

Why had she ever expected these people to be happy? Because they were comfortable?

What a fool she had been. She had figured the people of Littlefield would be balanced. Rich enough that they didn't worry about food and shelter and safety, but not so rich that they never worried about food and shelter and safety. Balanced. Especially because they were all in therapy, investigating their fears rationally, with the care and absorption of scientists. That, she had thought, was the secret of good quality of life. Rational balance. But instead she had stumbled onto the most unbalanced people of all: they were afraid of everything. They projected their fears onto everything. Everything they could do nothing about, but had the wit to recognize. The whole world surrounded them, a black forest crawling with beasts and creatures, phantoms, monsters.

Such a rabble, such a throng. She stared at the unfinished paragraph of her grant proposal. She'd had too much bad coffee, she could not hear herself think.

What had been neglected? What object overlooked?

You are a sympathetic person.

Her fingers trembled as she reached for her water glass just as a UPS truck lumbered by outside on Brooks Street, making the water in her glass tremble. Even the sunlight trembled, slanting through the windowpane beside her, falling warm as a hand on her bare arm.

21.

Soft lavender shadows stretched across the quieting lanes and byways of Littlefield; but the light, of course, was what everyone noticed. The dense honey-colored light of early June evenings, falling in broad bands across lawns, shining through the scissor-cut red leaves of a Japanese maple, illuminating cascades of purple rhododendron blooms, each leaf, each blossom with its own dusky corona of sunlight. A breeze settled into the trees, agitating the crowns. Lawns sank deeper into velvety shadow. The air tasted of wine. Such elegiac light, gilding every driveway cobble, every deck rail, gleaming along the curve of every outdoor grill. Flowing across the village and into the park, spot-lighting each milkweed tuft drifting across the soccer field, falling back just at the edge of the woods where ferns, tall and luxuriant, were joined by lady slippers and that most mysterious of plants: jack-in-the-pulpit, its knobby identity hidden under a striped curled jade-colored leaf. What force of nature could have dreamed of such a thing? The breeze picked up; the trees swooned with a deep watery rush and a bird sang out five notes like links in a silvery chain.

Bill was fixing a supper of pasta and tomato sauce from a jar for himself and Julia. Margaret was already at Duncklee Middle School – he had just dropped her off, her car was in the shop – doing a final run-through before accompanying the chorus in tonight's Spring Concert. Bill and Julia planned to attend the performance in half an hour.

In the kitchen he hustled from sink to stove to counter, heating the tomato sauce in the microwave while the pasta boiled, setting out baby carrots in a bowl, finding half a loaf of French bread in the breadbox, only slightly stale. As he moved about the kitchen, he kept thinking he saw the dark shape of Binx asleep in his crate in the mudroom. Every so often he thought he heard a small groan.

Poor crazy bastard.

Because he did not want to get tomato sauce on his white shirt, Bill wore a blue apron he'd given to Margaret for her birthday a few weeks before. The white letters on the apron read: *I'd Rather Be Playing Schumann.* Ordered online, from a company that would print whatever you wanted on almost anything: T-shirts, balloons, wallpaper. He was proud of this gift idea, gratified when Margaret said, 'Where on earth did you find it?' When he'd put on the apron five minutes ago Julia had actually laughed.

'I can't believe you're making dinner,' she'd said just now, sitting at the kitchen island with her glass of milk, long brown hair tied back in a ponytail. 'You're a terrible cook.'

'Says you. Sit back and watch the master gourmet.'

'Master of mess,' she said.

He was feeling a little better tonight; in fact he'd been feeling a little better every day, slowly coming back to life. He'd just got off the phone with Passano, who'd been looking at office space in the Back Bay for the consulting company they might start. Downing & Passano. It looked like Roche Capital might not be kaput after all. Last week a district court judge ruled that the electronic surveillance of their computers had been illegal and recommended the federal charges against Roche be dropped. Roche was quoted in the papers saying he was going to sue the SEC. A photo of him standing outside the courthouse in his shamrock tie: 'In the America of our forefathers, a man did not get punished for success and hard work.' Some punishment. Six months of sunning himself on a rock in Sedona. No way would Bill ever work for that old snake again, but it would help to have Roche more or less in the clear. A few of the old clients might come back. Passano & Downing. Money would be tight, especially at first, but what could you do but give it a shot? A couple of rooms with plain white walls and some cheap furniture, two guys in shirtsleeves answering their own phones, eating subs from Quiznos at their computers. *That's* the America of our forefathers.

As for him and Margaret, oddly enough, ever since she told him about George Wechsler, they'd been getting along much better. What they'd both been dreading had happened: one of them had finally thrown in the towel and now at least they had something to talk about.

They had a regular late-afternoon appointment with Dr Vogel now, four thirty on Thursdays. Often when they left her office they went across the street to the Tavern to continue talking. At that hour the Tavern was still almost empty; they sat at the back, always choosing the same dark booth, with a battered table and worn plush banquettes that smelled anciently of beer. The table top was made of rough pine planks stained a sodden-looking umber, the varnish pitted and gouged by forks and knives dropped clumsily or dug into the wood, the exposed mortise and tenon joints coming apart.

Over the table hung a framed print of people in red jackets on horseback amid a swarm of leaping hounds. Between them a candle flickered in a greasy bubbled holder of pinkish glass. Mostly they talked about Julia – what to tell her, when to tell her. Julia had hardly spoken to Margaret since Binx had to be put down, would not allow herself to be touched, looked at Margaret as if she were a toad or a frog. She was nicer to Bill.

Separation anxiety. That's what Dr Vogel said.

'She is separating me from my wits,' said Margaret.

It was all her worries about Julia, that's what she'd been seeing, she told him, when she thought she saw those dogs. She was very cogent about it now, almost businesslike. She did not believe in ghosts. It was all neurosis. Not sleeping, not eating, the difficulties they'd been having, trying to suppress her fears – all of that had made her unbalanced, so that her mind had shown her what she was afraid to see. Just as Dr Vogel said: anxiety. It wasn't madness – she wasn't going mad, thank God, though for a while she'd thought she was – but only anxiety, its next-door neighbor. She was going to get a prescription. There was a certain medication. Naomi knew someone, a psychopharmacologist.

'I can't spend my life worrying about Julia,' she said.

But some evenings they left off talking about Julia and leaned across the battered wooden table, faces aglow from the candle, and talked about what had happened to them; they went back to when they'd first met, and the ways in which their lives had been predictable and ways in which they were still surprised by how everything had turned out. How could it be that once they'd had no idea that life could be so hard?

He found himself listening to Margaret's voice as he hadn't since their early days together, when she used to talk to him about poetry and her English class.

Oh the after-tram-ride quiet, when we heard a mile beyond,
Silver music from the bandstand, barking dogs by Highgate
Pond . . .

'Is he in love with you?' he asked one evening at the Tavern.

'I think he's still in love with his ex-wife,' she said. 'She might move back in.'

'I thought you said she hated him.'

'Apparently living with her mother has given her a new appreciation for marriage.'

He shifted the metal-capped salt and pepper shakers on the table, sliding them next to each other and then drawing them apart. He did this several times.

'So is it over, between you?'

She sighed. 'It wasn't ever a real affair. More like an out-side interest.'

He'd glanced up from the salt and pepper shakers then, prepared to laugh at this small gift, this mordant joke, recog-nizing the way Margaret used to offer up news stories about disasters, to let him know that things could be worse. But from the stiff way she held herself, one hand at her brow half shielding her eyes, he saw the joke was too bitter to be meant for him. Her husband did not want her, her child did not like her. Even her lover preferred his ex-wife.

So he said nothing, just watched her across the table as she tried to hide her face; she seemed impossibly lovely to him again. The graceful turn of her slender wrist, the way her hair brushed her cheekbone, skin warmed by the ruddy light of the candle.

'Anyway.' She dropped her hand and sank back, away from the halo of light from the bubbled-glass candle holder. 'I don't know what it was. Anyway, basically, if you want to know,' she said, 'I was dumped.'

They were quiet and drank their wine.

'What should we do?' he asked at last.

'I don't know.'

'What do you want?'

'What do *you* want?'

'I think,' he said carefully, 'I might be starting to feel something again. So maybe we could see what happens. I think that's what I want.'

'You think that's what you want,' she said, putting a hand to her brow again. 'Well, that's something.'

She wouldn't say anything else after that, so he paid for their drinks and they drove home to make dinner for Julia.

A mayfly had somehow got into the kitchen and died by the blender. After looking at it closely, Bill picked it up by a hair-like leg and was about to drop it in the trash can when its delicate semi-transparent wings caught the pale light from the window above the sink. For a moment, the whole kitchen seemed semi-transparent.

'They only live for one day,' said Julia. 'We learned that in science.'

He was aware of her watching him.

'Isn't that sad?'

'Better than nothing,' he said, depositing the mayfly in the trash.

'They hatch and they mate. I don't think they even get to eat anything.'

'At least they get to mate.'

'*Dad.*' Julia made a revolted face and drank some of her milk.

He began to saw through the loaf of bread, staler than he'd thought, relieved to see Julia making faces. She seemed unnaturally responsible these days, doing her homework, once again practicing the oboe, all without being asked. Her attempt to impose order on the troubled atmosphere at home – that was Dr Vogel's theory. He was almost relieved when she went back to her old little-kid questions, a steady battery of best and worst. Who's your favorite Red Sox player? What's the meanest thing anyone ever said to you? If you had to spend the rest of your life eating only liver or broccoli, which would you choose? He always tried to answer honestly, feeling he owed her that. It was clear she was monitoring them, like a nurse watching patients' heart rates on screens at the nurses' station. Every hour or so in the evenings she hunted them down, wherever they were in the house, in the den off the living room, or in the kitchen talking about replacing the stove fan or why the celery kept freezing in the refrigerator's vegetable bin. Sensing some fibrillation, signs of a skipped heartbeat, a palpitation. Prepared to resuscitate any silence.

What was the best day in your life? What's your worst memory?

At last week's session with Dr Vogel the word 'cohabitation' had been introduced, tentatively, by Bill, along with a financial argument for such an arrangement, one that was logical and fair. Afterward they went across the street to the Tavern, ordering beer because the evening was so warm. They were about to continue their discussion when George Wechsler walked in. With George was a short woman wearing a red sun-dress, dark blonde hair pulled back, oversized sunglasses pushed on top of her head; from the brisk way she pointed to a table by the front windows and the docile way George followed her, Bill figured she must be the ex-wife. Square, compact, large-busted body. Athletic calves she clearly liked to show off; on one small shapely hand an array of stacked gold rings.

'We'd like a menu,' Bill heard her say to the bartender, in a not-unpleasant bray.

Margaret had seen them, too.

To give her a moment to collect herself, Bill gazed up at the old print of fox hunters and their leaping dogs that was hanging above their table. He thought of the fox, not pictured, perhaps huddled in a culvert just below the frame. Long nose quivering, eyes unblinking, listening to the baying overhead, the shouts and horses shifting their hooves. The timbered low ceilings of the Tavern began to shake. It was the trolley pass-ing outside, rumbling along the tracks.

'We can go,' he said quietly.

Her face had gone sharp and white. Once more her hand shielded her eyes, a gesture that now seemed theatrical, demanding.

'Well, it's up to you,' he said coldly. 'But I don't want to sit here like this all night.'

'Then don't.' Her lips barely moved.

More reasonably, he said, 'But I also don't want to leave you.'

She said nothing. He stared for a while at the table. In the unsteady candlelight flickering through the tall beer glasses, he had the brief impression of a raft afloat.

At last Margaret said, 'I can't bear it.'

She stood up and walked past the bar to the front of the Tavern where George and his wife sat by a leaded glass window, each square full of evening brilliance, looking at laminated menus. Bill stared into his beer. What was expected when confronting your wife's lover? His father once told him a story about a guy who'd found out his wife was sleeping with his boss. The guy drove to the boss's house, crawled in through a basement window, went up to the bedroom and worked his way through the boss's closet, cutting off the right sleeve of every shirt and jacket.

'How Freudian,' Margaret had said, when Bill told the story to her.

He pushed back his chair and got to his feet.

'Hello,' she was saying to the wife, whom George had just introduced.

'What a nice evening,' said the wife politely, squinting slightly in the bright haze of the window beside her. Bill couldn't tell by her expression if she knew who Margaret was; he could not bring himself to look at George.

'Isn't it? Just beautiful.' Margaret's cheeks were red. 'By the way, this is my husband, Bill.'

'Hello,' Bill heard himself say.

More weather-related comments were exchanged. Then Margaret was saying something about the Tavern, making a menu suggestion: the onion rings were good but the Caesar salad was limp. It was hard to find a good Caesar salad that wasn't limp, still the Tavern could try harder, buy fresher lettuce, because who wants a limp salad. Her back was very straight and she had rested her fingertips on the back of a third chair at their table, as if she were prepared to pull it out and sit down.

What agonies people put themselves through, thought Bill, feeling himself nod and squint at George's wife, who was nodding and squinting back at him. It was almost criminal. George sat with his forearms resting on the table, hands clasped, staring down at his wrists as if they were shackled together. Bill felt a spurt of fury. *Look* at this guy, with his stubble and his squat bossy wife. Who the hell did he think he was? He'd like to cut off both of his sleeves and stuff them down his throat. The next instant he felt only pity. How foolish it all was, how unnecessary and unwise, to go on nodding and squinting, three of them with ice in their guts – and the fourth, he could see by her glance at George's bowed head and the way her smile froze, just now getting the drift.

'Well, have a nice dinner,' said Margaret.

The next moment she was opening the Tavern's thick oak door, both hands on the heavy iron latch; there was a margin of golden light, a lively breath of spring air, and she was gone.

He'd had to return to their table alone to pay for the beers, barely touched, apologize to the waitress. When he passed George and his wife they were both staring out of the window, and by the time he finally made it to the sidewalk, Margaret had vanished.

'The point of mayflies,' he said to Julia in the kitchen, 'is to be part of the food chain.'

'Gross.'

'Well, mayflies don't see it that way.'

'How do you know? I think it's sad when something dies, no matter what it is.'

From the pantry came what sounded like a long, flat sigh.

'I don't agree. Mayflies are different. Think about it. For them every minute is as long as a year. That guy I just threw away was probably three centuries old in mayfly years. Empires had crumbled. He'd survived death two dozen times, fathered a thousand children. Seen mind-blowing sights. Flowers, bird baths, lawnmowers.'

She looked at him soberly. 'I still think it's sad.'

'Sad doesn't really apply to bugs. Anyway, it was his time to go.' He finished slicing the bread and put the knife down. 'And he died a natural death. By a blender. What else could a guy want?'

He was aware of trying to entertain, to be diverting. Aware, also, that the effort most likely showed.

'Who's Dr Vogel?' she'd asked a couple of nights ago, materializing in the kitchen doorway after they thought she'd gone to bed.

Margaret explained that Dr Vogel was a therapist, someone 'we're seeing to help us figure some things out'.

'Okay,' Julia had said. 'Whatever.' They waited for her to ask more questions. But she faded away from the doorway, her expression bland, tolerant.

She had been through so much this year. Bullying at school. Not enough friends. That awful accident on the ice. Babysitting that boy and losing him in the woods. Losing Binx. And now, soon to be her worst memory of all: Julia, honey, come sit down, Mom and Dad have something to tell you . . .

Okay. Whatever.

Across the counter she sat watching him, drinking her milk. Calmly she set the glass down. Picked up her paper napkin, wiped her mouth.

'What's for dinner again?'

Whatever it was, she'd eat it. She wouldn't complain. For a moment he braced himself against the counter with both hands, unable to breathe. Because there it was, his terrible fear, that Julia had lost every illusion, all her questions had been answered, and that somehow he and Margaret had done this to her, taught her far too early the saddest adult lesson of all: that so much of life was just something to get through.

22.

In the green and beige auditorium of Duncklee Middle School, boys and girls rushed up and down the aisles as if something were chasing them. Boys in white shirts, black bow ties and black pants; girls in black dresses, their hair neatly braided or held back with a black headband. No one sitting down, everyone talking, while from the stage Mrs Dibler, the chorus director, clapped her long, narrow hands and looked down her big nose. 'Chil-dren! Qui-et!' No one listened. She stood tugging at the bodice of her sleeveless green dress, arm flesh jiggling, bra straps showing, while Julia Downing's mother, at the piano (with sleeves), played a few chords from 'Chattanooga Choo Choo', which they were supposed to be rehearsing one last time.

Some children ran through the swinging doors and down the long school corridors, footsteps echoing, to peer giddily into empty classrooms. Outside the school windows, light seemed to be shining up from the ground, hitting the white dust on the windowpanes. 'Boo!' someone squealed, leaping out from behind a door, and then they were all squealing, rampaging back into the corridor.

Soon the seats of the auditorium would fill with parents, grandparents, brothers, sisters, even some teachers (Ms Manookian had been spotted in the lobby, with Mr Anderman!), while they, the chorus, waited backstage. There would be a final furious shushing from Mrs Dibler and this time they would all obey – grave with importance now – and even listen as she reminded them to keep their place in line, to walk quietly, with *dignity*, onto the stage. This is a *per-for-mance*! Smiles! No fidgeting! And they would look at her solemnly, also with contempt, because of course it was a performance. What else had they been practicing for all these weeks and months?

And then it really was time.

One by one they filed onto the stage. The lights dimmed overhead. Onstage the lights came *up*, right into their eyes. Dazzled, they managed to stay in line, to make their way to their appointed spots, row after row, on four levels of metal risers, listening to their shoes clang hollowly, their stomachs hollow, too, and the stage suddenly like the interior of a great seashell, while beyond its shining wooden lip waited a dark sea of hushed faces.

There was a tremendous pause, a vast insuck of breath.

Then Mrs Downing struck the first notes of 'Let the Earth Resound' and in perfect unison they opened their mouths to sing.

These concerts were always so lovely, everyone agreed afterward, milling in the lobby by the two sets of double glass doors, which someone had thoughtfully propped open to let in the evening air. Amazing, isn't it, still light at eight o'clock! Tables had been set up by the Parent Teacher Organization, laden with plates of cookies and brownies on white paper tablecloths with plastic cups for the bottles of pink lemonade. The children – so sweet – singing 'The Star-Spangled Banner' and 'La Bamba' – they were *good*, too – but how quickly they were growing up. It was kind of heart-breaking. One minute they were in kindergarten, drawing rainbows, astonished by the butterfly garden, by yellow chicks in an incubator, by *everything*, and the next, in middle school, shouting words on the bus that would make a rap star cringe. And yet they sang like angels. Soft cheeks, clear bright eyes – with that look, perhaps not of wonder any-more, but at least not of overmuch concern. Fixed ahead on something that no adult could see, something that went on and on, past the low horizon.

Having eaten all the cookies and brownies, the children dashed in and out of the crowd in the lobby – bow ties askew, braids coming undone – while their parents watched them fondly and talked among themselves, comparing summer vacation plans or sleep-away camps in Maine (do kids really need a Claymation studio? What happened to archery?), gazing out through the open glass doors to the school lawn and the parking lot. There was the usual mention, too, of whatever had been in the news: congressmen forced to resign for assaulting staffers, high schools installing metal detectors, new untreatable viruses.

Yet whatever they were discussing, what the parents really said to each other was: This moment will never come again. The setting sun will never catch just like so in the branches of that birch tree, planted in memory of that boy on the plane, or gleam exactly like this along the needles of the white pines by the parking lot, or turn those cirrus clouds that color of pink above the flagpole, the air will never again feel this soft and still.

Our children, our children. Oh, how *can* it be? – the earth is turning on its axis; we will all be left behind.

*

'A really nice concert,' everyone said to Margaret, who truly had done a remarkable job of accompanying those kids, even when they speeded up the tempo in Rodgers and Hammerstein's 'It's a Grand Night for Singing'. At the end of the performance, Margaret was called up on stage and given a bouquet of orange gerberas and yellow sunflowers in a beribboned cellophane sheath, presented by one of the children, in gratitude for 'saving the show', as Mrs Dibler put it, by filling in for the lost accompanist. And she had agreed to accompany the chorus next year! Bill and Julia clapped energetically at this presentation, as did everyone seated around them. Clarice Watkins and Hedy Fischman were one row ahead; they had come together – Hedy said she never missed a chance to hear children sing, claimed it cleared her sinuses – and next to them, Naomi and Stan Melman. Matthew was there in a ripped black T-shirt, satanic and mortified, slouched in a seat beside his mother, his mustache slightly thicker than when Bill had seen him last, holding a video camera.

But the real star of the concert was Hannah Melman. She'd had a solo during 'Seasons of Love' from *Rent*. Bill was astounded by the depth and complexity of her voice. A contralto. He'd always thought of Hannah as a silly kid who was obsessed with supermodels; but as she began to sing that night, pert freckly Hannah and her miniskirt faded away and a sixty-year-old black woman stepped forward, a woman who'd spent her life cleaning rooms in cheap motels off a Mississippi highway, humming church songs as she dragged a mop across cracked bathroom tiles. A woman who'd known love, loss. Mostly loss. Tears came into his eyes. Was suffering *always* there, ready to leap into any voice, no matter how unlikely?

'Wow,' he'd said to Julia when Hannah was done.

She frowned at him as he kept clapping. Naomi was blowing her nose and Stan had his arm around her. Even Matthew's mouth was ajar. Bill glanced over at Clarice Watkins in her violet turban to see if she had registered this phenomenon, but she was staring straight ahead and seemed absorbed in her own thoughts.

'Well, thanks,' Margaret was saying now in the lobby, looking flushed. 'It was fun.'

'You were really good, Mom,' said Julia shyly.

'Wasn't Hannah amazing? Such range!'

'*Won*-der-ful performance,' said the chorus director, tapping Margaret's arm as she passed by. 'Though the children were a *lit*-tle out of control. I don't know if you've met my husband, Eric.'

'Oh, no,' said Margaret, as she was introduced to a small man in a blue suit. He had a dark bony face and a dark goatee and at the sight of her he drew back his lips in a rabid smile.

'Pleased to meetcha. Great show.' Then he staggered away after his wife.

'What's with that guy?' said Bill.

Margaret shook her head.

It really had been a good show. Margaret had sat up straight on the piano bench in her turquoise dress, eyes so blue, slender and graceful, face serious, focused, alight, unhaunted, nodding every so often when the children managed a particularly high note. It was probably wrong to wish she would keep playing 'Seasons of Love' instead of Schumann, but maybe this concert would encourage her to mix up her repertoire.

As he watched Margaret receive congratulations from

children and their parents, smiling and cradling her bouquet of flowers, it came to Bill for the first time that maybe their problems were just problems, even if they were unresolvable. They had been married a long time. This summer, they would go back to Wellfleet (unless they did not) as they had for two weeks every summer, to the same gray-shingled cottage with dark green shutters and the driveway of crushed oyster shells. They would swim and walk on the beach. He and Julia would play Hearts, sitting on the sandy braided rug while Margaret read novels on the brown sofa that sagged in the middle. They would go into town and order fish and chips for dinner on the pier and afterward drive to the ocean and walk on the beach there, listening to the waves, the breeze against their faces mild and full of salt, each pebble throwing a long singular shadow onto the sand. And he would look out at the ceaseless swelling sea and know that whatever it was that was missing was going to stay that way.

But then Julia would ask for ice cream or Margaret would say something funny. The cottage was full of earwigs, but he was used to that now.

'So what's next?' he cried, suddenly exultant. 'Ice cream, anyone?'

No one was interested. It was almost nine on a school night and everyone was bent on getting home. Tomorrow was another day. In a few minutes the parking lot had all but emptied, and the Downings' car was joining a stream of headlights disappearing down Rutherford Road under a navy-blue sky crowded with stars.

23.

Such a hot morning. Only ten o'clock but already swelter-
ing. Even at dawn, when Margaret had sat barefoot in her
nightgown on the kitchen steps with a cup of coffee, watching the oak crowns turn from gray mountains to green
leaves and the pool go from black to mauve, heat had been
gathering, almost visibly, a solid muscular presence, and the
breeze brushing against her face had felt like fur.

'What do you want?' she had whispered aloud.

Now Naomi and Hedy were with her on the patio by the
pool, drinking iced coffee and fanning themselves with their
hands. Hedy's little dog, Kismet, was sitting on her lap,
though it was too hot for a dog in your lap, but try telling
that to the dog. Naomi had stopped by to pick up Hannah,
who had spent the night with Julia, and Hedy, hearing
voices next door, had walked over to see who was visiting
Margaret.

'Is it too early for wine?' asked Naomi.

Sunlight sparkled on the surface of the pool and the scent
of chlorine mixed with the dense sweet musk of Margaret's
roses in bloom by the back door. They were talking about the
'case', as everyone called it, which had at last been cracked.
According to a front-page story in the *Gazette* that morning –
Naomi had brought over a copy and was reading aloud – the
police had been right all along: someone had been trying to
poison coyotes. Acting on a tip last week, the police interviewed

a pest-control supplier in Mattapan who produced sales records showing that a ten-ounce package of arsenic had been sold the previous September to an Eric Dibler, of Littlefield, Massachusetts.

It was the environmentalist who had spoken at the town hall meeting last fall; Margaret recognized his name, and also pointed out that he was the chorus director's husband. When confronted by the police, Dibler confessed. He claimed the coyote population was out of control; since coyotes had no natural predators in the New England suburbs ('Other than the Massachusetts Turnpike,' interjected Naomi), he was attempting 'to complete the food chain and restore a natural order'. The dogs, he was also quoted as saying, were 'collateral damage'. He remained unrepentant about the dogs. They had no natural predators either. Charges had been filed. He had been fined two thousand dollars by the ASPCA. A civil lawsuit was also being considered.

'Well, thank God,' said Naomi.

Five dogs poisoned in all, Hedy noted, tapping her walking stick against the patio flagstones, making a monotonous calculative sound. Margaret interrupted to wonder at the strangeness of Eric Dibler being married to the middle school chorus director. An unsettling coincidence, Naomi agreed, adding that children in a middle school chorus had plenty of natural predators. But such a relief that the perpetrator had finally been caught; now they could rest easy, knowing that someone would be held accountable for what had happened to those dogs. Because it could have been anyone – friends, neighbors, all of them were suspect.

'Which really wasn't fair,' said Naomi.

It had been awful, hadn't it? For months they'd all been looking over their shoulders, the whole village, thinking something prowled in every shadow.

Margaret sighed and reached over to pet Kismet.

Hedy was still tapping her walking stick.

'Five dogs,' she repeated. 'Four of them died at the park, yes. But what about the sheep dog?'

'Boris?' said Naomi.

Boris had not been poisoned in the park. He was not collateral damage. He died on the sidewalk in front of the Dairy Barn, tied to a parking meter. Who could explain that? And the ugly graffiti, the outlines of which still clung to stone steps and storefronts?

A breeze rippled across the brilliant pool and scintillated into the trees; Margaret put a hand to her eyes as everyone fell to discussing theories about the graffiti. Hedy said the young Pakistani who had worked at the Forge was a candidate. Always seemed angry and why else return to Pakistan unless the police were on to him? Naomi confessed that in a dark moment it had crossed her mind that Matthew might be responsible for the graffiti, though of course that was nuts, he was a good boy, just going through a difficult period, fancied himself an anarchist (what teenage boy didn't?), but now that he'd started working at Radio Shack his mood had improved; he got good employee benefits, by the way. Also, he was shaving every morning. Frankly, her suspicions centered on Wayne, the Happy Paws dog walker, who'd always struck her as unstable. Economic resentment could have affected him: she'd spotted him at the Forge, reading Marx. The gardeners were not off the hook, either. But whoever it was – could it have been more than one person? A copycat, even? – he'd got what he wanted. Attention. Revenge. General unrest.

And yet, they all agreed, whatever the graffiti vandal had wanted, still there remained the question of Boris, a dog deliberately poisoned on a weekday afternoon a few days before Thanksgiving, outside an ice-cream parlor on a busy sidewalk.

As the sun rose higher the pool grew more dazzling, so that even when they looked away sunspots blinded them. They talked on with their hands shielding their eyes, Naomi offering various explanations and Hedy dismissing them, and as she listened to this discussion Margaret dropped her gaze to sprigs of wild thyme sprouting greenly between the patio flagstones and slowly realized that nothing they said mattered. It did not matter that the village was suddenly full of clean-shaven young men, or that last month's Clean Up Littlefield Day had been a success, with a record number of volunteers, every scrap of litter in the park picked up, new wood chips for the elementary school playground laid down and white boundary lines redrawn for the soccer field. It did not matter that a new petition for an off-leash park had once more been put forward, or that the aldermen were once again considering options and a trial period and preparing for a vote, or that a counter-petition was being filed. All that longing for rightness in the world, from every side of every issue, did not offset one cold fact: someone had liked the idea of poisoning dogs and had decided to try it. Not out of any conviction – even a wrong-headed conviction – but simply to see what it felt like to kill something that someone else loved.

In the same moment it also occurred to her that someone

who had tried something terrible once would probably try it again. No monster in the world was more frightening than a person with a taste for misery.

The scent of roses grew stronger. Above arched the endless blue sky. Kismet was panting.

Naomi was frowning at the pool. 'Well, clearly we've got to *do* something.'

But Margaret was thinking of Julia, of all the people Julia would meet in her life who could turn unpredictably cruel or crazy, and all the countless people who were just careless, people who would not find Julia miraculous in any way, who would not consider the world changed without her in it. Julia with her small, pale, sober face, her downturned mouth and lank brown hair hanging about her thin shoulders – who but Margaret understood the absolute astonishment of her?

'I wonder what Clarice thinks about all this,' Naomi was saying. 'Does she know? Is she home? Shall we invite her to join us?'

Hedy coughed. 'Clarice,' she said, 'is no longer with us. Went back to Chicago two days ago.'

'Without saying goodbye?'

Hedy coughed again. In a dry voice, she recounted the news that Dr Clarice Watkins, assistant professor of the University of Chicago's Department of Sociocultural Anthropology, had been doing research on *them*. Studying *them*. The residents of Littlefield.

'It is her theory – I am just repeating – that we suffer from delusions of being in touch with the rest of the world. But since we are too comfortable to share the world's worries, we are paranoid because we also can't do anything to make sure we are safe, since the world is such a mess, so that is why we are afraid of everything.' Hedy poked the rubber tip of her walking stick at a loose patio slate. Out scuttled a beetle.

'What else did she say?' Margaret touched the base of her throat.

'That we think our little problems are big problems, and every time we try to pay attention to the truly bad things in the world we are really just congratulating ourselves that they aren't happening to us.'

For several moments they were quiet.

'Well, that's one way of looking at it. Anything else under her turban?' asked Naomi.

Hedy pursed up her mouth as if tasting a newly decanted wine. 'Too many therapists and yoga studios and people online. Meanwhile our children are poorly educated and many of our attitudes are unconsciously racist.'

'We do have a lot of therapists,' allowed Naomi.

'That doughnut-baker gave her an earful. She went on and on about *him*. Stranger in a strange land. Do you know what is strange is Mr Skinny making doughnuts!'

In her lap, little Kismet whined.

'I can't remember everything she told me,' Hedy went on. 'She says we have proved that life in the Global Village is provincial. But she has decided not to write a book about us, even though she took a lot of notes. She says her findings are too problematic.'

'Well, thank God for that.' Naomi slapped at a fly that had landed on her arm. 'So how come she finally told you what she was doing here?'

Hedy gave a small smile. 'I asked.'

★

The morning came and went, and so did lunchtime and then more hours went by; it was one of those long, hot, breathless afternoons when the air was full of the meditative roar of air conditioners and no one could think of anything to do and even dogs didn't want to go outside. But by five o'clock it had cooled off a little and Julia and her mother set out for a walk around the village.

The walk was her mother's idea, Julia hadn't wanted to go. First of all it was weird to be walking without Binx. She kept seeing dogs like him everywhere; she hadn't realized how many black dogs there were in the world until she'd had one herself. Second, she did not like to be seen in public with her mother, who at any moment might call her 'sweetheart' or try to hold her hand. Two weeks ago, at dinner, her parents had told her they were going to try living apart for a while, 'to see what that's like, to see if it might make us all happier', both of them goggling at her like a pair of owls.

The dread she had felt that day in the woods and then for days afterward now seemed like a kind of trick, an extra betrayal. Her mother wasn't dying. She wasn't even sick. Julia's relief at this discovery had been so great that it turned almost instantly to fury. 'What's it like,' Mr Gluskin had asked during their final lunchtime meeting, 'knowing that your parents are getting separated?' She told him she didn't care.

'They're so annoying,' she said. 'Especially my mother.'

But in a week Julia would go to an all-girls canoe camp in Canada (Mr Gluskin's daughter was a counselor there and said it was empowering). Until then her mother insisted it was 'mother–daughter time'. They'd already gone shopping at the mall twice and visited the dentist. Hannah had gone home after a sleepover and Julia was bored of reading about people's favorite cereals on Facebook, so when her mother suggested going for ice cream, even though it was before dinner, she had agreed, reluctantly, to come along.

In many yards the grass was already looking singed and the flowers parched and drooping. On the radio it said the temperature today could reach ninety-nine degrees, a record for the third week of June. A peppery scent wafted up from the hot sidewalk mixed with the smell of cement, but in yards where a sprinkler had been set going there was the cool refreshing scent of wet grass. Here and there on the sidewalk was etched a brown leaf-shape where a dead leaf had lain under the snow all winter, leaving behind a perfect skeleton.

Her mother paused to admire droplets of water that had caught on a spider's web strung between two tree branches in a yard with a sprinkler. 'Look at that. Isn't that lovely?' She said that if you walked through a spider's web on a garden path in the morning, it meant you were the first person to have walked on the path that day. Julia refused to admire the spider's web and kept walking; her mother had switched into isn't-the-world-*fascinating* mode, which lately she turned on whenever she was particularly worried about something.

They passed a house with a shaggy vine climbing on a lattice above the front door. Her mother described a wisteria vine that grew over the back porch of her mother's house when she was a girl and how she would stand under it pretending to be Juliet waiting for Romeo. After that she told a story about visiting her grandparents' farm in Indiana and lying in bed at night listening to trains whistle past the cornfields.

'Such a lonely sound,' she sighed. 'But so beautiful. The world is full of beautiful things. Sometimes you can hardly stand it.'

I can stand it, thought Julia, keeping her head down and praying they would not meet anyone they knew.

Just before they reached the park they passed the house of an old lady on Endicott Street who grew pink peonies in a bed of mulch at the end of her driveway. Her mother first pointed out that the peonies were lovely and looked like old-fashioned bathing caps covered with white rubber petals, and then that someone had backed into the peonies with a car and flattened half of them.

'What a shame. Mrs Beale must be so upset. Peonies only bloom for a week. But while they last they're the most gorgeous, dauntless things in the world.'

As they stood contemplating the flattened peonies, Julia spotted Anthony Rabb on his front lawn a couple of houses down. He was cross-legged in the grass, whittling something with a knife. The blade flashed. His blond hair looked almost white under the hot sun.

'Let's turn around,' she hissed.

'What? Why? We're almost at the park. I saw a fox on the soccer field once, did I tell you? With a long red tail, it was so –'

'*No*,' said Julia. But it was too late. Anthony had seen them and put up his hand to shade his eyes in their direction. After a moment he gave a small wave.

'Who is that boy? Do you know him? He looks cute.'

Her mother kept walking; it was too awkward to be left standing alone on the sidewalk, so at last Julia followed her.

Anthony squinted up at them from the grass. He was

269

shirtless and barefoot, his legs covered with mosquito bites, some of which were bleeding. Something greenish was smeared on his chin. He got up, still gripping his knife and the piece of wood he had been carving.

'Hi, Julia.'

Her mother smiled. 'So how do you two know each other?'

'He's in my class.' Julia felt she was speaking another language, probably Latin.

'How *nice*.'

The three of them stood facing each other on the flaring sidewalk, as if rendered insensible by the heat of the day. Julia thought she might actually black out.

'So what are you carving?' she heard her mother ask.

Anthony held out the piece of wood. Julia couldn't tell what it was, but it looked like it might be obscene. 'It's a totem.'

'A totem,' repeated her mother. 'To protect you from bad spirits? How interesting. Is it a bear? A jack rabbit?'

Anthony said he did not know yet.

'Julia hasn't told me your name, by the way.'

Anthony didn't say anything, so Julia made a muttered introduction.

'Well, we were just on our way to get ice cream, *An*thony.' Her mother was using the chummy voice she usually reserved for greeting repairmen at the door. 'Would you like to join us?' Julia really did black out. But she came to in time to hear Anthony say, 'Sure,' and see him fold his penknife and stick it in the pocket of his dirty khaki shorts along with his totem. He was so beautiful it seemed wrong to look at him.

'I'll walk on ahead and see if there's a line at the Dairy Barn.' Her mother smiled.

Unbearable! Horrible! Why did parents even exist? Once they had procreated they should be exiled forever to someplace far away, like Texas, to live among themselves, and rattlesnakes, where they could do no harm.

Julia had dropped her head, limiting her peripheral vision to her own hair. As she walked along she counted sidewalk cracks, stepping on each one.

They were in front of Walgreens when Anthony said, 'So was it like totally weird?'

'What?'

'Going under the ice that time. Was it weird?'

Julia walked along looking at the sidewalk cracks. 'Yes,' she said finally. 'I thought I was going to die.'

But this was said for effect and because people seemed to expect it. She had not actually thought she was going to die. She had not thought of anything for the minute or two after the ice broke beneath her, being entirely preoccupied with not dying.

'Worse things have happened,' she said as they passed the Forge Café. Which was what her mother said these days whenever she broke a plate or forgot to pick up milk; she'd said the same thing at dinner during the 'living apart for a while' speech.

'But it was really scary,' she added.

'Cool,' said Anthony. Then he said, 'Did you know Ms Manookian is leaving to go teach in Lebanon?'

'Why?'

'I don't know. Maybe for a change.'

'Weird.'

'Really weird.'

At the Dairy Barn Julia's mother treated them to double scoops, Rocky Road for Julia and plain vanilla for Anthony.

'I don't like flavors,' he said. 'I've got food issues.'

Julia wondered if anyone from school would drive by and see her standing in front of the Dairy Barn having ice cream with Anthony Rabb. A cocker spaniel was tied by its leash to a parking meter. Julia stooped to pet it. Her mother said that people shouldn't leave their dogs tied to parking meters, didn't anyone ever learn anything? She looked up and down the street for its owner. Anthony licked his ice cream like a cat, neatly and with complete attention, making sure no ice cream got on his fingers, and then he threw the cone away with ice cream still inside. The cocker spaniel watched him with a shocked expression.

'Well, bye,' said Anthony, walking away.

'He didn't say thank you,' observed her mother.

'He's kind of annoying,' said Julia.

But on the way home she told her mother about Mr Anderman coming into the cafeteria on the last day of school wearing a gorilla mask and the school nurse calling the police, afraid he was a psycho killer.

'That sounds upsetting,' said her mother, missing the point as usual. 'And very irresponsible of Mr Anderman. Oh, Julia. Look at that big horse chestnut tree. Did you know that its flowers change color once they're pollinated? To let the bees know. Isn't that interesting?'

'No,' said Julia, though she thought it was, actually.

24.

A storm blew in just before five o'clock. It rained hard for fifteen minutes, enough to wash away the humidity; afterward the air cooled suddenly and the corners and edges of things stood out sharply. By seven the sun was shining again. Margaret had dried off two of the Adirondack chairs with a dishtowel and was once more sitting by the pool, watching light dripping off the oak trees. In her lap was a book. A biography of Clara Schumann, which had looked interesting in the library.

That afternoon she'd switched on the waterfall for the first time all year. The pump had broken last fall; the hose had needed to be replaced; the filter was clogged. The pool specialist had finally arrived after lunch, a tall fat man with tattooed arms and a crease at the back of his shaved head who fixed the pump, the hose and the filter. 'Like open-heart surgery,' she'd said when he was done, but he hadn't laughed; probably he thought she was remarking on the bill, when she'd only meant to be complimentary. (Why was the simplest gesture so complicated?) For weeks, she'd been waiting for the waterfall to get going again, looking forward to the soothing sound of water coursing down the rocks, and yet now as she sat with her unread book in her lap, she found the burble of water irritating.

She was waiting for Bill to come home.

From an open window of the Fischmans' house came the

noise of a baseball game on the radio. Since Marv died, Hedy kept the radio on all day. Over the roaring crowd, an announcer said, 'He was batting a buck fifty in May but June's a whole different story!'

She thought back to her first meeting with George, their walk in the woods, how she had wanted to tell him about her marriage and Bill. She thought of the night she had kissed him in his car when the creature had reared up at her, which she understood now to have been only a projection of her own fears and unmet needs. *What do I want?* she'd asked herself so many times since. *What do I need?* Whatever it was, she'd never really thought it could be supplied by George. And yet from the beginning there had been something between them, a sympathy, if not kindly, exactly, then almost fraternal, a recognition of wanting what the other was missing.

Do you understand? he had asked, when he told her about Tina.

A companionable sound, Bill's father used to say of the waterfall when he visited in the summer. Margaret's Niagara.

She had selected each stone herself from an old quarry in Gloucester she and Bill had visited one weekend, after her last time in the hospital. Filled the back seat and the trunk of the car with stones, some showing veins of iron ore, some plain granite, a few pinkish quartz.

Bill helped, but she'd wanted to choose the stones herself and even quietly put back a few he had selected; in her mind hung a picture of how the waterfall would look. At home she read a book about the way people used to build stone walls, without mortar, each stone placed with an eye to symmetry and balance, no single stone holding too much weight or too little. She bought an electric pump and one blazing afternoon Bill's father, who had been a contractor, cemented it in at the far end of the pool, and did the wiring and hooked up the hose. While he worked she brought him glasses of lemonade, noticing how the sun reflected off his bald head. She kept offering to get him a hat.

'Don't bother,' he said. 'I'll wear one later.'

It took a long time to build because she kept taking it apart. She couldn't get the stones to fit exactly as she wanted them; she made mistakes, left gaps and jagged places. Sometimes it looked just like a pile of rocks, like the collapse of something. For two days while Bill was at work, his father had ferried stones with her, back and forth, from a tumble on a tarp by the pool. But finally she was impatient to have it done and so she decided the waterfall was finished. It had turned out well enough, especially now that moss had grown onto some of the stones, and a little green creeping vine that wasn't ivy; she kept forgetting the name. When you turned on the switch, water ran down the stones and made a babbling noise that wasn't so different, if you shut your eyes, from the real thing. Right at the center was an oblong stone, heavier at one end, quartz with a dark artery; sometimes in the evenings it looked ghostly and alive.

Bill was late.

He was supposed to be home by seven. All day she had thought about what she would say when he came home. All day, since this morning, even while sitting with Hedy and Naomi by the pool talking about the dogs and then the surprising news about Clarice Watkins (which wasn't so surprising, looking back). All day, while taking her walk with Julia and meeting that boy, all day, behind the daunt-lessness of peonies and horse chestnuts and the rain and the sun coming out, behind everything she had seen and done and thought about, she had been waiting. Sometimes it seemed as if her whole life had been waiting, that she had been operating from within a dream of her life, waiting to wake up, and now the moment had finally arrived to do something before it was all gone.

She had made a simple cold dinner, just to get it out of the way. A salad, with a plate of sliced tomatoes and some cheese and bread. A bowl of strawberries. Half a bottle of pinot grigio in the fridge.

It was both reassuring and depressing that there had been no final blow-up. No scene. No grand denunciations, hyster-ics, drama. Only calm discussions in Dr Vogel's office, a reasoned inventory of their separate failings. Followed by their declaration to Julia. Followed by a hesitation. A deci-sion to decide nothing. *It's up to you*, Bill had said. He said it again last night, as they sat together, at the end of the bed, making the mattress sag as they pulled off their shoes. *We don't have to do this. You decide.*

She leaned back in her Adirondack chair, waving away the gnats, listening to the birds and watching light glisten in the trees.

'Children adjust,' Dr Vogel said at their last session.

A mourning dove was calling out from somewhere in the trees. Where was Bill? What was keeping him? Why tonight, of all nights, did he have to be late? She sighed, shifting her legs. Had he thought of her today, of what she might be thinking? Probably not. She wondered if this was, finally, one of the main differences between men and women: that men rarely wondered what women were thinking, unless they were with them, while women always wondered what men were thinking, and never seemed to know.

A slip of paper in her pocket rustled; she put her hand to her pocket, drew out the paper and looked at it.

milk
eggs
orange juice
Cheerios

She refolded it and slid it back inside her pocket.

'Bill,' she would say.

But she would wait until he got himself a drink. Maybe point out the sun setting behind the trees, the beauty of the evening, the dove. A list of small marvels, although she was finished with trying to make herself interesting to him. Such a lovely time of day; they'd called it the witching hour when Julia was younger. That was what she would do, and tell him about walking to the Dairy Barn with Julia and meeting that boy.

Not a very nice boy, but it was good to see Julia with someone her own age. She hadn't been spending much time with her friends, not even Hannah; yet she didn't seem unhappy exactly. Mostly sullen, although today had been better. When they got home they had talked about Julia packing for Canada – Margaret thought she should start getting organized – and then laughed together over the list on the camp's website: 'What You Need and What You Don't' (a good book, a flashlight, a warm sweatshirt, 'absolutely NO iPods, iPads, cell phones, MP3 players, electronic devices of ANY kind! Where you're going, you won't need them!').

'Where am I going,' Julia had said, 'a crypt?'

A white space was forming in Margaret's mind; slowly it took on dimension and color, like an instant photograph that develops as you watch: three people walking on a beach, shadows trailing them, and beside them a flat gray sea. Was this a sign? If so, a sign of what? Again she shifted in the wooden chair, straightening her back, crossing her legs; she thought about going in to pour herself a glass of wine. But she wanted to be sitting outside when Bill came home. Out in the cool air, listening to the waterfall, watching the sunset. The days seemed so beautiful lately she was almost afraid of being inside, of missing any of it. Her roses by the back steps. The pink geraniums. Was that a bat over the pool?

On the cover of her library book was a painting of a woman bent over piano keys. Shades of blue, with brown for the piano, gray for the woman's long dress; on the windowsill, a small red vase in a low stroke of light. A suggestion of evening, the woman playing for herself. Raptness indicated in the tension of her body, fingers suspended above the keys. Not rapture, something more labored, a deep attentiveness.

The paper in her pocket rustled like a dry leaf.

'Julia?' Margaret called. 'How are you coming along?'

From Julia's window came a heavy sound, like furniture being moved. Someone's dog began barking from the end of the street.

'Julia? Can you hear me?'

It was almost dark.

Where was Bill? He hadn't even phoned to say he'd be late. After all that had happened, all their talking. He was working again. She had made dinner. Nothing was very different. But she could hear a difference, all the same, a complex movement in the leaves overhead and the water on the rocks and in her own breathing.

The sky was pink and orange. The breeze smelled of honeysuckle. That mourning dove was calling. She would never be loved passionately. Her life was not what she had hoped. She was going to worry about her child to the end of her days, her child who might grow up to be disappointed or afraid, or alone, or not, who might instead get almost everything. Her child, whose neck was as slender as a stalk, whose life was opening like a flower. What I want to tell you, she would say (someday), is that sometimes things don't work out very well, no matter how much you worry about them beforehand. But (my darling, my darling) that is the least of it.

Light was sifting through the darkening trees like a great golden net.

Was that Bill's car in the driveway? Her heart was beating so violently she couldn't hear.

'Bill?'

She knew what she wanted to say, first the dove and the net and – what was the rest? It was so hard to keep hold of it all. I have been waiting, she would say. Waiting and waiting. I have thought it all over. And I have to tell you –

Already it was almost gone.

Trees, leaves, light, bird. And the breeze and the bat over the pool.

'Bill?' she called out again, almost in terror, thinking she heard a car door creak open. 'Bill, is that you?'

Something was moving in the deep blue twilight, under

the oak trees, moving toward her or moving away, it was too dark to tell. What else could a person do, she thought, staring hard at the darkness, but try to be happy? However confused and wrong-looking the attempt might be. And then whatever happened afterward all you could do was bear it, because whatever you could not bear you had to carry.

'Hello?' she called, to whatever it was.

Trees, leaves, light, bird.

Acknowledgments

I am grateful to the MacDowell Colony for granting me a residency during the summer of 2012 and to Ann Stokes for two weeks at her Welcome Hill studios. Heartfelt thanks to Suzanne Matson, Eileen Pollack, Phil Press and Joan Wickersham, all of whom read drafts of this novel and offered tremendously insightful and useful suggestions. Maxine Rodburg's help was, as always, simply invaluable. I'd like to thank Marjorie Sandor for her marvelous and uncanny friendship; my wonderful and patient agent, Colleen Mohyde, who accompanied this book from its first pages; and Juliet Annan, for her steady encouragement and wise guidance, which have mattered more to me than I can ever say. Thanks also to my husband, Ken, my daughters, Avery and Louisa, my sister Evie, and to all my family and friends, without whom I would have long ago gone to the dogs.